Life Rewired

Also by Lynn Galli

Something So Grand

Mending Defects

Finally

Full Court Pressure

Blessed Twice

Uncommon Emotions

Imagining Reality

Wasted Heart

Life Rewired

Lynn Galli

Penikila Press

ISBN: 978-1-935611-24-0

Part I

Falyn

1

The low fuel indicator blazed to life on my dash like a bright warning beacon for so much more than just a dwindling supply of gasoline. The four hour drive had given me a long time to contemplate this move. Too much could go wrong, but I was hoping more would go right. My outlook switched back and forth with every change in altitude on the endless mountain pass. The miniature gas pump icon served as a taunting reminder that I could be making the second biggest mistake of my life.

I rolled down the window, letting the crisp, cool air flow around me. Even two years out, I still wasn't used to being able to get fresh air anytime I wanted. The breeze and what it represented prompted me to take stock. So I only had $100 to my name—well, $58.13 after gassing up and stopping for a snack on the road. So it had to last me until my first paycheck. So if I got fired from my new job I wouldn't have enough money for the return drive to Denver to beg for my old job back. A lousy job working a chicken packaging line, but a job. Even minimum wage was better than nothing. Especially for an ex-con.

Another ski area? How many were there on this road? Five, six? And how many more curves and aspen trees would I need to get through before I saw this damn town? Okay, I get it. The town is called Aspen for a reason. Enough with the trees already.

I shook my head. Sarcasm was a slippery slope to cynicism, and being jaded was what got me into trouble the first time. Until I felt sure I wouldn't follow sarcasm to that end again, I had to disrupt it from the start. Best just to focus on what I had here and now. Clean mountain air, unmatched scenery, new town, nonjudgmental friend, all leading to what I hoped would be a better life.

I was pretty sure I made the right decision coming here. Not like I had much of a choice. Two months behind on rent at my old place, eviction couldn't be more than a day or two away. If that weren't bad enough, my place was the first stop for three moronic detectives anytime they caught a burglary case. On parole, I could do nothing but endure their searches and accusations. Off parole, I knew nothing would change. Either I let them question me or I became suspect number one in their cases. With police, once a criminal, always a criminal. Not for me. It might be true for others, but I had no plans to repeat the biggest mistake of my life. Five years in prison beat the criminal out of me. Moving was my only option, and without first and last month's saved up, options were limited.

Finally! The town-limit sign. Were they serious with that population count? I'd be lucky to find more than a dozen streets in this place. On the non-sarcastic side, I'd be able to bike those twelve streets and save on my now depleted gas budget.

I fished out the directions once again. I'd double-checked them at every merge and turn on the trip. My gas tank wouldn't allow for doubling back. It wasn't long before I was taking the turn off the highway onto a one-lane road. A driveway shot off to the left, leading to two homes mostly hidden by trees. Down the road, I spotted a two-story home with a barn and horse corral. A sweeping curve through more trees took me past a small cabin. My tight grip on the wheel relaxed at the faint sound of nail guns firing in the distance. I'd finally found it.

I parked behind one of the trucks lining the gravel driveway and looked up at the house under construction. The build was smaller than I expected. Two stories but compact. Sheets of plywood enclosed the framing, but no house wrap or windows yet. That put the project at a month in already.

I wanted to be here for the foundation pour in March, but my asshole parole officer denied my request to relocate. I could have checked in with him by phone for my final month, but no, that would have diminished his authority somehow. As if that weren't dickish enough, he'd flaunted his remaining power over me this morning by pushing our final meeting back a few hours without telling me. I sat on that rigid plastic chair in the dingy, underfunded government lobby waiting for his ego to deflate. It took every ounce of patience I had to keep from ripping his fingernails off when I was finally shown into the office to complete my release paperwork.

I'd driven off the anger, but I was bummed that I was late. I wanted to get that awkward first day on the job out of the way with a half day of work.

"Falyn," a voice called out from the work tent beside the structure.

Natalie Harper traversed through the equipment with a pretty redhead at her side. Only the third time I'd seen her in almost ten years, I was again surprised by the changes I spotted in my friend. The first time we met she'd been sixteen trying to pass for eighteen. Her light brown hair used to be longer and her frame two inches shorter. She'd really come into her beauty over the past decade with stylish chopped hair, sleek longer body, and fully mature face. When she was sixteen, she never drew attention to herself and shrouded her femininity to keep the guys on the construction crew in line. She'd obviously found a great balance between staying one of the guys and ramping up her hotness.

I stepped out of the car, my knees and back cracking. It felt good to stand and even better to see Nat again. Last time was a chance meeting in a Denver parking lot. The encounter was too brief to really catch up, but long enough for her to offer me a job on her construction crew. Based on the unassuming Natalie I knew, I anticipated a two-person shop that tackled small repair jobs. It turned out she had a lean but full crew that could use an electrician to help build a custom home. I jumped at the chance to get back into construction after being denied for years.

"How was the trip?" Natalie asked and reached forward for a hug. Even with the two inch growth spurt in her late teens, the top of her head only came up to my mouth.

She'd been like a little sister to me when we first met, especially once she confessed to her true age and the fact that she was on her own because of homophobic parents who kicked her out. At that point, I always tried to watch out for her on the jobs we worked together. I also taught her everything I could. She'd soaked it up and now had her own construction company. One she had no problem risking to hire on an ex-con electrician. Something no other construction crew had been willing to do.

"Long, but it's good to be here." I smiled and tried to scope out her girlfriend without making it look like I was checking her over. Conventionally pretty with bright blue eyes and an engaging smile.

"Meet Glory, my friend and your landlord," Natalie indicated.

Oh. So not the girlfriend then. "Hi, Glory."

"Nice to meet you." She gripped my hand with both of hers. Short thing, even more than Natalie, but pretty and off-limits based on the flash of gold I caught on her finger. No doubt straight anyway. "I was dropping off your key, but now I can give it to you."

I reached to take it. I hoped the place wasn't a dump like my apartment in Denver, but it was free and Natalie was paying three times what I made on the packaging line. I'd take a tent for that wage.

"Let me know if anything comes up while you're there," Glory told me. "I better run. The house looks beautiful, Nat." She waved and went off to her car. Already, she seemed ten times better than my last landlord.

Turning back, I caught Natalie staring at me. A blush hit her cheeks. "Your hair is lighter and you lost the braid."

I huffed in amusement. Until two years ago, I kept my dark blond hair long and braided. Feminine tomboy, perfect for construction sites, but I wanted everything to change when I got out. Now my hair stopped just past my collar, and the shorter style added body to the thick strands. "You saw me a few months ago."

"I was too excited about running into you to notice. Did you possibly get taller, too?" She grinned, and I felt my tension dissipate at the longstanding tease. At five-ten, I was as tall as most of the guys on our old crew. She always resented that my height made it easier to blend in. Blending was her constant goal on the jobsite.

"At least half a foot," I kidded back.

"Thought so." She tipped her head toward the house. "Do you want to take a look before we get you settled into your new digs?"

"Sure."

I followed her around to the front of the structure. It was a cottage style home, but it had elements that tied it to the house down the road and the cabin nearby. We were building it for Natalie's girlfriend, who owned the cabin I'd passed and whose brother lived in the other house.

"Thought I heard a new voice out here. This the new fritz?" A solid guy with sheered, black hair and a wide nose appeared in the front doorway and strode down the steps.

"Falyn, this is Miguel. He's the crew chief when I'm not around."

"Damn glad to meet you." His smile was kind as he pumped my outstretched hand. "We've really needed an electrician on the crew. Nat tells me you're the best."

My eyebrows rose. It had been years since I'd done electrical work. Long enough that I had to reestablish my license when I got out. I wanted so very much to live up to Natalie's expectations.

"Let's show her what we've done so far." Natalie moved ahead of us into the structure.

It was still in the open frame stage. Anyone without construction experience would have a hard time seeing the layout. I was happy to note that I could spot all the major elements almost as fast as when I'd been doing this work day to day. Perhaps I wouldn't be as rusty as I feared.

We hadn't been looking around long before two women stepped through the front doorway. One was short and a little plain except for the trendy but clunky glasses. The other was beautiful, closer to my height with long, chestnut brown hair that fell in waves around her face and shoulders. Even without the bright smile for Natalie, I knew the gorgeous one was her girlfriend. Holy smokes, I mean, Natalie was hot, but this woman was walking fire.

"Hi, babe," she said softly, leaning in for a quick hello kiss from Natalie before tapping Miguel's shoulder in greeting.

"Hi, Vivi," Natalie answered, keeping her hand on the woman's arm. Her eyes flicked to me as she stepped back and introduced us. "Vivian Yeats, this is Falyn Shaw."

"Falyn, it's so great to have you here. Natalie's been looking forward to it." Nothing about her statement sounded insincere, but Natalie must have told her about my history. She had to be worried I would ruin her girlfriend's company. Hell, I thought I might ruin her girlfriend's company.

"It's wonderful to meet you, Vivian."

She introduced me to the other woman as her assistant, Samantha. Then she had Natalie catch her up on the day's progress. Her questions proved she had a lot of construction knowledge to go with her design talent. Normally the designer did nothing but make things more difficult for the people who made their designs come to life.

"Fos," Natalie said to me, and a flush crested her cheeks as she realized my initials just spilled out of her mouth. She hadn't called me Fos since our last job together. Falyn Ophelia Shaw. Yes, Ophelia. Blame my mom. "Do you mind looking over the electrical plans and drawing up a supply list? I was waiting for you to get here so we wouldn't miss anything."

"Sure," I said, happy to help somewhere today after getting here so late.

Miguel and Natalie went out the back door opening as Vivian and Samantha discussed some design elements in the great room. Everything seemed calm and efficient. I'd worked many construction crews and seen almost every dynamic. This felt different somehow, but of course, it wasn't her whole crew yet.

The sound of an engine outside made me glance up from my scribbles. I watched as a striking butch stepped down from a compact pickup. She was tall, probably as tall as me but with a little more muscle than on my trimmer frame. She had short, espresso colored hair in a perfect wave that pushed back from her face and ears. The determined line of her mouth matched the intense stare of her dark eyes as she moved toward the house. Confidence dripped from her every stride. There wasn't a doubt in my mind that she was a lesbian, which given the population, I found surprising. I feared there might not be any others in town.

A smile formed on my lips as I considered dating again. I hadn't given it any thought since getting out. Parole wasn't exactly conducive to dating. The occasional one night stand served my infrequent needs. If there were more single lesbians in town, I might have to pull out my charm and dust it off. See if it still worked. Not on this person. She wasn't my type, but if I could find someone else.

She stepped up into the house and greeted Vivian with a tight hug. The smile slid from my face as she leaned back and kissed her. On the mouth. In broad daylight. In front of Samantha and, although she didn't know it, me, friend of the person who loved the woman she was kissing. In a house the woman's girlfriend was building for her.

What. The. Hell?

2

I ducked out the nearest doorway, wondering what kind of messed up drama I'd stepped into here. Natalie gave me the impression that she and Vivian were exclusive. She was building a frickin' house for the woman. She got all moony when she talked about her. They had to be exclusive. Could she really be okay with someone else kissing the woman she loved? She better know about it. I sure as hell didn't want to be the one to break it to her, but I couldn't just ignore it.

"Nat?" I called up to where I'd heard her walking on the roof.

She poked her head over the side, spotted my perturbed look, and came down the ladder. "What's up?"

Prison pretty much beat all the social elegance out of me, so I blurted, "Your girlfriend's with a fine butch inside. You okay with that?"

Natalie's face scrunched up in confusion. Her eyes didn't even flick towards the back door opening. Like she didn't think what I said was possible. "Molly?"

"Didn't catch her name. Just saw her kiss your woman."

She tipped up onto her toes to look through one of the window openings. "That's Molly. They've been friends a long time."

"You're okay with it?" Confusion soaked into my sizzling brain.

She let a laugh slip then noticed how serious I looked. "Viv and I are together."

Like that explained everything. I knew they were together. That's why I was out here fuming over seeing what I saw. "You're okay with kisses from women who clearly like other women?"

"I don't have anything to worry about. Viv loves me, and she's her own woman. She and Molly have been friends a lot longer than she and I have been together." She squeezed my arm. "C'mon, let's say hi."

"Hey, Nat," the over-affectionate greeter known as Molly said when we walked through the back opening. She no longer had her hands on Vivian, and in light of Natalie's attitude, appeared as harmless as Nat seemed to think she was.

"Hi, Molly," Natalie said and gestured to me. "This is Falyn. She's an old friend and now works on the crew."

Molly's dark eyes cut to me, a smile erasing what had looked like a slightly irritated face. Her chin tipped up as she extended her hand. "Molly Sokol. How ya doing?"

I shook her hand, expecting a crushing grip. The soft skin and firm but nonthreatening hold was a pleasant surprise. "Falyn Shaw. Good to meet you."

"Molly is an outdoor guide in town. You're still big on biking, right?" Natalie asked me before turning to Molly. "Maybe you could show her a few trails? She's new to Aspen."

"Absolutely," she offered kindly as Vivian stepped over and slid her arm around Natalie's waist.

Now I saw it. Too many years inside made me suspicious of everyone. Or maybe too many years with an ex-girlfriend who loved making me jealous. Vivian only had eyes for Natalie. Almost as important, Molly knew and respected that. I shouldn't have jumped to conclusions and felt like an idiot for doing so.

"Sorry," I whispered to Natalie.

Vivian eyed me with interest, but Natalie didn't explain. "We're headed out to practice for the pool tournament."

"You guys have fun." Natalie stroked the hand gripping her waist.

"Maybe I'll stop off at your place on my way home. Two nights alone is too many," Vivian sighed dreamily.

"Gawd!" Molly breathed out in exasperation and shot me a conspiratorial look. I liked her instantly because of it. As happy as I was for Natalie, it could get a little nauseating watching a new couple be new together.

"All right, all right." Vivian leaned in for a quick kiss that looked far more involved than the hello buss she'd given her friend. "Call you later." She gave me a wave and led Molly and Samantha outside.

"Let's get you settled in at your place," Natalie said to me before calling out to Miguel that we were leaving.

I followed her outside and got into my car, waiting for her to swing her truck around first. I peeked into the backseat again to check on the beasts in their cat carrier. Still sound asleep. They'd be hyper tonight, but I wouldn't mind. They'd managed the long trip beautifully.

Natalie took us out onto the highway and into town where we turned off into a residential neighborhood. When she parked, I pulled in behind her. I glanced at the house then at the one nearby. This couldn't be it. This wasn't a crappy apartment. It wasn't even a rundown house. This place was beautiful. One of four homes on the street, not big like the others, but a decent size. It couldn't be the place. We must have gone to Natalie's house first.

"This is it," Natalie encouraged me out of the car.

I managed to keep from shaking my head in disbelief. "Looks nice." I reached into the backseat and grabbed the cat carrier.

"When did you get cats?"

"A year ago. Will the guys mind?" I was going to be sharing the house with two other crewmembers. She tried to give me an accurate picture of the guys, but after taking a step into the house, I could already see that cleanliness wasn't a priority.

"I doubt they'll mind. They like my dog." She shot me a guilty look. "I asked them to do a little straightening before you got here. At least I cornered the master for you." Her hand waved down the hall past the kitchen. "I was here when the boys landed. They were ready to beat each other senseless to get that room."

My brow lifted. I'd get the master and she somehow made it okay with the housemates? This was getting better and better.

"You do not want to share a bathroom with those guys," she explained as she started down the hall to the master.

I set the carrier on the bed and opened its door. Dancer sprang out right away, stretching and licking her paws before sniffing along the bed. Tusk came at me next, bumping against my hand for a scratch. They were both all black with yellow eyes. I'd been leaning toward an orange tabby when a volunteer came by and told me that the all black cats had the hardest time being adopted. The news made me want two of them.

"It's beautiful." I looked around a bedroom that was a palace compared to my dinky studio apartment back in Denver. I nearly wept when I saw the five piece bathroom. I couldn't remember the last time I got to take a bath after a hard day at work.

"We're remodeling the place after the summer. Glory wants to use it as a vacation rental whenever her family or friends aren't visiting."

That must have been the deal she struck. Whatever the terms, I was fine with it. Free rent for the summer for a little work in the fall sounded fine with me. She probably hadn't told the landlord about my record. I doubted if Glory would be fine with leaving me in her house, even if it wasn't up to the standard for homes we used to target.

"This place is spectacular. Thanks again." I should be kissing her feet and agreeing to indentured servitude for not only offering me a job with a livable wage but providing summer housing for free.

"I'm just happy to have you here and on the crew."

"What are they going to think?" I jerked my thumb toward the other rooms. They couldn't be thrilled to share a house with a stranger, especially a woman.

"All they care about is steady seasonal work to pay for their skiing habit. Last year, they stayed in a rented trailer for the summer. They wouldn't care if you had twenty cats."

The front door crashed open and a guy about my height with curly, blond hair came through. "Yo, Harp! She here?" He pulled up short when he spotted me. His brother smacked into him from behind. The brother was an inch taller with the exact same hair. Same broad nose, wide brow, and strong chin, too.

"Falyn, these are the Sweeney Brothers, Curtis and Cole." Natalie gestured to them.

"Yo," the first guy said.

"Whaddup," the second guy said.

They looked like beach bums without a beach, which might be the definition of a ski bum. They each had dimples on opposite sides of their faces and dark blue eyes. Probably late twenties. Jeez, frickin' babies I'd be living with, but it was free, bigger than I'd seen in a decade, and if Natalie said they were all right, that was all I needed.

"Hi, guys," I greeted, surprised when they each thrust a hand at me to shake.

"You like video games?" the one with the left dimpled cheek asked.

"Haven't had a lot of time for them."

"We've kinda taken over the television out here for showdowns. Hope you don't mind." He gestured to the flat screen TV in the living room.

"Fine by me." I planned to spend most of my free time out on that great wraparound porch or in my huge bedroom. I had my own small television. The guys could take over the rest of the house for all I cared.

"Coolio," right dimple said.

"Hauling time, Sweeneys," Natalie told them and started toward the front door.

I was going to protest, but the guys were already out the door. I followed behind. There wasn't much to bring inside, but I wanted to handle my bike. It was the only splurge I'd made since getting out. The expensive car I had before being caught paid for my legal bills, my less than precious used car, and this amazing bike.

"This it?" Cole, I think, asked.

The backseat and cargo area of my Outback was packed with boxes, but I guess for someone my age, he expected me to be driving a moving truck. Since my ex pillaged my condo as soon as I went in, I had no furniture or many possessions really. If I hadn't sold my Porsche to pay my legal bills, she probably would have tried to take that, too. It still amazed me to realize just how wrong I'd been about so many things at the time: girlfriend, so-called friends, must-have gadgets, and top of the line everything. None of that mattered. It only took five years in prison and two years on parole to drill that lesson into me.

"I travel light."

"Coolio," Curtis said again, grabbing three boxes from the backseat.

I rushed to the back and unhooked my bike from the rack. I wheeled it to the garage door that Cole opened for me. He headed back to grab more boxes than his brother had. At this pace, we'd be done in two trips.

"They're handy," Natalie said as she watched them disappear into the house. "Hope they don't drive you nuts."

"Please," I scoffed then realized she didn't have any idea what I'd lived with. Nuts was a cellmate that chewed sunflower seeds and spit out the shells wherever she wanted in your six-by-nine cell every day. Nuts was a celly that made wine in the toilet water and forced you to wait to use the toilet. Slobs who played video games weren't going to drive me nuts.

"I'm glad you're here." Natalie was suddenly serious. "I wish I'd known—"

I held up a hand. I didn't need her guilt. She'd stuck by me when she heard what I did. Sent letters and at least one care package a year when everyone but my mom turned away.

We hadn't even been working together when I got caught. Snitched on, actually. That was hard to get over. If I'd been caught burglarizing a house, I think I could have lived with the sentence. Instead, they'd caught one of the other guys on the crew and he flipped on the rest of us. Still, it was my fault whether I got caught in the act or told on. I'd gotten off track with the friends I was keeping and the people I worked with. I thought I had everything I needed. Turns out, I didn't have anything I needed or wanted.

"Anyway," she said, looking away. She'd never asked me why I'd done what I'd done. Never looked at me like I was stupid for doing what I'd done. Everyone else had, even my mom who loved me through all of it. My mom had to know why, needed a viable reason to explain my moronic behavior, but Natalie never did. "I'll swing by to pick you up tomorrow morning."

I wanted to protest, but I wasn't sure I could backtrack to the site. I probably didn't have enough gas to get there anyway. "See you in the morning." I gave her a gentle shove to get her moving. She didn't need to spend all of her Monday night helping me.

3

Even with the guys playing video games late into the night, it had been quieter than I could remember in years. The paper walls of my lousy apartment never allowed for continuous sleep. Not so here.

When I walked into the kitchen, I found Cole, of the left dimple, making scrambled eggs. Coffee percolated in the maker to his right and bacon sizzled in the pan next to the eggs. He had on a dark green t-shirt with Natalie's company logo. I was wearing a heather green version of the same. Six others in varying colors sat on my dresser after Natalie left. I would have been happy enough with one. That's what I used to get on other crews, one large, men's t-shirt with the company name stamped on the back. These were women's t-shirts that fit and had cool designs to display her company name. Free, too. Every other crew made us buy the shirts we were required to wear, which was another clue that Natalie ran things differently here.

"Morning. You like eggs?" Cole lifted the pan and moved it toward the three plates he'd set out.

"Uh," I started because I didn't know how to handle this. Money was tight right now. Putting in for combined groceries with these young guys could blow my grocery budget every week.

"Take him up on it when he cooks." Curtis joined us then bumped into the into the breakfast bar as he slid a company t-shirt over his head. "We can figure out grocery runs later."

I shrugged. Natalie had also left groceries for me, the little sneak. I wouldn't be living on ramen noodles until my next paycheck. "Thanks." I held out a stopping hand as he reached to add bacon to the eggs he'd just dished onto my plate. "Vegetarian."

The guys exchanged a look then shrugged. "More for us."

We sat and ate together, which was a nice change for me. The past two years had been pretty solitary. Nobody really talked on the line at work and my personal time consisted of trying to pick up handyperson work to help pay the rent. A normal breakfast filled with easy conversation was both entertaining and a treat. So far, I was getting a good vibe from them.

"You guys mind if I let my cats wander the house when we're not here?" I asked when I cleared our plates into the dishwasher.

"No probs," Curtis said, and it set the tone for our house sharing experience. They were casual and cool with my cats. I'd do what I could to be a decent roommate for them. It was a relief really. Being a shitty roommate bothered me as much as it bothered my roommates and cellmates in the past.

A horn sounded from outside. I finished packing a lunch and shoved my thermos under the facet to fill. On the way out the door, I picked up the five gallon bucket where I kept my limited supply of tools and the new hardhat Natalie had left for me. I shook my free arm and let out a slow breath. Time to start my second chance at a decent life.

Natalie waved me up to the front seat. The guys loaded into the backseat with Natalie's dog, a cute herding breed that seemed at ease with them and familiar with this morning routine. She got the truck in motion and headed to the end of the street, pulling into the driveway of the nearest house. Before I could ask what we were doing, the front door opened and an Asian woman stuck her head out the door and waved. Natalie waved back but Cole brought down his window and shouted hello.

A black man a little older than the woman appeared beside her and kissed her cheek before making his way to the truck. Was this guy really on Natalie's crew? He was seventy if he was a day.

"Yo, Owen," Curtis greeted while Cole went into a long, "Oowenn."

Natalie introduced us as she backed out of his driveway and got us on the road to the site. The boys yammered the entire drive. By the time we arrived, I could tell they had nothing but respect for Owen and what he could do with woodworking. Interesting crew Natalie had here.

Ten seconds after we stepped out of the truck, someone called out from inside the structure. "Harp's here!"

The front porch suddenly filled with Miguel, two other Latino guys, and a white dude. All sported various versions of Natalie's t-shirts and looked cohesive as a unit.

"Q-king Owen in the house," one of the Latino guys called, rushing down the steps to bump fists with the older man.

"New chick," the white guy said.

"Falyn, this is the crew," Natalie said introducing each as Luis, Ramón, and Tyler.

"Hey, guys." I tried for nonchalant. I'd perfected this attitude in prison where it was dangerous to show any emotion when meeting someone.

"Damn glad you're here," Luis told me. "No more dealing with Anton the Putz."

"The electrical subcontractor," Natalie supplied with a smile. I hoped I lived up to her expectations. Even if all the guys turned out to be assholes, working with Natalie again, living in the beautiful place she arranged, and making a livable wage was enough.

Natalie gathered everyone around the work table with the plans and gave out the day's instructions. She carefully explained things that were often missed without making it sound condescending or like an order. She, Cole, and I would start wiring the house while the rest of them would get working on the roof. The crew listened intently, a few asked questions, but none of them gave her any grief. She'd told me she hired only the guys she'd liked working with on the crew she came from, but this was a little amazing. Ordinarily someone was grumbling by now.

My group started drilling through the studs where we'd run the wire. It didn't take long to figure out the cheap drill I'd bought to pick up extra work on the weekends wasn't going to cut it on a real jobsite. Natalie swapped mine out with hers without a word or letting Cole see her do it. She was saving my ass everywhere now.

After the mid-morning break, we were making good progress on the first floor. Vivian appeared in the doorway, giving Natalie a bright smile and nodding at Cole and me. No kiss for Natalie this time. I hid a grin as I watched them put on their professional faces.

"Will you run through the electrical plans, Viv?" Natalie asked. "We're picking up the supplies later."

Vivian walked through each room we'd worked on. They discussed adding more boxes to a few additional locations and asked me about codes and such. She was more than just a designer. She knew what she was doing architecturally, design wise, and on a construction site. I felt a twinge of envy that Natalie had found herself a real winner here.

"Lunch!" someone yelled from outside.

I checked my watch not able to believe the time had flown by so quickly. Days at the chicken packaging plant stretched out endlessly. Cole tore through the room we were in toward the front door. Guys started clanging down the ladders from the roof. Lunch must be a group thing, too.

"Owen barbecues once a week," Natalie explained, ushering us out the door to the work tent where he'd been slicing reclaimed wood into roofing and siding shingles all morning.

The guys lined up at the grill where Owen was dishing out burgers and brats. It looked good if I still ate meat, but years of being forced to eat meat-like objects in prison turned me into a vegetarian. I started toward my stashed cooler, but Natalie grabbed my arm and shook her head.

"Grilled cheese okay?" Owen called to me.

All but the Sweeney brothers turned to look at me. My mouth dropped, not believing Natalie would remember the one time I mentioned now being a vegetarian. "Great, yeah, thank you, Owen."

He held out the plate with the grilled cheese sandwich to me. "I can make another if this isn't enough?"

"Oh, no, thank you. This will be plenty." I felt a lump form in my throat. This little act of kindness piled on top of everything that Natalie had already done got to me. I didn't normally get choked up unless I was backed into a corner that I didn't have the power to get out of. It happened so often in prison and on parole. Getting choked up for a good reason was a new experience for me.

Natalie's hand squeezed my shoulder. I used to do this to her when we'd worked together. A way to make sure she knew that I had her back among some of the assholes we had to work with. Now she was doing it to me, and I felt the ton of bricks I'd been carrying on my shoulders throughout parole slip away.

I found a bowl of pasta salad and a stack of grilled corn to add to my plate and took a seat next to Cole to enjoy a loud and happy lunch. They talked like they were a group of friends at a bar not just work colleagues. Cursory questions were tossed my way throughout. Natalie obviously hadn't told them about my record. I felt bad about it for maybe a second. In fact, I felt more like the woman I was when I'd first known Natalie. The woman I'd liked before I became someone motivated by the wrong things.

"Let's go pick up those wiring supplies," Natalie said to me as we finished lunch and everyone got back to work. "Head up to the roof, Cole. We'll grab you when we get back," she told him and let Owen know where we were going. She looked at me and explained, "Miguel's a good foreman, but he's not as good at playing the bad guy if some of them start screwing around. Owen steps in when necessary."

"Is he onsite every day?" I asked as we loaded into her truck.

"Two days a week. He loves working with wood and grilling, but he's in his eighties, so he doesn't have the energy for it every day."

"Wow," I said, amazed that he'd even want to be there.

She started the engine and backed out of the drive. "He's a great guy. His wife, too, but I see Owen a lot more."

"And they're my neighbors."

"Along with his granddaughter and your landlord, yeah."

I shot wide eyes at her. "The cute strawberry from yesterday plays for our team?"

"Yep." Nat laughed at my shock.

"Well, damn, that means there are at least six lesbians in town now."

"More. Viv and Molly can introduce you."

I caught the mysterious smile she tried to hide as she sailed down Main Street. There must be something about one of them, and for the first time in years, I was actually looking forward to meeting anyone she or her friends wanted to introduce me to.

We pulled around the side of the building supply store and parked. As we got out of the truck, I recognized Molly walking toward us. Was this how it was in small towns? Mention someone and ten seconds later, she appears?

"Hey there," she greeted, coming to stop before us. Despite it being a cool late April day, she had on cargo shorts and short sleeve polo. Muscular biceps peeked out from under the cuffs of her shirt. Her calves were just as toned. Tan, too, which contradicted the season and elevation. Overall, she was an impressive total package for someone who went for that type.

"Hi, Mol. Viv said you got in some good practice for the pool tourney last night."

"We might even take James and Spence this year." Delight at the prospect animated her serious face. "Good to see you again, Falyn."

"Hi." My eyes lingered a bit. Definitely impressive, and if she went for the same kind of woman I did, major competition.

"You up for a bike ride on Sunday afternoon?" She somehow remembered Natalie's request about showing me the bike trails. Damn, she was nice, too. Now I'd never be able to compete.

"Sounds great," I agreed, already looking forward to it. For the first time in two years, I wouldn't be hanging out in a building store parking lot hoping to pick up a day job.

"We'll get some others to join us and find a scenic trail. Nothing too demanding. Should be fun."

"Great, thanks, Mol." Natalie squeezed her arm.

"I've got a tour group leaving in ten minutes." She pointed to a shop two doors away.

"Hike?" Natalie guessed.

"Horses, which means lots of griping about sore behinds. Yee-haw. I'll see ya." She tipped her head and moved past us.

Natalie glanced at me and must have read something in my expression. "She's great. You'll like her, really."

"I overreacted yesterday. I get that now." I had to stop it. With my conniving ex and the hypersensitive convicts, overreacting was a way of life. Before both, I was more reasonable and mellow. I wanted to work toward achieving that Zen again.

"It came from a good place." She pushed us into the store where she waved at the woman behind the counter and steered me to the power tool section. "Let's get you set up."

My feet reacted for my pocketbook, stepping back. I knew she was right because everything I had was low grade. They wouldn't last long on the job. I just couldn't afford to replace them now. "Listen, I'm a little short."

She nodded. "On me."

That pesky lump lodged in my throat again. "I can't do that, Nat. You've already done too much." Way too much.

"We'll work something out."

Swallowing hard, I tried to remember if the help I'd given her as a young woman compared to this. I didn't think it did, but I wasn't in a position to reject it anymore. "Thank you."

With my show of gratitude, a vaguely familiar feeling ran through me. Trust. After being ratted out by someone on the burglary crew and my ex-girlfriend taking advantage of my incarceration, it was hard to trust again. Prison didn't foster the feeling and parole was even worse. I trusted Natalie and she trusted me. Both felt better than anything I'd experienced in years.

4

The Sweeneys and I headed into the bar together. Natalie had offered to take me, but I knew she'd rather go straight from work with Vivian. It was nice of everyone to include me. This first week on the job had been long but satisfying. I was ready to unwind and have a day off.

"Sweeneys!" half the bar shouted when we walked inside.

A laugh escaped for probably the hundredth time this week. More than I'd laughed in the last eight years total. These guys were funny, childish sometimes, but funny. Apparently their antics were known everywhere.

Cole pulled on my arm to make sure he didn't lose me in the crowd we were slaloming through. My initial instinct was to yank my arm back, but I recognized in time that the gesture was thoughtful in this setting. In prison it would have been threatening.

"Hey, guys," Natalie greeted when we made it to the pool tables in back.

Vivian was lining up a shot. Molly and two guys were standing next to her table with cues in their hands. The rest of the tables were occupied by other teams competing in what Natalie told me was a charity tournament. The boys had entered as a team. I was here for moral support.

"Hey, Falyn." Glory appeared at my side with her partner.

"Good to see you, Glory. Hi, Lena." I nodded at the woman I met last night as she was walking her dogs past the house. Like with her grandfather, it only took a short conversation to know we'd get along fine.

"Have you met Vivian's sister-in-law, Cassie?" Glory asked, gesturing to the blonde behind her.

I hadn't but I'd met her husband when he came to check on his sister's house yesterday. "Nice to meet you."

"Nat's so happy you're here," Cassie bubbled, bumping her fist against Natalie's shoulder.

"We're up," Cole told me as he brushed past. "Sure you don't want to play?"

"I'm good."

"We could play for Joanna and Brandy," Natalie suggested to me. "Believe me, they're more concerned with who they'll be going home with than winning enough to stay in the tournament."

"I'm okay to watch." My eyes instantly searched for the two she mentioned. There were three female pairs at the tables. One of them did indeed seem more interested in the people around them than the games. If they were the pair, Natalie was wrong. They most definitely wanted to keep playing for the attention.

"Beer?" Natalie asked as she took a step toward the bar.

"Thanks," I responded, not wanting to be rude. Alcohol was a luxury item on my budget. I'd gotten used to being without it in prison. Same with caffeine. The fewer addictions you had inside, the easier you passed your time.

I glanced back over at Vivian's table. Molly was lining up the eight ball. Her two opponents looked perplexed at getting bumped in the first round. The Sweeneys were setting up at the table next to them. Glory and Cassie were stepping up to Vivian and Molly's table to take the next game. Odd pairings considering none of them were playing with their significant others. Never would have happened in prison or among my friends back in Denver. The women I've dated thrived on jealousy.

Natalie handed me the beer when she came back. She waved to get Vivian and Molly's attention. "Nice shot, Molly," she told her when they reached us.

"My donors are going to be pissed again this year." Vivian wrapped an arm around Molly's shoulders.

"They can't be surprised anymore." Molly didn't seem bothered that Vivian's sponsors might have been duped into a larger donation because of her billiards expertise. "Oh, hey, there's Tessa."

"Viv!" A blond woman pushed through two guys to get to us. "This place is packed." Her long, blond hair swished forward, covering her face for a moment when she came to a stop in front of the table. "Hey, all."

"Tessa!" Molly called out to a woman who wasn't the one standing in front of us.

"How'd you do, Joanna?" Natalie asked the nearby blonde.

"Lost the match, but whatever." Her blue eyes flicked to me then away then right back. "You're new."

"Falyn, this is Joanna. Oh, and Brandy," Natalie said, pointing to a second blonde who stepped up behind Joanna, squishing into our little space.

"Newbie." Brandy raised her brow at Natalie then shot a look at Joanna before extending a hand to me. "Hello."

"Hi." I shook her hand and nodded at Joanna whose eyes slithered over me. I stiffened before remembering that someone checking me out here wasn't a bad thing. I glanced over at Natalie just to be sure. Her easy gaze told me this was exactly what I thought it was and probably the reason for her mysterious smile when she mentioned meeting other lesbians. Something about these two reminded me of attack dogs.

A woman bumped into Joanna, brushing her against me. Not exactly subtle, but it was a crowded bar. "Sorry, Jo," the woman said.

"Hey, Tessa." Joanna's head barely turned to acknowledge the new woman.

"How ya doing, Tessa?" Molly asked, full of concern.

"Getting by," she responded and took the chair that Molly vacated for her. This blonde was short and cute. The other two were taller and hotter.

"Still not crying over that bitch, are you?" Joanna asked her.

"Jo!" Vivian scolded.

"What? Kathleen dumped her with no warning."

I glanced at Natalie again. She shrugged but gave me nothing else.

"I can't believe it." Brandy threw an arm around Tessa, who hadn't yet noticed that there was a new person at the table. "She was, like, the perfect girlfriend, right? Did you guys ever fight? She always paid whenever we all went out. She sent you flowers at work all the time. Ideal girlfriend."

Tessa's eyes filled. Molly's hand started rubbing her back as she shot a death glare at a clueless Brandy. "I don't know what happened."

"We're sorry." Vivian scowled at Brandy. "Breakups are really difficult."

Molly nodded, edging closer and adding her other hand to rub Tessa's arm. Her eyes looked as sad as Tessa's. "They always take you by surprise."

"No, I mean I really don't know what happened. We just got back from a wonderful vacation, and all of a sudden, she says it wasn't working anymore. I honestly thought she was joking, but the joke was on me."

"Did she give you the, 'I love you, but I'm not in love with you,' speech?" Joanna asked.

Tessa's face flamed as a tear raced down her cheek. "That's just it. She never actually said the words."

Molly straightened next to her, pulling on Tessa's arms to face her. "What words?"

"It's stupid, I know. She showed me all the time. I never thought about not hearing it. I just assumed she had a hard time saying it."

"What?" Joanna asked as confused as everyone else.

"I'd tell her I loved her all the time. She showed me but never said the words."

"Hold on, sister," Brandy said. "You guys were together three years, and she never once told you she loved you?"

Tessa sagged against Molly whose eyes had turned lethal. Interesting. She either really didn't like Tessa's ex or she was a lot more involved in Tessa's peace of mind than she first appeared to be.

"She didn't, did she? Christ, Tessa, there's a big clue for you," Brandy scoffed.

Whoa. That sounded insensitive to me, and I dealt with some pretty mean bitches over the years.

"Back off, Brandy," Molly barked at her.

My eyes flicked to Natalie again. She was wearing the same incredulous look I was. Even I, a complete stranger, was starting to feel sorry for Tessa.

"Fine. Let's talk about your new friend here, Natalie." Brandy gave me the same once over that Joanna had.

"She's an old friend, actually."

"What kind of friend?" Brandy asked while Joanna asked, "How old?"

"Knock it off," Vivian said, clearly exasperated by these two.

"Fine," Joanna said. "We'll let you get settled in, but we'll come visit you soon enough."

They both winked at me then turned and headed to the bar. Subtle as two skunks in a rose garden.

"Are they a package deal?" I asked Natalie.

She laughed and pushed at my shoulder. Molly chuckled, and Tessa sniffled a laugh. "Are we all set for the ride tomorrow, Mol?"

Molly nodded, squeezing Tessa for a moment. "Want to come? We're going to take Falyn up Government Trail."

"Don't think so." Tessa wiped her eyes.

"Oh, c'mon. A bunch of us are going. It'll be fun."

"Maybe. I'm waiting to hear back from those California buyers tomorrow."

"You work too hard," Molly said.

"That's what Kathleen always said."

Molly flinched, clearly upset at being compared to what sounded like a pretty dickish girlfriend. "Take a day off."

"I'll let you know."

Molly didn't look satisfied with the answer, but she was smart enough to realize that pushing harder might bring on additional tears. Tessa looked like a wreck at this point. She needed a tub of ice cream, a package of cookies, and a dozen episodes of some chick show to drown in for a while.

I wasn't sure if it would be more entertaining to have sad Tessa along for a ride with a bunch of people I didn't know. I might be able to figure out just how badly Molly had it for this lost cause, but it might be a little too much drama for an afternoon off.

"There's Rachel. I better go say hello," Tessa told us, giving Molly's hand a squeeze and moving toward the entrance.

"Did you know that about Kathleen?" Vivian asked Molly.

She shook her head, surprise rounding her eyes. "Three years and she never once told her she loved her? What kind of cold bitch is she?"

"Pretty cold."

"You never really liked her, though, did you? We all thought she was the perfect girlfriend, but you never seemed fooled."

Vivian shrugged. "Tessa vented about Kathleen a few times. I had a hard time moving past that."

"You were right."

"I don't like being right about stuff like that."

"You can say that again."

"I'm just glad I never have to worry about that, right, babe?" Vivian smiled at Natalie.

"Never," Natalie confirmed, leaning in for a soft kiss.

Molly rolled her eyes before landing on mine. She shrugged and smiled. Again, I found myself comfortable around her when I'd only just met her. A week in and things were a thousand times better for me already.

5

The gang Molly assembled for the bike ride ranged in skill from okay to expert. I liked them all, especially the two that slowed us down most of the afternoon. Dwight, another designer that Natalie worked with, and Kelsey, a friend of Molly's, made us laugh the entire day. Vivian added to their comedy routine by goading Dwight with tales of their design school days. Everyone got along, despite being a mixed bag of friends. I tried keeping track of who was whose friend and why their significant others weren't on the trip, but it only mattered that there was no sign of the drama from the bar last night. Of course, sad Tessa had skipped the bike ride.

"You're hardcore." Molly slipped back beside me on a mountain bike slightly nicer than mine. Her eyes skated over my pumping thighs.

"You're not even winded," I pointed out. I knew my cheeks would be red with exertion, but Molly looked like we were enjoying a ride on a neighborhood street instead of a rugged mountain trail.

"I wouldn't have a job if I were."

"There's no one crazy enough to do that job but you, Mol," Dwight called out from the back of the herd.

"You deal with rich d-bags who remodel their homes every year like they're playing in a dollhouse and you think I've got the crazy job?"

"Your rich d-bags ask you to ski them off a cliff in the winter," Kelsey piped up.

"My rich d-bags give you great tips, Kelsey. You should be on my side."

Her giggle turned into a groan. "Can we stop, please?"

"Mol's showing off," Dwight teased loud enough for everyone to hear.

"Shut it!" Molly barked but didn't seem truly bothered. She slowed her pace to a stop, so we could step off and take a look at the view.

"Got her." Lena nudged Dwight's shoulder as they chortled together.

Molly just shook her head, exasperated. "You want to stay sane in this town?" She drew a questioning brow at me. "Don't hang out with him." Her thumb jerked over her shoulder at Dwight.

"I'm your best friend," Dwight teased.

"You're my best pain," Molly teased back.

"Kids." Vivian stepped between them. "We're trying to make Falyn want to stay, not give her a reason to leave."

"Please," Natalie agreed. "She's only been here a week. She hasn't had to put up with any rich d-bags yet."

James, who was either Vivian or Dwight's friend, piped up, "I'm a rich d-bag."

"You're a city worker," his friend Spencer pointed out. That was how he'd introduced himself to me when I met him coming out of the house next to mine. Curtis later told me Spencer was actually the mayor.

"What's your story, Falyn?" Kelsey asked as we all took seats on an overhanging rock that looked out at one of the ski areas.

I felt my heart rate kick up. I never liked this question before I went to prison. Hated it after.

"We worked together back in Boulder," Natalie supplied for me, probably recognizing the panicked look on my face. "She was the only other woman on the crew. Remember that one guy?" She looked at me before continuing. "We had this foreman who spent half the workday taking bets on the stupidest things."

"Yeah, like how many times the klutz on the crew would drop his drill before morning break," I inserted, relieved that Natalie was giving me a "story" without giving the story.

"And the rest of the day smoking, drinking spiked coffee, and flirting with the lunch truck lady."

"No one flirts with me," Kelsey pouted as everyone laughed.

"Every man that takes one of our tours flirts with her when she drops off their catered lunches," Molly supplied for me. Both she and Natalie were helping to keep me from feeling lost in this tightknit group. It was a sweet gesture from a woman who didn't know me but must have felt obligated because she'd cobbled the group together.

"Every man in town flirts with her," Lena added.

My eyes roamed over Kelsey again. She was cute enough, but it was the big boobs that must prompt the excessive flirting.

"Exaggeration," Kelsey groaned.

"Ha! The last time you catered my client's post-reno housewarming party, you got two marriage proposals." Dwight slung an arm around her shoulders and squeezed until they were both laughing. He seemed to have that effect on everyone. "By the way, Natalie, darling, sweetie, lovely woman—"

"Uh-oh, I know that tone," Molly said. "Make a break for it while you can, Nat."

"Don't," Kelsey moaned and rubbed her thighs. "I can't move yet."

"As I was saying," Dwight sighed dramatically, making everyone smile. "Would you have time to stop by my project for a teensy, tiny, little job?"

"How is that a 'by the way?' And you never do little jobs," Vivian teased.

"We failed our last inspection. I'm desperate."

Everyone turned to James. "Don't blame me for Burt's incompetence. Time to get a new contractor."

That was the city work he did? A building inspector? Crazy. No contactor I'd ever worked with would spend two extra minutes with a city inspector.

"I would, but *somebody* keeps hogging the best contractor in town." Dwight shot blazing eyes at Vivian.

Everyone turned to look at her. She smiled smugly and wrapped her arms around Natalie. "Damn right I am."

"Please tell me I didn't look that sickening when Glory and I were getting together," Lena joked.

"Worse," Spencer retorted, getting a laugh. "She used to conveniently need to walk her dogs every night just as Glory was sitting out on her porch."

"Dogs need routine," Lena huffed, looking irked that Spencer had seen through her ruse.

Amusing group. No wonder Natalie hadn't bothered to move back to Boulder when her boss decided to expand to Aspen for a housing development project.

I frowned. That was about the time I met the guy who convinced me that breaking into homes would be a good way to add excitement and riches to my life. Before that, Natalie and our other friends kept my outlook and attitude in check.

"Eh-hmm, eyes back to me," Dwight kidded again. "So, Nat? Got time for a bid to save your good buddy's stellar behind?" He lifted to one side and showcased an admittedly nice butt.

She shook her head. "I'm watching every inch of Viv's home go up."

"Our home," Vivian inserted and kissed Natalie on the cheek.

"But you've got more people and a wonderful, talented electrician who can do my little job with her eyes closed. Surely you can find time to loan some of them to me?" He clasped his hands and pleaded with her.

She smiled as Vivian sighed. "If Falyn doesn't mind being tossed onto another site."

My eyes widened. No boss had ever asked if I cared where I was working each day. "I go where you tell me."

"Wonderful. It's settled then." Dwight clapped his hands before Natalie could say one way or another.

"You're in line behind me," Lena spoke up.

"What? No." Dwight looked at Natalie for confirmation.

"It's for the drama club," Lena told him.

"Oh, well, okay then. Everyone needs a good drama club."

"You're your own drama club," Molly muttered.

He looked both affronted and amused and about to start a verbal war that I knew I wouldn't be able to follow, so I asked, "What are we looking at?"

Molly pointed toward the mountain with skiers swishing their way down the slopes still abundant with snow. Very few traces of snow were left anywhere else. It was as if the mountain took it all from the rest of the town. "That's Snowmass." Her hand darted to the base of the mountain. "That's the Village."

"Good skiing for intermediates. How good are you?" James asked, assuming anyone who moved to Aspen would ski.

"Haven't been in a while." A long while, and given how inflated most prices had gotten, I doubted I'd be able to afford it if I stayed through the winter.

"You're welcome to join us on the bunny slopes with my nephews this winter," Vivian offered with a smile.

The statement warmed my heart. My boss's girlfriend wanted me to stay on past completion of the project I'd been hired for. This past week had been the best I'd experienced in eight years. Hell, probably fifteen since the years before prison weren't outright enjoyable either. It would be incredible to stay on Natalie's crew among these warm friends and engaging outdoor activities.

6

The house party was more of a rave than a party. When Brandy and Joanna came by the site to invite Vivian, Natalie, and me, I thought it might be a gathering of a few people, some bites of food, and a variety of wine. Instead, I walked into a raging mass of bodies, loud music, kegs, and flailing limbs on a makeshift dance floor.

"You made it." Brandy appeared at my side. "Come dance with me."

"Let her breathe first, B." Joanna took up my other side. "Grab a beer and we'll introduce you around."

I wondered again how old these women were. They acted as young as the Sweeney brothers, but the crinkle of skin around their eyes told me they were closer to my mid-forties.

People vied for their attention as they walked me to the keg. They did a masterful job of keeping everyone happy while continuing with the squeeze on me. It might have been a mistake coming here. Large gatherings weren't my thing, and this was as crowded as the yard on a rainy day when all the blocks emptied out at once instead of in shifts.

Joanna handed me a beer and curled her hand around my elbow to lead me toward a more private corner. I wasn't sure that was such a good idea either. Natalie said she'd try to make it so I wouldn't be here alone, but she wasn't much for crowds either.

"Hey, Falyn," Molly called as she appeared through the crowd.

Relief rinsed through me when I saw her. It wasn't that I knew her well, but I was out of my comfort zone here. Any familiar face would help.

"We were just taking some time to get to know her, Mol." Brandy's voice had a little edge.

Molly flicked her eyes between us before landing on mine in question. Well, that was sweet. She was looking out for me. "I'll go find Tessa," Molly said to me, blatantly ignoring Brandy's warning. "See you later."

"She's going to flip when she finds out we invited Kathleen," Joanna said to Brandy.

Even I started at that. Seemed a little callous. Picking sides after a breakup sucked, but it seemed like Tessa was the more entrenched with their group of friends than Kathleen had been.

"Are they really close?" I asked of Molly and Tessa.

"Wouldn't say close. Vivian and Tessa are close because of their work, and Molly's tight with Vivian."

So they didn't see it? Molly couldn't be this attentive with everyone. Then again, maybe I was imagining things like I had with Molly and Vivian.

"Excuse us a sec," Joanna said and dragged Brandy away.

I took a sip of beer and immediately looked for a place to spit it out. The food options looked as cheap as the beer. I could probably slip out and join the boys at the bar they said they were going to, but I needed to make an effort to get to know more people.

"Hi, Falyn," Dwight greeted, coming to a stop before me. "Bit crowded in here, isn't it?"

"Hey there. Didn't know this was your scene." My eyes slid over his party getup. His slim frame was sheathed in designer casual. I hadn't put as much effort into my appearance, not having the clothing budget he clearly did. Maybe in a few months I might be able to afford a full off-work wardrobe, but for now, my one pair of khakis and two button-down shirts were how I rolled.

"J&B have a way of corralling all the single people in town."

"This is every single person in town?"

"I wouldn't be surprised." He reached for a loaded cracker but his brain must have thought better, stopping his hand halfway. "Hey, did Molly tell you that next weekend is river guide training?"

My brow drew down. "No. Why would she?"

"When she trains the other river guides, she needs willing volunteers to fill the boat. Free rafting trips on the Roaring Fork all day. You up for it?" His brown eyes revealed his excitement.

"Sounds fun, but I'd have to hear from Molly first."

"Hear what?" Molly appeared at that moment with Tessa by her side.

I nodded hello to both as Dwight said, "I was telling her about the training."

"Oh, yeah, great. What do you say? I'm trying to get Tessa to go, too." She looped an arm around Tessa's shoulders.

"Sounds fun if Nat doesn't have something going with work." It also sounded a little dangerous, but I wasn't about to wimp out without even trying it. Not when Dwight was jumping out of his pants to raft and Molly offered the trip as nonchalantly as she would a Sunday drive.

"Cool. Let me know."

"Oh my God," Tessa breathed, her eyes darting away from the front door.

"What?" Molly asked, following her line of sight. "Shit. What's she doing here?"

I turned and saw a voluptuous brunette making her way through the crowd. By the angry look on Molly's face, I'd guess this was the infamous Kathleen. She didn't look as broken up as Tessa was, but then again she'd been the one to end things with a woman she never claimed to love.

"I need to talk to her." Tessa jerked forward.

"Tess," Dwight said as Molly grabbed her arm to keep her from leaving.

"No, I need to talk to her. She hasn't returned my calls."

Molly lurched with Tessa, but Dwight stopped her with a shake of his head. He took over the escorting duties, probably seeing the anger tightening Molly's muscles. At least he was smart about it, leading Tessa to the balcony. If she was going to make a scene, better to do it outside alone.

"Those stupid bitches," Molly growled, her eyes glaring at Joanna, who was walking toward us until she caught Molly's look and pivoted to talk to someone else. "You got dropped into the middle of some drama."

"Seems so." I was used to it. She didn't know drama until she watched a prison love triangle play out.

"J&B love doing crap like this."

"Really?" Seemed like J&B were a hazardous combination of egotism and mischief making.

"They find it amusing."

"They do something like this to you before?"

She scoffed, took a sip of her beer, made the same face I had and forced a swallow. "I'm a favorite victim of theirs."

"Give me an example," I pushed because she didn't seem too upset about it.

An amused snort left her lips. "When Lena first moved to town, J&B told me she'd seen me at work and thought I was attractive. They gave me her number and said she was waiting for me to ask her out. When I called, not only was she not interested but she didn't even know who I was."

I whistled softly. "Tundra. Is that their deal?"

"I've known them for years and still don't know the answer to that." She leaned back against the wall next to me and picked an imaginary piece of lint from dark jeans that fit her well without being too tight. Her lightweight sweater clung to her just enough to show her fit frame. I'd always been the fittest one of my friends. That wouldn't be holding true here. "Piece of advice?"

My eyes rolled over her, assessing. Did I want to hear this? "Sure."

"They're going to be all over you until you give in or push back. They get upset when you choose. Tourists can choose, but someone who lives here can have both or neither. Don't show preference for one or the other."

"Seriously?" Now that wasn't a situation I ran into every day in prison.

"I've seen it a few times. It's a big competition for them."

"Yeah, that's not weird."

She smiled at my sarcastic comment. It transformed her face. Her resting expression looked hard, but her smile brightened her eyes, softened her mouth, and augmented her cheekbones. The tiny silver hoops in her earlobes glinted with the slight movement of her jaw, drawing more attention to her femininity. I wouldn't go so far as to call her pretty, but she definitely had appeal. Far more so than Kathleen. Too bad Tessa was too wound up to see it yet.

"Did you learn the hard way?" I asked, now fascinated by the behavioral patterns of the local lesbian Lotharios.

"Not me. Thought about it, but it could make a small town even smaller, you know?" Her brown eyes conveyed sincerity. "Not trying to influence you one way or the other, especially if you're not sticking around. Are you?"

"That'll be up to Nat."

"Thought she really wanted you here?" Her interest seemed genuine, which wasn't something I was used to.

"She has to have the work. I'm not going to be dead weight on her crew."

"You know her and Viv's last project was for a reality television personality, right?"

"Some of the guys mentioned that." And the crazy reality star they had to deal with. It sounded equal parts insane and exciting.

"Probably going to get a lot of referrals once those episodes air."

I felt my eyebrows rise. "Hope so for Nat's sake."

"It will be nice having another outdoorsy type to hang with. Viv's been a bit busy of late."

I could bet she'd been busier and what she'd been busier doing. "Vivian seems great. Good for Natalie, too."

"Natalie is wonderful to her. Sweet lady."

"You should have seen her when she was a kid."

"You go back that far?"

I realized that Natalie might not want her history known. She'd never told anyone else on our old crew about her parents kicking her out when she was barely sixteen. "I say kid, but she was a young woman. Kept her head down, did better work than anyone on the crew, and way too sweet for someone working construction. Way too sweet for someone working in a candy shop, really."

Molly laughed three short bursts of sound that warmed the energy around us. "Anyway, hope you stick around." She bumped my shoulder and headed toward the balcony.

I wanted to shake my head, seeing her situation for the train wreck I thought it might become. By the look of the conversation Tessa was having with Kathleen, it didn't matter if Kathleen was done with her, Tessa wasn't. Poor Molly was in for the uphill climb of her life if she kept pursuing this.

7

Lena walked down the auditorium's center aisle toward us. "How's it going?" She directed her question at me after watching Natalie do the same the night before.

"On track," I replied, not sure how much Natalie wanted me to say. My old crew chiefs would bite my head off if I got specific on timelines or problems. They liked to use the chance to up their fee or extend the deadline. I hadn't seen anything like that with Natalie, but then again, we'd only been working on her girlfriend's house.

Cole, Natalie, and I were on our second night revamping the electrical setup in the high school auditorium. The rest of the crew was back at Vivian's working to get the house dried-in. Given a choice, I'd much rather be here than hanging off a ladder affixing thousands of cedar shingles as siding.

"I brought dinner." Lena set the bags on the stage.

"You didn't have to do that again," Natalie told her.

"Did Tamiko cook?" Cole shouted down from the rafters where he was hanging a spotlight. He'd asked the same thing last night when Lena walked in with pizza boxes.

Lena beamed, causing Cole to clamber down the steps faster than he'd moved all night. Having tasted her grandmother's cooking on Sunday night, I knew this food would live up to his enthusiasm. "You're saving my school budget for the next two years. It's the least I can do."

My brow rose involuntarily at the reminder that Natalie was donating the labor for this job. It didn't matter that they were friends and Lena was the principal here. The money she could make from a government contract like this could help meet all her revenue goals for the quarter. Natalie explained that Lena was one of the people who encouraged the start of her company. That and Glory's continued help with the financial side of her business was enough payment for her. Three weeks on the job and I was still amazed at the woman Natalie had become.

Cole was busy pulling containers from the bag, inspecting each as he set them on the stage. I twisted the locknut onto the cable clamp in the box I was finishing before the aroma called me to join him. He grabbed a chicken dish and poured half the container onto his plate. Natalie elbowed him and salvaged some for herself and Lena. I went for the stir-fry veggies, noodles, and rice before Cole could wipe those out, too. We'd worked out a fair system with the food we shared at home, but sometimes their appetites got the better of us all and we had to shop more often. I didn't mind, especially since they put in twice as much as I did for the grocery tab.

Halfway through dinner, the auditorium doors opened. Vivian, Molly, and Glory walked in chatting happily. Natalie mentioned having evenings plans, so I figured they were here to pull her away. She'd put in a full day at Vivian's house, unlike Cole and me, and deserved some free time tonight.

"Tamiko's?" Molly called out as she walked down the aisle, her eyes sparkling.

"Yep," Cole said through a mouthful of noodles.

"There's extra," Lena told her.

"Score! Hand it over," Molly said.

"We just came from dinner, Mol." Vivian shot her a disbelieving look.

"I've always got room for Tamiko's." The way she said it made it sound like it was a restaurant in town. She grabbed a tempura zucchini and chomped on it happily, taking the space on the edge of the stage next to me. "How's your stomach?"

I swallowed a forkful of rice and grimaced. "Fine."

The rafting trip last weekend had been a lot hairier than I anticipated. I'd nearly been pitched out twice from mistakes the new guides made. The experience was enough to make me queasy. Molly tried to assure me that it wouldn't be that scary the next time I went, but it was good that the mistakes occurred while she could correct them.

"I'm not fine," Glory told her. She'd sat opposite me and went through the same hairy experience. "Ron's not actually hiring those guys is he?"

"Wayne and I have to ride with them their first few times. If they don't improve, Ron will have to find others."

"He must be desperate for guides if he thinks those two are anything like you and Wayne."

"Summer help is always spotty." Molly shrugged not bothered by what could mean a more rigorous work schedule. I knew how she felt. Whenever a boss added extra crew to get a job done, it seemed like my workload doubled trying to help them or fix their mistakes.

"Maybe I should run a spreadsheet for him to show the benefit of not hiring incompetents." Glory smiled brightly.

Everyone laughed at the idea that a spreadsheet could be as convincing as she thought it would be. Apparently she was very good at her accounting job, but it would take a pretty sexy spreadsheet to make a business owner walk away from potential business.

"When are you done here?" Molly asked me as the others started talking about the movie they were going to see later.

"We've got another three days at least."

"Then you'll be back on regular hours?"

"Should be. This was a special deal." Cole and I were starting our work days after school let out and working until midnight. The schedule took a day to get used to, but I didn't mind the odd hours.

Molly nodded, finishing a gyoza dunked in teriyaki sauce. "I'm taking groups out almost every evening for hikes or biking the trails if you ever want to join us. In the summer, it's the only way I get to see my friends sometimes since I work day and evening tours on weekends. My boss doesn't mind unless it's a private booking. Lena, her friend Kirsten, and Glory's business partner Brooke join me a lot. Some of the others you met last time come occasionally, but you seemed like you really enjoyed the ride. You'd probably like everything else we do, and it's a great way to learn the trails around here."

The offer felt good, like so many other things since moving here. Molly was a comfortable person to be around and liked being outdoors. Even when I felt like I'd been flush with friends back in Boulder, I didn't have anyone who enjoyed outdoor recreation as much as I did. Based on the biking tour Molly led, I got the impression that no one else in the group was like that either. I'd have to take her up on her offer. She was cool enough that I didn't feel like I needed Natalie as a buffer anymore.

8

The backpack was starting to get heavy. How did Molly manage this with so much ease every day? Not only that, she was now carrying Tessa's backpack as well. I didn't know what the tiny blonde was thinking, showing up with a backpack the size of a small bear, but she'd hauled it up the mountain okay. It was the last part of the downhill trek where she'd run out of steam.

"How long are you in town?" one of Molly's tourists asked Joanna.

Brandy snickered beside me. Molly hadn't told us to lie to the people taking her tour, but Joanna and Brandy seemed to relish playing someone they weren't. They'd made up some story about getting in one last spring ski run before jetting off to their homes in the Riviera. Honestly. The Riviera. And neither of them had accents.

When Molly called at lunch to see if I wanted to round out her small tour group this evening, I jumped at the offer. Curtis and Luis bummed invitations when they heard me talking to Molly. As casual as she was with allowing them to join in, I was still surprised to see Joanna, Brandy, Tessa, and Dwight loading into the van when we arrived at the shop. Molly's friends outnumbered the tour group seven to three.

I packed a few water bottles and the first aid kit into my backpack to help ease Molly's usual load. She said no one ever brought enough water, and she was required to bring a pretty involved first aid kit every time. At only half her normal load, my backpack with the snacks and extra sweatshirt I'd packed weighed almost as much as my new toolbox. It prompted a more thorough perusal of her figure. Her calves and thighs were well defined and her ass was a thing of beauty, both for its musculature and shape. I had no doubt under the polo she had a powerful back and visible abs. When she'd hefted Tessa's backpack onto one shoulder, I had a moment's pause, wondering why I'd never gone for a woman with her build before.

"Just the week," Joanna was telling the flirtatious woman. Her hand with its outrageously colored manicure gripped the woman's forearm as if she needed help walking down the trail. "How about you? If you're staying the night, we should grab a drink. I know all the local hotspots that tour books don't tell you about."

Considering the woman had started her flirtatious ways with Luis, I wouldn't have guessed she'd be interested. But apparently, Joanna and Brandy didn't let a thing like sexual preference bother them.

Brandy didn't try to hide her amused snort this time. The dark red manicure on her nails didn't match her skimpy halter top or tiny shorts, but it was starting to resemble the color of her skin at the base of her neck and tops of her thighs where the breeze attacked. Even in May, the evening air could grow chilly. She had to know that being a local, but she'd forsaken warmth for sex appeal. That had never been my thing. Sure, I was in shorts, but they were much longer and I was in layers on top with a backup sweatshirt. Of course, I wasn't trying to seduce one of Molly's tourists. Or one of her friends.

Her painted fingernails rubbed down my arm. "Looks like Jo's going to be busy tonight. I'll have the apartment all to myself. Want to keep me company?"

Molly's head turned to cut a look at Brandy and me. Her lips pursed, holding back a smile. I joined in her amusement. This was the third time Brandy tried to sound casual in her invitations for sex with me. Joanna offered twice before I'd even gotten into the van tonight.

I gave Brandy another once over. Her blond hair was twisted into some fancy style that kept it off her face and neck. Before getting involved with my ex-girlfriend, I would have gone for her in a second. Boulder was big enough for casual hookups. Aspen really wasn't without making sure the casual nature of the relationship was reciprocal. I knew Brandy wanted casual, and it was tempting, but I trusted Molly's judgment more than I wanted casual sex with a beautiful woman who could turn crazy.

"Can't, thanks. Early morning."

Her hand gripped my elbow as she fluttered her eyelashes at me. She stumbled when she realized it wasn't a good idea not to pay attention while traversing rough terrain. "C'mon, Falyn. We're only here for a week, remember?" She grinned, reminding me of the lie she and Joanna had told to the tourist lady.

I shook my head, hopefully putting an end to her pressure tonight. My eyes shot to Tessa, worried that Brandy may now make a play for her. I didn't want to inadvertently screw up Molly's deal. Tessa glanced back at me, a smile on her face. Didn't look like I needed to worry. Joanna and Brandy's antics must be well known to every lesbian in town.

When Brandy slipped back to double team the single tourist, Dwight sidled up next to me. "Good call, lady."

I shrugged because I wasn't entirely sure I could keep putting either of them off. It had been seven months for me, and these two were hot and ready.

"Chances are high that Jo would come home at the worst possible moment and get pissy with Brandy."

"Seriously?" I laughed. It didn't matter if they were hot and easy. Best just to avoid spectacles like that.

"Seriously. Wait for the softball league in Glenwood Springs to start. Your prospects will increase tenfold."

That sounded promising and smart, but damn Brandy had all the right curves and it had been a long time. Better not, though. At least not tonight.

"You play?" Molly asked, taking up my other side. In her professional capacity she proved informative, encouraging, and entertaining. The whole trek up she'd given the three tourists as much attention as they wanted without becoming obnoxious about the activity or the area. I'd learned a lot about the town, the resorts, and what to look out for while hiking in the area.

"Not recently." Or in years. It wasn't like softball was added to the prison activity schedule each spring.

"It's mostly for fun. I'll tell our coach if you're interested."

Softball, women watching, beers after the games, yet another aspect of my old life falling into place. Even when I had my girlfriend, I never missed a Sunday game. With Molly on the team, it might be a lot of fun. It was plain to see why Vivian considered her such a good friend. She could easily become that for me.

"Yeah, why not?" I felt the enthusiasm I used to feel starting to come back to me. Why not indeed. How my life had changed in the space of a month. And all for the better.

9

Molly's sofa was really comfortable. Any sofa would be comfortable considering I rarely got to sit on the one at home because the boys were always lounging on it playing video games. But Molly's was especially comfortable. Suede or microfiber, whatever the material, it cradled every part of me.

"Water or coffee?" Molly called out from the kitchen.

I pushed deeper into the formfitting cushions and propped my overworked feet up on the ottoman. They throbbed a little from the hike today because Molly could work a trail down to a rut. The dull ache felt good. Having a buddy who liked the same kinds of activities I liked felt even better. That she didn't judge me for being in prison, or worse, ask what it was like being in prison was amazing. Who knew people would be so curious about life inside when they were never in danger of going to prison?

"I brought you both." Molly sat next to me, placing two mugs and a bottle of water on the coffee table.

"Thanks." I reached for the water.

This was becoming a bit of a habit. Molly would call whenever she had a small tour group. I'd join her on the hike or bike ride, then we'd head to a bar for a couple of drinks to end the night. Tonight, we'd had one too many to drive, so we walked back to her place to sober up before I drove home. It surprised me how quickly I fell back into the more than once a week drinking habit now that I had a decent paycheck.

"You might just want to crash here. I've got more beer and plenty of bad TV. Or the Rockies are probably on."

I thought about going home and finding the boys wearing out the Xbox or having some of the other guys over to watch the same baseball game. I'd rather watch the game with Molly then a bunch of loud dudes. Crashing here might be fun.

I gestured to the remote. Molly smiled and flicked on the television. She settled in next to me and again I thought how nice it was to be relaxed around someone. Relaxation didn't happen in prison, and friends after prison were hard to come by.

"Glad you moved from Boulder?" she asked.

"Denver, and yes."

Her brow furrowed. "Natalie mentioned Boulder."

"That's where we worked together. After I got...uh, moved to Denver." I was shocked at what almost jumped out of my mouth. I'd never actually said the words. *After I got out of prison.* Everyone who knew me before already knew. Only Natalie had stayed the same. My other friends dropped me. A few tried to keep up the pretense of politeness until I got the hint with all the unanswered phone calls and canceled plans. The few acquaintances I made at work would put in for other schedules when the dickhead line manager made a point of letting my ex-con status known. I hadn't met anyone I wanted to tell or needed to tell since. Yet with Molly, I'd almost just blurted it out. I couldn't chance that she'd react like Natalie. I didn't know her that well yet, and I liked her too much to lose her friendship. I felt conflicted about keeping this from her but not conflicted about how good it felt to have someone give me the same consideration as she would anyone else.

"Never lived there," Molly continued, oblivious to my internal debate. "I go in every once in a while. Only place to find more than ten lesbians."

I laughed. According to her, I'd met pretty much all the lesbians in town, but Joanna and Brandy rounded up the tourists better than an escort service. I'd met more lesbians over the past five weeks than I had in my two years in Denver.

"How'd you connect up with Nat again?"

"She was dropping someone off at the airport, and we ran into each other." Not at the airport, but Molly didn't need to know the embarrassing truth. Natalie was picking something up at the building supply store, and I was loitering in the parking lot with twenty other desperate for work guys trying to make some extra cash on the weekends. Having her see me in that situation had been pretty mortifying, but she made it okay for me. Like she was making this restart on my life okay for me.

"Lucky."

"For me, very." Understatement of the year. She'd saved me from many impending hardships given my financial situation and employment outlook.

"I was just curious when I asked this before, but now I'm invested. You are planning to stay, right?"

A smile crept across my face. It was nice hearing she enjoyed our budding friendship as much as I did. "I'd like to. Affordable housing is going to be a problem. Nat pays more than my last job, but Aspen is more expensive than Denver."

"One of my neighbors is thinking of moving out. The landlord would give you a good rate because you're handy. She'd rather have a no hassle renter for less income than her other tenants who call her when a light bulb needs changing."

"I won't know until we finish the house and Nat picks up more work, but thanks. Let me know if the neighbor leaves." I finished off the bottle of water, already starting to feel the buzz leave me. I could safely drive home, but I didn't want to. I'd rather celebrate the normalcy of hanging with a good friend. Of all the things I missed in prison, this luxury was at the top of the list.

"Did you decide what to do about J&B?"

I snorted at the recurring topic. Sometimes I brought it up, and other times she did. One or the other of them called to try to make plans at least once a week. The game they'd started had become somewhat amusing, especially since I could make fun of their efforts with Molly. "Nope. They know how to pour on the pressure though."

"Wait until they drop by your work for a tour. That's when you know they're really getting serious. They aren't the least bit interested in design or construction work."

I chuckled, glad I'd listened to Molly's first warning. I couldn't know just how involved they'd get in trying to one up each other if I slept with one or the other. "So," I drew out because Molly was having a little too much fun at my predicament. "What are you doing about Tessa?"

She whipped her head around. Suspicious brown eyes bored into me. "What about Tessa?"

"C'mon, Molly, I'm an outsider. You can tell me." She needed to tell someone. If she talked it out maybe she'd see how difficult her quest would be.

"Tell you what?"

Her earnest tone gave me pause. I didn't want to force her to talk about it, but I wanted to let her know she could trust me. "You like her, right?"

"No. I mean, sure. We're buddies and she's going through a rough time." She couldn't keep my gaze.

"A rough time that includes crying over a chick who never loved her and being willing to take that chick back when another chick is pining for her."

As convoluted as my observation was, she seemed to follow it. She held up a hand to wave me off. "No way, man."

"Like I said, I'm an outsider. If you need someone to talk to, I'm your woman."

She seemed to consider that for a moment. "I'm not hung up on her."

"She's single, she's pretty, she's your type." I counted each point on my fingers.

"How do you know my type?" Her gaze came back to mine with that familiar playful smile on her lips.

"Tessa, Glory, J&B. You like the pretty ones but not the gorgeous ones like Vivian, or I assume that's why you never made a play for her."

Her head dipped back, eyes large and amused. "They're the only ones in town."

"There was Nat."

"Nat's hotter than pretty."

"That's for sure," I agreed. "Which brings us back to Tessa and your unrequited longing."

Her laugh was a sharp bark this time. "Zip it, sister."

"All right, but I'm a good listener."

She sighed and admitted, "Kathleen's a bitch."

"Is she a bitch for what she did to Tessa?" I gave her a second to ponder that before posing, "Or is she a bitch because she can get Tessa back in a second even being the bitch she is?"

Molly's gaze pinned me in place. That one hit home. "Let's talk about you. Ever have a thing with Natalie?"

I choked in surprise. "She was way too young when I knew her." When I met her, I should say. We'd established our relationship as big sister and little sister. No way I'd screw that up even when she got all hot and stuff.

"Otherwise you would have been all for her?" Molly's teasing tone resurfaced.

"I like the pretty ones, too." Which was why I'd never gone for the toned, non-girly types like Molly. When pretty was around, all other types got lost in the background.

"And Nat's not pretty?"

"She's hot, alluring, magnetic." Sexy androgynous rather than pretty.

"Sizzling and very attached."

"Yep, and I'm really happy for her." Envious, too.

"Me, too, for Viv."

"So, we're just two chicks happy for our close friends who are madly in love and looking for love ourselves?"

"In a tiny town with almost no singles around, yep." She raised her coffee mug to mine to clink. After taking a swig, she settled back next to me.

I didn't get nervous that we'd run out of things to talk about while the game was on. I didn't get nervous that it would be awkward to get this couch ready to crash on tonight. I wasn't even nervous about seeing her in the morning after taking advantage of her hospitality. We had that kind of camaraderie now, and it made me very happy.

10

No one should have as much fun in a Bobcat as Molly was having right now. As soon as Tyler stepped out of the rented mini-loader, Molly swung herself up into it. She'd been taunting Tyler for over an hour while he joined the rest of us planting, raking, and shoveling in the front and backyards. She got to relocate trees, unload materials, and push things around all while sitting down. Tyler looked dejected. I'll admit to being a little envious, but honestly, she was helping Vivian out and we were getting paid. It was the least we could allow.

"Ty, stop whining, dude," Luis scolded him. "Move some of that river rock over here."

"Mol can do it." He shot another longing look at the Bobcat as it whizzed by us.

"Use your shovel." Miguel made the motion of digging into the pile of rocks.

"I shoulda called in sick today," Tyler griped as he plowed into the pile and scooped out a shovelful for the wheelbarrow.

I kept my chuckle silent. Six weeks on the job and I hadn't seen one person call in sick yet. I wondered if they knew how different they were from every other crew I'd ever worked with. They didn't show up late without first calling Natalie, they didn't leave early without first telling Natalie, and they didn't just not show, ever.

"Be glad Nat is letting us do this in May instead of waiting until August," Miguel said. "I'll take 70's and breezy over 90's and blazing for landscaping any day."

"Yeah, or we could be getting screamed at by Mini-Cal right about now," Ramón told Tyler.

"Hell no, man. We barely escaped that nimrod."

"Who's this?" I asked.

"Our old boss's son. Dude hadn't ever picked up a drill, and he becomes project manager the second he clears high school."

That would have sucked. I'd worked with some real assholes in Boulder, but at least they all had construction experience. "Must be great to be out of that mess, huh?"

"You know it, Fos," Luis confirmed.

"Thought I'd miss the overtime, but I'd rather have the comp time to coach my kid's soccer team," Tyler said.

"No screaming fits," Ramón inserted.

"The boss works the job with us instead of showing up for a half hour and yelling," Miguel pointed out.

"No working outside in the middle of winter," Luis said.

"A whole week off after every major job," Cole spoke up.

"Paid!" Curtis joined in.

"Paid!" Ramón agreed.

"Oh, yeah, gotta love that consistent salary!" Luis bumped Cole's fist.

Sure did. Even when I was making a lot more doing only electrical work, no scheduled job for the day or week meant no paycheck. Natalie annualized the salary and paid every two weeks whether we worked or not. The guys told me they'd had three paid weeks off in less than a year. She promised another as soon as we were done with this house.

"Guys, we've got one more shipment of materials coming in fifteen minutes," Natalie said as she approached with an empty wheelbarrow.

"That means stop yakking and start shoveling," Miguel interpreted.

"Samantha needs another set of hands in the backyard." She switched to the other wheelbarrow we'd been filling with rocks.

"All me," Luis jumped forward before anyone else could ditch the shovel duty.

Ramón slapped Cole's shoulder as they both watched him dart around the house to the backyard. "He should just ask her out. He's making a dweeb of himself flitting around her like this."

The Bobcat came to a stop beside us. Molly grinned down at everyone. "Damn, this thing is fun."

"Yeah," Tyler muttered.

"Paid," Miguel reminded him

"You tried this yet, Falyn?" She gestured me up. "Nat? Want to get in on this action? It's your rental."

"I'm good. You keep doing what you're doing." Natalie hefted the handles in front of her and pushed the wheelbarrow into motion.

"Was she always a workaholic like that, Fos?" Tyler watched as the shortest and slightest person on the crew maneuvered easily through the native plants we'd already planted.

"She never liked just sitting around, that's for sure."

"Fos?" Molly looked down at me.

"My initials," I supplied.

"Give it up, sister." Her eyes twinkled, and I was beginning to realize just how many of her emotions they revealed.

"Oprah," Ramón guessed.

"Opie," Tyler submitted.

"Olive Oyl," Miguel put in.

"Osiris," Curtis offered.

"Oligarchy," Cole said.

We were all laughing by the time everyone had a go. I never guessed there were that many "O" options.

"Well?" Molly asked.

"Ophelia. Do not quote *Hamlet* to me, please."

"It's…" she searched for the right word.

"Cute," Curtis kidded while Cole said, "Darling."

"Sweet," Tyler added to prolong the torture.

"Adorable," Miguel joked.

"Precious," Ramón said and got the biggest laugh.

Molly shook her head at them and shared a look with me. "Distinguishing."

"That means 'freaky,' right?" Tyler asked.

"Be nice or you'll never get on this thing today." Molly grinned down at him. "You're probably a Michael or a David."

"How'd you know?"

"I swiped your wallet at the bar last week."

His eyes widened as his gloved hand reached around to his back pocket. The panic left his gaze when he felt the bump of his wallet. "Bobcat stealing, fun having killjoy."

She held her hands up and hopped down from the machine. "It's yours till the next truck comes."

"Oh, yeah." He raced up into the controller seat.

Molly grabbed up his shovel and stood next to me, digging into the diminishing pile of river rock. "You've been out here a while. You should see the progress they've made in the backyard."

"Last wheelbarrow full. I'll give Nat a break and take a look." I glanced at her. "It's really nice of you to help out."

"It was this or watch daytime TV and fold laundry."

"Daytime TV," Ramón voted, taking a long swig of water from his thermos.

"How many times do you really care if the guy turns out to be the baby-daddy?" Molly asked him, attacking the rock pile with vigor.

"My favorite is when they've been fighting all show, calling each other names, and once he finds out he's the baby-daddy, he's all loving and kissing and stuff. You can't script entertainment like that," Ramón told us.

I studied him because I couldn't tell if he was serious. Those kinds of shows were very popular in the community room at prison, mostly because it gave the women a reason to shout at men. This was the first I'd heard of men liking them.

"He's just hoping to be invited on one of the shows some day," Miguel told us.

"You guys up for an ATV trek Saturday night?" Molly asked. "We had eight people going but six just canceled. They already paid for the rentals." She got confirms from three of the guys then turned to me. "Falyn?"

"Sure," I agreed. It had to be better than the horseback riding last week that made my rump ache for hours. Probably as much as my arms and shoulders would ache tonight after shoveling most of the day.

"Viv and Nat are taking me to dinner tonight for helping out today. You should come."

"Nat never buys me dinner," Ramón grumbled.

"She just bought you lunch," Miguel reminded him of the barbequed chicken Owen had put on today.

"It's not dinner," Ramón said.

"Who's whining now," Curtis joked.

Molly leaned into me. "You deal with this every day?"

"These guys are angels compared to some of the people I've worked with," I told her in a low voice.

But Ramón managed to hear me. "Got that right. Angels with wings and everything."

We all laughed again. Compared to some of the other electricians and everyone I had work detail with in prison, these guys were angels. And I enjoyed every minute of working with them.

11

Black curls blew into my face from the breeze on the bar's patio. The woman who sported the black curls was leaning into me, whispering something in my ear. Whatever she was saying made no sense. The words were slurred and out of order from all the wine she'd consumed. I stared at her friend wondering why she wasn't doing something to protect her from being taken advantage of, but she was busy flirting with the third basemen on our team.

Molly caught my stare and turned a knowing smile toward the two women who were trying to get her attention. I shook my head as the woman gripped my neck and brushed her lips against my ear. She must really want to get her point across. Our entire outfield was staring at her draped over me. They were wide-eyed and grinning. Men and their fantasies.

When Molly suggested we join a Wednesday night co-ed team instead of her usual Sunday night all women's team, I was a little hesitant. She couldn't get Sunday nights off this summer, so she wanted to play with a few of her friends on this co-ed team instead of finding a women's team. I agreed to fill in occasionally, not wanting to commit to something permanent.

"You're the hottest wingman Kirk's ever had." Peter leaned into my other ear. "He's going to get lucky with her friend, and she's climbing all over you."

Peter played beside me in left field and seemed decent, but like most men, seeing a woman on another woman made him forget the decency. His eyes kept darting between me and Molly. The two women trying to win her favor were at least standing a few inches away from her. I was practically wearing drunk lady.

I pushed at the woman leaning onto me, blowing her curls out of the way. "You've had enough, hon. Time for you to get a cab home."

She whined far longer than any person over the age of five should whine. "You could take me home."

I wasn't sure what planet I was living on, but since moving to Aspen, I'd been hit on by three pretty hot women. My ex-girlfriend hadn't been anywhere near as hot as Joanna, Brandy, or this woman. She'd been pretty enough but not really hot. Her other qualities were what I'd liked until some of them encouraged me to do things I shouldn't have done.

Molly somehow recognized a look she'd never seen in my eyes before because she leaned forward on the table to say, "She's my ride home, sweetheart."

The curls swished around as her head turned to look at Molly. "Oh, are you two together?"

Flames shot from the eyes of the Molly groupies before she chuckled and said, "No."

The rest of the outfield swung their heads back and forth watching the conversation play out. Peter's brow rose in question toward me, like I'd have a different answer for him. I wouldn't have let this woman drape herself all over me if Molly and I were together.

"Next game?" the woman asked me.

I felt my pulse kick up at the prospect. She was the look I generally went for, but I wouldn't even consider taking her home if she got sloppy drunk again. I tilted my head and smiled, not wanting to give a promise.

"I'm going, Francine. You staying?" she was talking to her friend who had her tongue down Kirk's throat. Francine waved her off. "Walk me out?" she batted her eyes at me.

I had no doubt she'd try to coax me into the cab with her. If I was sure a sloppy drunk could make her way through the bar and into a cab on her own, I would have declined. A breath pushed out as I kicked my chair back to stand.

"We'll both walk you out, sweetheart," Molly spoke up, receiving startled groans from the two hopefuls at her side. I bit back a smile as Molly gave them each a cheek kiss and slapped the hands of our first baseman and pitcher before joining us.

"Mmm, lucky me." Drunk lady slipped her hand through Molly's elbow and locked her other around my waist, dragging us toward the door. Maybe she thought she'd coax us both into the cab.

My mind immediately flashed on a threesome with her and Molly. It's definitely been a while if I'm considering something I've never been into and with someone I never would have considered a bed partner. But now the image flittered through my system, sparking nerve endings along the way. My sex drive had died in prison out of necessity. I barely managed to resurrect it after I got out. Now it was flaring so hot I felt perspiration spot my upper lip.

Molly studied me for a second, curious at my apparent lack of focus. She mouthed, *this okay?*

I nodded and let her lead us out of the bar. As wingmen went, Molly was pretty great. If I'd wanted to leave with this woman, she would have backed off and found another ride home. Who could ask for more with a good buddy?

We loaded the woman into the cab, her clinging to our hands until we could finally shut the door in her face. Since she was able to give directions to the cabbie, I didn't feel guilty about the chances of her making it home all right.

"Her breath smelled like an open box of wine," Molly said as we watched the cab roll away. She swiped a hand through the bangs that normally succumbed to a natural cowlick and stayed off her forehead. The cap she wore for the game ruined her perfectly coiffed wave.

I chuckled, watching her second more persistent pass through the offending bangs. "You didn't have her breathing right on you for the good part of an hour."

"Hey, I thought you were into it. She's not going to play mind games like J&B." She studied my expression. "Guess not. We could come back on Sunday to meet some of my old teammates?"

Molly the Pimp. Amusing. "Not this week."

"Too intense?"

Intense? No. Too much? Maybe. That word came up often in her speech, almost like she felt it was a complaint about her. I liked Molly's intensity. I never felt like I didn't have her attention when she spoke to me. It was a refreshing change from the distraction-filled world I now found myself living in.

"No, it's been fun. Just tired." I glanced at her, realizing that I might have messed with her plans. "You sure stirred up those ladies."

"Like I can shut this down." She gestured to her body with a cocky look that broke into laughter almost immediately.

I laughed with her. It had been a long time since someone could make me laugh this much. "Must be a hard burden to bear."

"It is, but I soldier on."

When we reached my car, I offered, "It's okay if you wanted to finish the night with one or both of those women. I can find my way home."

"I'm good right where I am." She acted as if she'd never dream of ditching her buddy for a woman. The way she attracted women at the softball fields, I found it hard to believe she wouldn't have gone off with someone in the past. Yet here she was seemingly unbothered by missing out on sex with one of those women.

"Whatever you say." After all I'd walked away from sex tonight, too, and I wasn't bothered by it.

She watched me unlock her door and step back. "Did you lose your key fob?"

"Bought it used and the guy didn't have them." Six years used with high mileage, one set of keys, and a suspect smell in the backseat. It took two upholstery shampoos before I could bear to take a drive. All of that helped make it affordable for my limited after prison resources.

"Sucks. Then again you'll never lock your keys in your car."

I slid into my seat and looked over at her. "You like the bright side, don't you?"

"What's not to like?" She smiled, and I wondered why I'd ever thought her face looked angry when I first met her. Even when she was angry, she masked it pretty well. That smile, though, was pure allure, and I was lucky enough to see it often.

"Buckle up."

"Boss me around," she muttered with a huge smile and reached back for her seatbelt as I pulled out of our parking space. "Want to keep the theme going tonight? Watch a little Rockies for some inspiration?"

"Sure." I didn't feel like going home. A few more hours with my friend would be a great way to spend the evening.

It didn't seem to take as long to get home as it had to get to the field. Not having a ton of anxiety probably helped that perception, but in almost no time, we were stepping out of the car at Molly's condo complex.

"Do you need a shower as much as I do?" Molly read my mind as she let us into her place.

"Could I?"

"Be my guest. I'll order pizza and get the game on."

"You can do half veggie this time," I suggested. Everyone had a favorite pizza, and I was betting that Molly's wasn't vegetarian. "What do you like?"

"For pizza? Almost anything. The veggie tasted good last time. Never thought artichoke hearts would taste good on a pizza or at all for that matter."

I reached out and squeezed her shoulder. She was kind enough to embrace my chosen eating habits consciously and without complaint. The boys ate veggie when I made dinner, but they often lamented the loss of whatever meat was missing.

She went to retrieve a fresh towel out of the hall closet for me. I grabbed clean sweats from my duffle and took the towel. Contentment filled me with how easy I was here in her home.

"Pizza should be here in twenty minutes," Molly said when I surfaced from her bathroom, feeling fresh and relaxed. "The game's already on. I'll be ten minutes." She headed to the bathroom for her shower.

"Take your time." I sank down onto her couch and fought the urge to fall asleep all cozy and warm.

The knock on the door woke me up. Molly grinned down at me as she rounded the sofa to answer the door. She shook her head and droplets of water from her wet hair helped wake me from the snooze I'd taken.

"Hey," I protested, wiping the drops from my face and sitting up so I didn't immediately succumb to the comfort of her couch again.

"Pizza's here." She grabbed money from the counter and passed it off to the pizza guy when she opened the door. Seconds later, she was back sitting beside me. "Hungry or just sleepy?"

"Didn't mean to fall asleep, but damn your couch is comfy." My hand rubbed the back cushion, the motion lulling me into a daze.

"I know. I crash out here almost as much as I sleep in the bed." She handed me a slice and gestured toward a beer she'd placed on the coffee table for me. She brought another slice up to her mouth and took a bite.

My slice was gone in six bites. I didn't realize how hungry or tired I was. I'd spent the day installing reclaimed wood floors in the upstairs of Vivian's house. Natalie let me leave an hour early to get to my first game. I didn't think I was taking advantage because she let Tyler leave an hour early every other day to coach his son's soccer team, and the Sweeneys took a day off last week to meet with their ski team sponsor. The workday and expended energy worrying about playing softball for the first time in years had worn me down. I'd be lucky to finish another slice and drive home without falling asleep again.

"Stay here tonight. You're dead on your feet, lady." Molly's hand patted my thigh. "I had the day off. You were tired before we even started the game."

"You wouldn't mind?"

"Not at all." She turned back to the screen and made a gesture at the TV when the Giants first baseman looped a line drive into center, scoring the go ahead run.

I watched her annoyance with amusement. She didn't feel the need to fill the silence between us with useless chatter. After being forced to listen to cellmates yammer on to abate their boredom, it was nice to find a friend that cherished the quiet when merited.

An inning later, it was clear the Rockies were going to lose unless they had unprecedented scoring in the ninth. Molly clicked off the television and shook her head in disgust.

"At least we won," I reminded her of our softball victory. "It's a good team you've got."

"Been playing with them a few years. The guys aren't arrogant pricks, and they can play. The women are fun. Not as good as my Sunday squad, but now that you're around we might win a few more."

"Thanks." I wished I could be as free with compliments as Molly was. She had a way of making all her friends feel better with a simple positive observation. It was a skill I now coveted.

She glanced at me. "You're bushed. Get some sleep."

I would have protested if she weren't right. I watched her get up and go over to the closet for extra sheets. We worked together to get a makeshift bed ready. I tucked in the bottom sheet as Molly ran back to her bedroom and grabbed a pillow.

"Thanks, Mol." I took the offered pillow, sitting back down. "I think I would have fallen asleep on the way home."

"You're always welcome to crash." She speared me with an intense stare to make sure I understood how genuine she was with her invitation. "Sleep well."

She leaned down for a hug. I was still getting used to the physical contact, having been so cautious over the past seven years. It felt good to drop the fear, and I looked forward to the hello and goodbye hugs from Molly.

Pulling back, she said, "Goodnight, Falyn."

"'Night, Molly."

She swooped in for a peck. I expected to feel a flicker of softness, a hint of moistness, a fleeting pull of suction. That's what hello and goodbye kisses were. That's what kisses from friends felt like. That's what a quick peck on the lips was supposed to be.

What I got instead was a thunderbolt that went from my lips to my chest to my stomach to other points south. Holy smokes. That did not just happen.

I was taking stock of my elevated pulse and audible breaths as I glanced up at Molly. Her dark brown eyes glittered, but I couldn't tell if it was shock or alarm. It definitely wasn't indifference.

Before I could chalk up my reaction as something unexpected, Molly knelt onto the couch next to me. My heart rate kicked up as she reached forward and slid a hand along my jaw.

Her lips parted, eyes searching mine. She cupped my face with her other hand. "Jesus, Falyn."

I barely registered her anguished tone before she listed toward me, bringing her mouth to mine again.

12

An entire lightning storm touched off inside me at the second press of her lips to mine. They glided across mine in slow motion, pulling here, pressing there. I grasped the back of her neck and tilted my head, wanting to wring every single sensation out of this.

Her mouth coaxed mine open. My stomach took a plunge with the surge of her tongue inside. Mine was there to meet hers, teasing and taunting her need to lead. My smile was immediately swallowed by her roaming mouth and an unexpected moan. She stiffened at the sound, clearly shocked that she'd made it. I took advantage of her surprise and pushed against her, making her drop to her rump on the cushions.

"What are we...?" She didn't finish her thought before her hands were grabbing my face and bringing it to her mouth again.

I couldn't have answered the question had she finished it. She was my friend whom I'd never had one sexual thought about. She might as well have been a man for all the sexual interest I'd shown in her. But dammit she could kiss, and dammit again, my body didn't seem to care that she wasn't my type.

She pulled me against her, wrapping her arms around me as her mouth made love to mine better than any full-on sex I'd had. My breasts molded to hers, thighs now interlocked. If my head was going to stop this, it had to act now. But my mouth and hands weren't listening.

I pushed again. She resisted my getting her horizontal. In the next second, she was pushing against me. I would have smiled if her tongue hadn't just started this twirling thing with mine. It was distracting enough that she accomplished her goal of pushing me back. Her body leaned over mine. Her face pulled up and flashed a triumphant grin.

I see how she thinks this will go. "Not so fast, hot stuff."

"What?" She swooped in for another kiss.

"I know what you're trying to do."

"Me?" she mumbled, dragging her mouth down the column of my throat.

I arched up, all thought leaving me. What was I protesting? Oh yeah, she was trying to top me. Well, actions speak louder than words. I levered my hips and swung her up and over onto her back.

She barked out a surprised laugh. "What are you trying?"

"Same thing you were." I leaned down and nipped her lower lip. "Looks like we're going to be taking turns."

Her hands slid up and grasped my breasts. Her eyes twinkled as she squeezed. "Is that so?"

I squeezed my eyes shut as her fingers flicked my nipples through my shirt. "Hmm?"

"We could just do this my way." Her fingers went to my waist and ducked under my shirt, drifting up until they crested over my breasts. She let out another moan that drowned out my hiss of pleasure.

"Hmm?" I repeated, not sure what we'd been talking about. Something important enough for me to attempt a discussion when her hands and mouth had the potential to give me an orgasm without going anywhere near my pants.

"Yeah, let's just do this my way."

Oh, yes, her topping me. Nope, not going to happen. At least not all the time. "Turns, Molly. If we're doing this, we're taking turns."

She leaned back to look at me. Light glinted off her deep brown eyes. "Twist my arm."

I slid my hands under her shirt and up to take her nipples between my fingers. Her face tilted up, jaw clenching. I twisted the hard buds through her bra, laughing at the much louder moan I got from her this time. "Twisted enough?"

She grinned again. "Twisted just enough."

I went to pull her shirt off. She perched on one arm and helped me get it over her head. Chiseled shoulders and arms blended into a contoured chest and countable abs. Her breasts were small and tucked into a sports bra that did nothing to deflate my excitement. I never thought I'd undress a woman who wore sports bras.

She pulled at my shirt, and I sat up to help her. Her eyes roamed over my torso, hands skating everywhere her eyes went. She managed to release my bra with only two fingers, showing just how much game she had.

"Falyn," she whispered, her eyes taking in my stiff nipples.

I leaned over and kissed her again. My hands stroked down her back, biting into the flesh. She pulled at her bra, taking it over her head, messing up her hair. I ran my fingers through the thick strands as my eyes zeroed in on her breasts. Small, firm, perfectly shaped with dark red nipples. My mouth started salivating with the single purpose of wanting those nipples. While she was still sitting up, I took advantage and locked my mouth around one of the luscious pebbles.

She moaned and gripped my head as my tongue lashed at her. Her body tilted into me, seeking the pleasure my mouth was giving. I found myself drifting backward no longer caring who was on top. My hands squeezed her waist, bringing her down to grind against me. My knees came up and pressed against her hips, shoving at her mesh shorts to bring them off. I added a hand to the mix, tearing at the waist to slide them down her legs. Her legs tried to help, but she ended up sitting and pushing them off. Her eyes landed on mine and with one tug, she had my sweats and panties off.

I took in every silky inch of her naked skin. Her thighs were just as muscled as her arms. Her narrow waist and hips were almost as tantalizing as the rippled abs and beaded nipples. The dark brown hair at her apex was trimmed almost to the point of shaved. My fingers inched to drag through the trim to feel the addictive bristles.

Her fingers slid down the center of my chest. She followed the path of her fingers with her mouth, smooching loudly. It both tickled and drove me wild.

I stopped her mouth just before it could land home. I needed her up with me. I wanted to look into her eyes.

"I was just getting to the really good part." She surged forward and pressed her lips to my core for a fleeting kiss.

I moaned and tugged on her shoulders. Based on that teasing touch, I knew she'd have me done in a minute if I let her continue. "Get to it later. C'mere." I pulled her down on top of me.

Her hips dragged up against me, drawing groans from both of us. She straddled my raised thigh and slid her hand down to cup me. A smile tugged at the corners of her mouth when she felt how wet she'd made me. Not one to let her have all the fun, I pulled her down onto my thigh. My smile wasn't as subtle as hers when I discovered her excitement painting my leg.

She stroked two fingers through my swollen lips. My hips bucked up against her hand. Her body rolled with my movement, but I wouldn't let her lift her hips. It was amazing how easy it was to anticipate her actions because I used a lot of the same moves. She wanted me to come first. I'd always wanted the same with my partners. Wonder who would win this round.

Her mouth wrapped around a nipple, sucking in and biting softly. Her fingers glided through my creases, working me into a snit when she wouldn't hit the spot I needed them most. She looked up, pinning my gaze as her fingers finally grazed over my throbbing clit.

I let out a small cry and watched that smile appear again. I pulled on her hips, dragging them down my thigh. She bit back her cry of pleasure as she skated back up my thigh and down again.

Her gaze grew hazy when she rocked against me once more. She tilted forward to kiss me as her fingers pressed harder and dipped down. They circled, hovering, waiting. My pelvis jutted toward her. My fingers gripping her hips. Both should have been enough to let her know just how much I wanted this.

"Inside?" she asked and I felt my heart trip at the question. She guessed that I wasn't into penetration, which I wasn't, but with her, apparently anything goes.

I nodded because I would have embarrassed myself if I tried to say anything. Seconds later, her probing fingers pushed inside, stretching and filling, satisfying every need I had. I reached up to cup her breasts, pinching her nipples between my fingers. It seemed to take forever for her to seat fully inside me. I tried to split my attention between playing with her nipples and experiencing a fullness I'd always lacked in sexual intimacy before.

"Mmm, you feel so good," she said on a breathy moan. Her hips had taken over the rocking on my thigh. It became clear neither of us would last long. She added her thumb to my clit, tapping and twirling while keeping up a slow thrust inside.

"You feel amazing." My voice was raspy as I held on to the climax of a lifetime. I needed my hands on her first. I continued with the assault on one nipple while I slid my other hand under her thrusting hips. She felt engorged and slick and perfect. My thumb pressed against her clit as we lunged together.

"Harder," she coaxed.

I applied more pressure and more when she told me again. I worried that I might be pressing against her swollen, tender flesh too hard but she pressed down even more, riding my hand and thigh. It was demanding and insistent and wonderful. I stopped worrying and just went with it.

"Come, Falyn."

"You first," I said through a clenched jaw, knowing it wouldn't happen. "Ah, yes, Molly!"

My orgasm smashed into me so hard I seized up every muscle, jerking and pulsing through the contractions. I pulled Molly down, gripping her to me as I heaved and shuddered beneath her.

She sped up her thrusts on my thigh. My fingers tightened on instinct. Molly jolted to a stop and groaned my name, climaxing in a majestic display of tremors and twitches.

I recovered seconds before she did. Her boneless form sprawled over me. I lightly kissed her neck and dragged my fingernails over her back. She shuddered and squirmed over me. It was almost as good as the sex she'd given me.

"Like that?" I asked.

"Hate it," she said, squirming against my hands to recreate the fingernail drag.

I nibbled on her ear and tried to keep up the afterglow. Before she'd kissed me goodnight, she was my friend and only ever going to be my friend. Now she was sprawled out naked over me, having delivered the best sex of my life.

"Not tired anymore?" Her words breathed out over my chest where her head lay. I heard the teasing in her tone and rose to the challenge, dropping all concern about the change in our relationship for now.

"Ready for round two." I flipped her under me before she could protest. "My turn to be on top."

Her beautiful eyes flared and joined her smile. She was looking forward to round two as much as I was.

Part II

Molly

13

Not my best move pretending to be barely awake when she left. I'd hustled women out before. Sure there was a bit of the morning after awkwardness, but it was based on bedding a stranger and all the unknowns that go with that in the light of the day. This had been entirely different. Never, in all my years, had I slept with a friend. One I'd only ever thought of as a friend—well, a buddy, really, which was worse. Who sleeps with her buddy? A buddy that is not my type. A buddy that I don't find attractive. Well, until last night.

I had to give it to her, though. She could have crept out the door without saying anything to me this morning. She left for work earlier than I did. It was the perfect excuse. With our schedules this week, we could have avoided each other for days until the awkwardness faded. Instead, she'd gently woken me to say that she had to get to work and tell me she'd had a good time. Of course, she said she had a good time when we sat around watching baseball, too.

This was seriously screwed up. I finally had a buddy in town who liked to do all the things I liked doing and had an open social schedule, and I might have blown it by sleeping with her.

But damn, the sex had been amazing. Beyond compare, actually. Who knew sleeping with another non-femme would be so off-the-charts? I'd had good sex before, even wild sex, but this was like blasting for avalanches. I expected the explosion and cascade, but I might not be able to contain it.

My phone rang as I was stretching out my overworked muscles. I silently prayed that it wasn't Falyn, which was childish, but I really didn't know where I wanted this to go yet. I had to figure that out before I could face my buddy. A buddy who had the cutest combination yip-moan when her right nipple was tweaked just so. I really shouldn't know that about my buddy. Nor should I know that her breasts, a size larger than mine, were slightly upturned, permanently shaped to negate gravity.

I reached for my cell and saw my boss's name on the screen. "Hey, Ron, what's up?"

"I know you're not scheduled till later, but we had a private booking and Wayne is nowhere to be found. Can you take it?"

"What kind of tour?"

"Fly fishing on Fryingpan."

Of course, the one activity we offered that I didn't like doing. Although, if I wanted to prolong the childishness, it would give me an excuse to be out of cell range all day. "Fine. I'll be in soon."

I went into my bathroom and looked for any signs that Falyn had stayed over last night. No extra towel, not discarded makeup sponge, perhaps she'd ducked out as soon as she woke up. Ah, but the shower stall was wet. That meant she'd used the shower and either dressed without drying or took the towel to my laundry room. The sheets on the sofa were probably in the washer already. She'd done that before.

I flipped on the shower and tried not to remember how much her lean body had turned me on. I'd always liked some soft flesh on my women, voluptuous or curvy, but Falyn was lean, firm perfection. My height, too, which was also off for me. I liked leaning down to kiss my women and being able to maneuver them easily onto a bed. I liked women who liked me doing that to them. Falyn was as much a top as I was. Taking turns turned out to be as thrilling as being the aggressor at all times. More so, if I were being honest.

I soaped up my torso, ducking my head under the spray. If I knew Ron, he already had the tour group in, selling them rods and full-length waders. I jerked back when my hand ventured lower. Damn, I was sore. Falyn's concerned face floated into my vision as I remembered telling her that I needed her thigh and hand harder. I'd actually asked for it. *Harder.* I almost begged for it. I'd never pleaded for anything during sex in my life. She'd been concerned that she might hurt me. I'd been concerned that I wouldn't climax, which happened too often with lovers. I must have been on some sort of mission because I wasn't going to miss out on any she'd give. And she'd given four before we finally fell asleep in my bed. Hence the soreness.

I finished with the shower and went into the kitchen to make coffee. Falyn didn't drink coffee. Random thought. Now I was thinking about non-sexual things with my formally non-sexual friend when I should be freaking about the sexual things I'd done with my non-sexual friend. But here I was thinking that I'd never met anyone until Falyn who didn't drink coffee. She didn't drink tea either, so I wondered where she got her caffeine. I'd have to find out. No, I wouldn't because she was my non-sexual buddy whom I wanted to stay a buddy because I didn't have any real buddies now that Vivian was in a relationship and Dwight was more interested in where his next client or guy would come from. Falyn had been great, and now we'd slept together because I'd stupidly given her a simple goodnight brush of the lips that had set mine on fire.

Suited up in my cargo shorts and shop polo, I grabbed my wading boots and headed down to the parking garage where I'd get my pole and waders from the storage locker. My thermos was filled with much needed caffeine. I'd stop at the quick mart for a few extra snacks. Our tours always got catered meals from Kelsey, but no snacks. Normally I had snacks, but Falyn and I had the game last night instead of hitting City Market like we sometimes did on Wednesdays after work.

My cell rang again. I cursed when I saw the display. "Hey, Tessa, what's up?"

"I was hoping we could get lunch before your tours start today."

My heart pumped a little harder as it usually did when I heard from Tessa. Or at least it had for the last few months since she'd broken up with that bitch. This morning, though, it didn't feel as intense. Perhaps the guilt of sleeping with someone else when I'd been slow playing a move on Tessa was the root cause.

"Sorry, can't do it. Ron just called me in for a private booking this morning. Rain check?"

Normally I didn't sound like I blew people off when I talked to them. Hell, most people thought I was more intense than a CIA interrogation. Tessa probably couldn't notice it, but I felt guilty just the same.

"Oh, okay." She sounded really down. I'd let myself down, too.

"Everything all right?"

"Yeah, I just had a couple fire me from their house hunt because they weren't ready to buy. It never feels good. Thought I could get you to cheer me up."

An unexpected flash of irritation hit me. I never minded before when she needed cheering up. As a friend, that was my job, wasn't it? So why did I feel like this time I was being used? That she'd been using me as her tissue fetcher for months? Sure, I'd let her do it. Hell, I'd welcomed it if it meant a pretty, sweet lesbian was now single and eventually available once she got over that bitch of an ex.

"Sorry. Maybe Dwight's up for lunch." I knew I was throwing my other buddy onto tissue patrol, but I had to at least offer up an option for my disheartened friend.

"I'll give him a try. I was just hoping to see my Molly-Bear."

Like a teddy bear only life-sized and named Molly. She told me that once. I thought it was cute at the time, but now, I didn't find it as endearing. Vivian had warned me once that I tended to romanticize the relationships I had with women I found attractive. She didn't want me wasting time with women who would never return my affections like Glory, or women who would never be a good fit with me, again like Glory. She knew I'd crushed on that cutie and was worried I'd get hurt when Glory wasn't into me. I knew my attraction was one-sided but looking and sighing never hurt anyone. I hadn't told her about Tessa, though. She'd probably slap my hand for this one, too.

"Sorry, Tess. Maybe next time. I'm just pulling up to the store. I'll call you over the weekend."

"Have a good tour."

At least that sounded like she meant it. She'd been so focused on her breakup that care for others had passed by the wayside. Now she was at least wishing me well whenever we parted, which was a step in the right direction.

I grabbed my pack and headed into the shop. Sure enough, Ron was ringing up a bunch of unnecessary purchases he'd goaded the tourists into. I shouldn't judge. He paid a good wage for me to do things I liked doing, but these people would never fly fish again. Instead of renting the equipment, he was getting them to buy it. Gullible tourists.

"There she is," Ron called as he handed over the credit card slip to the silver-haired dude with the black card. "Everyone, this is Molly Sokol. She'll be your guide today."

Silver Hair gave me a long once over as if he couldn't decide if he should protest. He expected a man. It was a man date with his fishing buddies, after all. Shouldn't another man be their guide? Now they'd have to be on their best behavior because a sensitive woman would be within earshot. Or he could be wondering if I really was a woman. My haircut sure didn't let him know, nor did my makeup free face and androgynous clothing. His eyes went to my chest. Yep, he was trying to figure out if Ron had a male guide name Molly. What a dimwit.

"Are we ready to catch some trout?" I watched Silver Hair and one of his buddies lean back with raised eyebrows, my voice giving more confirmation that I was a woman.

"Is she experienced?" Silver Hair flashed his black credit card at Ron, like throwing more money at him would make Wayne appear in the store to take them out instead of being stuck with me.

"She's the best around," Ron confirmed and I smiled. Not for the compliment but because he actually meant it. I dug my boss. He was a good guy that didn't take advantage of his employees. Except to call them in when he booked last minute private parties. I knew he'd give me an extra day off soon to make it up to me.

The four men in the group introduced themselves to me as Ron and I loaded up the company van with their newly purchased gear. A car pulled up next to us. For a second I had hope that it was Wayne showing up for his shift. Instead I heard Kelsey's voice.

"Perfect timing," Ron praised.

She jumped out of her car with a smile. "Hey, Ron."

She was unnecessarily introduced to the men in the group, but Ron knew how best to satisfy his customers. A pretty brunette with a great rack did wonders for four aging men with too much money to burn and even bigger egos. They fawned all over her and what she'd made for lunch, each tipping her individually and slipping her their business cards. She played her part perfectly, flattered and impressed with just enough flirtation to change their tips from ten dollars to twenties.

"Hi, Molls." She handed over the packed cooler after the men had finished looking through it. "Packed your favorite sandwich."

"You're the best, Kelsey."

"Jenna and I are ditching her hubby and my boyfriend for brunch on Sunday. Wanna come? Jenna hasn't met your buddy Falyn yet. You could bring her."

Heat touched my face. I hadn't blushed in twenty years, but one mention of a woman who was supposed to be my friend whom I'd somehow turned into a lover had me blushing. Okay, maybe not a full-on blush, but I bet I looked embarrassed. "Working Sunday, but you guys have fun."

"Sometime soon, then. Have a good tour." She reached out to rub my arm before zipping back into her car.

I looked up and found all four guys staring at me. Silver Hair had a curious look on his face, his eyes flicking down to my arm. Right, right. They flirted and gave her money, but she touched me. Perhaps they didn't hear the part where she mentioned her boyfriend. Or perhaps they were the kind of people who didn't care what that word meant.

"Ready?" Ron asked as I stowed the cooler in the cargo area.

"All set. Gentlemen?"

"We have to stop for beer," one of them said. He looked pretty insistent that no fishing trip was complete without beer. They didn't seem to get that fly fishing was a two handed activity.

"No problem. Molly will stop on the way to the river spot."

And we were off. My once free morning now filled with four corporate blustery types who thought beer in the morning was a must have. At least I wouldn't have much time to dwell on the sleek and now sexy body of my one-time platonic, unappealing because of the platonic thing, buddy.

14

Vivian gave me her widest blue-green stare. A beautiful blue-green stare. Truthfully everything about Vivian was beautiful, but she was looking at me in disbelief. It was the same look I'd been giving myself for two days.

"Yes, you heard me."

"Molly, I mean...Mol." Her halted speech spoke volumes about what she thought of my dilemma. Vivian could speak eloquently in the most uncomfortable situations.

"I know," I sighed and glanced around the café. The couple at the table next to us was having a snippy discussion about whose job it was to clean the guest bathroom. Any other day, it would provide great amusement and opportunity to mock. Any other day I wasn't telling my closest friend that I'd done something really stupid with my newest friend.

Vivian's head bobbed, lips pressed tight. "But, really, do you?"

"What do you want me to say? I'm an idiot?" Because I was. Definitely an idiot.

"No, of course not." She reached across the table to squeeze my hand. Viv did this, touch to soothe, touch to connect, touch to show affection. "I just, well, she's not your usual get."

No, she wasn't. Women with long hair and lush boobs and swishy hips who wore high heels and cloying hairspray and bothersome lipstick that smeared when I kissed them. Women who wanted to be coddled and fished for compliments and expected me to be their handsome stud. That's my get. Safe and familiar and expected. "I know, I know. What can I say?"

"How do you feel about it?"

"I don't know. That's the weirdest thing." I shook my head still not able to pack my actions with Falyn into a nice neat box.

Sex with tourists, sex with part-time snowbirds, and although a lot more rare, sex with girlfriends could all be classified. I knew how to handle the event and the aftermath. This was something entirely new. I felt one way about Falyn—buddy, chum, pal, friend. Period. Then the sex and now I didn't have those same feelings. Sex didn't do that for me. Sex was sex whether it was with a one-night stand, a vacationer, or a girlfriend. Sex didn't change my feelings for someone. Even with the one serious girlfriend I'd had. Sex with her at first was physical and that was it. My feelings for her changed but not because of sex and, more importantly, not during sex. That did happen with Falyn, and I wasn't sure how I felt about it.

"I didn't know you liked her like that."

"I didn't."

"Do you want to tell me how it started?" She gave me an encouraging smile.

I didn't, but I had to talk to someone about it and Vivian was the best option. "We got back from our first softball game and watched some TV. She was dead tired, so I suggested she just stay over."

"Like she has a few times, right?"

"Yeah, so I make sure she's all set with sheets and everything for the couch. I lean down to give her a quick peck goodnight, and it was like someone struck a flare inside me."

Vivian rocked back against her chair. "Wow."

"Yeah." A flare that burned so hot I couldn't think but for the heat.

"Did she feel it, too?"

Falyn's expression after I'd bussed her goodnight flashed in my mind. Surprise and delight, a breathy inhale, then all I could see were her full, pink lips. "Pretty sure. She looked as shocked as I felt."

"So you jumped her?"

"Viv!"

She grinned, easing the tension I felt. "You kissed her again."

"Yeah, or she kissed me. I don't know. I just know it was a real kiss that never ended and somehow our clothes are off and we're on the couch—"

"Okay, I get the picture." Her hand came up from mine, waving in front of me.

I grinned now. She was a romantic. She didn't go for details of other people's sex lives.

"And was it good?"

"Sensational."

Her mouth came open as her eyes blinked. She was trying to hide a smile. "And now you don't know how you feel?"

"I know what you're thinking, and you're wrong," I insisted, knowing she thought I could be falling for Falyn. Vivian had looked for and, well, needed love her whole dating life until she finally went out with Natalie. Now she had it and, like most new lovebirds, thought she could see it everywhere.

"I didn't even suggest it. You did. You had unbelievable—"

"Sensational," I corrected. And unrestricted. I kept that little chunk of truth to myself. I'd let Falyn do whatever she wanted with me. Everything I'd done to her and more. For the first time in my life. Sensational might not actually cover it.

Vivian's lips pulled into another smile. "Sensational, astonishing, mind-blowing sex with a woman who has never fallen into your physical or emotional type before and who has been your main hang for two months."

"What's your point? And I didn't say it was mind-blowing."

"No, you didn't, but it was, wasn't it?" She waited for the smile I couldn't hide. "My point is that she's not the woman you've been with in the past, she's not the woman you've had in your mind as the woman you'd be with in the future, she's not even the woman you'd think of for a one-nighter."

"That was a point?"

"Smart mouth." She shot me a mock glare. "The point is that you've been looking for someone to settle down with for what, two years now? You went from having fun with tourists who were all the same type, to having fun with snowbirds who were all the same type, to dating any single lesbian in the area that was your type in hopes of finding the one. You never once mentioned that the sex was anything but good. And now, you've fallen into bed with a woman who isn't your type, who was just a friend, and the sex was sensational and made you feel things."

"I didn't say that," I rushed to deny the truth she'd somehow guessed.

"You didn't have to. Think about what it would be like to sleep with another pretty tourist and the sex is just good."

My face fell. Jeez, put that way, I was destined to be disappointed forever. Oh, that was her point. Well, shit.

Vivian could see the thoughts as they passed through my head. She managed to keep from looking smug when she said, "Want to talk about the l-word again?"

"Shut it."

That pulled a laugh from her. "How is she feeling?"

"I've been working." I have. Really. Way too busy to deal with Falyn and these convoluted feelings just yet.

Her brow rose, but she was polite enough not to grin. "You're avoiding."

"What would you do?"

"Not my sitch, darlin'. I knew I loved Natalie before we slept together."

Wouldn't that be nice? Still, Viv always had good advice. "In my sitch, what would you do?"

"She's nice, she likes doing the same things you do, she's got a job, she doesn't seem to take much for granted, she thinks of your feelings before making a decision that affects you both, and she's great in bed? Is there really a question?"

"Yes, dammit. She's not my type." I doubted she had a girly blouse or high heels anywhere in her closet. She'd probably never get scared enough to tuck her face against my chest when we watched a scary movie. And there was no way she'd get excited to the point of screeching about something I did for her. Girly, she is not, and that's what I'd always wanted.

"But she was once, and she's obviously rocked your view of types."

"Like for real, though?" It was so hard to make sense of this. I'd been so certain I wanted one thing. Could I just walk away from that certainty? "You know I've been wanting to find someone all permanent like for a while now."

"And you're not sure if she's the kind to go for that?"

I shrugged. That was the thing about buddies. Deep, emotional discussions about wants and dreams didn't happen. "I don't even know if she's staying in town after she finishes your house."

"What?" Her eyes popped wide. "Does she think she's going to be fired?"

"No, she thinks that Nat took her on as a favor and won't be able to maintain the workload to keep her on full-time. She's not going to put Nat in that position."

"Wow," she repeated. It seemed like she wanted to say more, but she didn't.

"So, yeah, I could be getting into something that might end sooner rather than later."

She nodded her head and looked as grim as I felt. "Natalie will do everything to keep her on, but she might think the effort is too much and try to alleviate that for her friend."

"That's my thinking."

"Well, Mol, I don't know what to say." She took a sip from her lemonade and gathered her thoughts. "I do know that this is the longest discussion we've ever had about someone you're interested in, other than how to deal with J&B originally. And that says you think more of this than anything you've had in possibly ever. Am I right?"

"I had a talk with her about J&B, too."

"Avoiding," she accused.

"Mouth. Shut." I brought my hand up and slammed my fingers down onto my thumb to emphasize my order. The gesture just made her smile wider.

"I'm right."

"Yeah, okay."

"Good talk." She grinned wide and long. "You never needed romance like I did. You want someone who'll see you for who you are, not what they think you should be. Falyn seems like she's got that right."

Helps that she's been my buddy and would know that particular pet peeve of mine. Just because I'm butch doesn't mean I'm going to tend to every single whim of my girlfriend. Just because I'm butch doesn't mean I don't want someone to recognize that I like a little pampering, too. And just because I'm butch doesn't mean I'm not vulnerable sometimes. Falyn does seem to get that.

Even if she isn't my type.

15

She looked beautiful, not in the traditional sense, but beautiful nonetheless. Her hair would be considered short by most, but longer than mine. The natural wave didn't push it off her forehead or form loose ripples like mine. Her wave added volume to her entire style. I'd never dated a woman without long hair before, but I sure liked the look of it now. Dark blond, too. Normally I preferred champagne blondes or honey blondes. Falyn's was a shade shy of light brown, but the sunshine-infused, golden highlights snagged my gaze every time. Her hazel eyes weren't the piercing blue I usually favored. But forget drowning in a sea of blue. Falyn's brownish green hazel had the power to paralyze.

"Hey," she said, stepping back to gesture me into her house.

"Hi." I wanted to kiss her hello but knew that wasn't a good idea.

"Molls," Cole greeted from the couch where he, his brother, and Luis were fighting it out on some video game. Falyn's cats were curled up in his and Luis's laps, perfectly content to be jostled by their controller movements.

"Yo," Curtis called.

"*Hola*," Luis added.

Falyn hid a smile and nodded her head toward the kitchen.

"Fos, beer me, please?" Cole asked. "I'm in the middle of crushing these two."

She chuckled and didn't seem to mind grabbing beers for all of them. I had a feeling it was to keep them from wandering near us while we talked. Had the talk, I should say.

"Want a beer?" she asked me after placing three on the table and bringing over the open bag of chips.

I wanted to say yes, but beer had helped put us in this situation. Then again, beer might ease the tension a bit. "Thanks."

"Guys, I'm stealing one of your beers."

"Beer is communal. You know that," Curtis said and immediately swore as someone pinned him with gunfire on screen.

"It's not. They always pay for it," she said to me.

"You rarely drink it. It's communal. You buy us eggs and peanut butter."

"Yuck," I reacted to the combo.

"Not to eat together, Mol, jeez. You will die now!" he shouted at his brother.

"Lovely atmosphere," I commented, actually happy to have the buffer tonight.

"They're entertaining."

"We're like her TV," Cole told me.

"Go back to your game, kids." Falyn gripped the top of Cole's head to turn it back to the screen.

"Kids," Curtis snickered.

She shot me an exasperated look. "He doesn't believe I'm forty-four."

My eyebrows rose. I knew she was older, but I thought maybe a year or two at the most. Five seemed impossible. She didn't look it. Not her face or her tight, hard body.

She handed over a beer and took a bottle of OJ out of the fridge. "Porch okay?" She led me out through the sliders to the chairs that Glory practically lived in before she moved to Lena's next door. It looked like this was Falyn's new spot.

After taking a seat, I sniffed involuntarily. I could smell smoke. Not heavy, just lingering, like maybe one of the guys smoked regularly and had recently been sitting out here. I glanced around and saw an ashtray on the deck next to Falyn's chair. There was a single cigarette crushed inside.

"You don't smoke?" I would have tasted that when I kissed her. I know I would have. It's kind of a thing with me.

"Occasionally."

That shocked me. I hadn't tasted it. I'd only had a few beers that night. I didn't think I was drunk. Was the whole experience a blur because I'd been inebriated? "Really?"

"Used to, once a week, but not for months now. I thought I had quit."

My eyes cut to hers. Yeah, she was as twisted about this as I was. She'd quit and now she was smoking again, all because we'd gotten carried away the other night. "Think you'll take it up again."

She shrugged and glanced away. "How was your weekend?"

I didn't hear any accusation in her question. It had been four days with only one call between us, but she didn't sound upset about that. "Busy. The summer tours are taking longer and longer."

"You like it better than the winter stuff, right?"

We'd already had this conversation, but we needed something to start us off. I nodded and took in a deep breath to let out and begin.

"Hey, guys," Mei called out as she walked toward us from the house next door. I'd known her for years, but she didn't often join our group of friends when we planned outdoor activities. Most of our contact was limited to when I made plans with her husband, Spencer, or her best friend, Glory.

"Mei," I greeted. "Where's the hubby? Doing mayor stuff?"

"He'll be home soon. I was headed over to Glory's." Her finger gestured down the street.

"I saw her pull in about a half hour ago," Falyn told her.

"Thanks. I'm going to catch her before dinner. See you on my way back."

"See ya." Falyn waved and focused on me. "They work together, live next to each other, and still see each other almost every night. Wouldn't that get tiresome after a while?"

"I'd think so," I confirmed. "Viv and I have been friends a long time, but I couldn't work with her and live next to her every day."

"Little too much," she agreed.

Although, I could suddenly see that situation with Falyn. Maybe not the business part of it. I didn't want to own a business, but the seeing her every day and living close by or together, yeah, that might work.

She flicked her green tinted hazels at me and let out an audible breath. "So…I'm not your type and you're not mine. What next?"

A laugh escaped because she'd blurted what I'd been thinking. "I've been trying to figure it out." For days now and I still didn't know exactly how to feel.

"I meant what I said, you know. I had a good time."

"Me, too."

"It was unexpected."

"Yes."

"Nice, though."

"Yes."

"Say something other than 'yes,' will you?"

"Okay." I laughed and she joined me.

"What would you like to do?"

"Don't know."

"Me, neither," she said with a sigh, almost like she was disappointed. I was a little disappointed, too. I was hoping she'd have a clearer idea of what she wanted.

Like tell me she wanted a relationship, or she thought it was a mistake and we should be friends, or she really wanted a relationship. Oops, said that already.

"I didn't expect..." That it would be sensational. That I'd be rethinking what I thought would be great relationship material.

"Same here. Like I said before, I usually go for—"

"The pretty ones. Not that I'm not pretty," I joked.

"Definitely," she agreed with a smile. "But I didn't have you in the potential g/f category, you know?"

"Same here. It's kinda thrown me."

Her soulful eyes watched me for a moment. "In a good way? Like you want to explore a friends with benes situation, or I'm freaked and really need to go back to watching a baseball game with my buddy way?"

Friends with benes? Now that I hadn't considered. I already had too much emotionally going to be a booty call and not come out damaged at the end. Kinda hoped she did, too. "Never done that."

"Bene friends? Me, neither. My partners always wanted something more."

"Same here."

"So?"

"I guess we could try it." What was I saying? I could just call her up whenever I wanted sex and see if she was in the mood? Then we part ways and have a beer over a ballgame the next time? Not if we kept having the same kind of sex we'd had at first. No possible way. I'd be in love in a week, if I weren't already, which I wasn't because I wasn't like Vivian who equated sexual intimacy with romantic feelings.

"Don't sound so enthused," she joked, tapping two fingers against my shoulder.

"It's just so clinical. Like 'let's finish dinner, we'll have sex, and after we'll clean out the garage.' Not really something I've done."

She laughed and the sound rumbled over me. I liked her laugh. Full but not loud or startling. "Okay then, friends. I much prefer friends to benes."

Well, that bites. Guess I hadn't rocked her world as much as she'd rocked mine. That's a blow to the ego.

"Not to say that it wasn't great," she said when she must have seen a crestfallen look flit across my face. "I just meant I'd rather be friends with you than have sex complicate things, if that's how you feel."

"Yeah, sure."

She gave me a penetrating look. For a moment, it looked like she didn't believe me. Like she could see right through what I was saying and spot my fear that I could fall for her if we continued to sleep together.

"Fos! You gotta come ref," Cole yelled from inside.

An amused huff left her mouth before she opened the sliders and called back, "You know how I'll ref."

"Dude, shut up. She'll just turn off the Xbox," Curtis said.

I joined her amusement. Sounded like a good way to solve an argument.

She turned back and stared at me for a bit. "So, friends then?"

"Friends."

"Good." She relaxed against the chair. "Just don't give me another goodnight kiss."

That stabbed at my heart. I expected to be hurt by her decision to forgo a sexual relationship, but I didn't think she hated the kissing that much.

"Your kisses are dangerous." She shot me a grin before getting up to go inside and check on the boys.

And my stabbed heart suddenly felt like ten thumping hearts had taken its place.

16

Falyn and I were watching a baseball game at her place. We'd pretty much exclusively hung out at her place since falling into bed together two weeks ago. It seemed dangerous to be alone in my apartment. Not just for me. I'd caught her giving me a longing look at the movies the other night. Maybe this friends thing wasn't the right way to go.

The doorbell rang and Curtis went to answer it. Luis was coming over to watch the game with us. We'd all been hanging out together as yet another safeguard against my and Falyn's apparent lack of control.

"We're looking for Falyn Shaw," a voice at the doorway said.

"Fos," Curtis called as we turned to see who was there.

Two police officers stood at the door. I didn't recognize either, which was odd because I knew quite a few officers in town.

Falyn stiffened beside me and jumped up as soon as one of the cops took a step inside. "That's me. We can talk outside."

Strange, but not more than the officer's hard look. "May we come inside?"

"We can talk outside," Falyn repeated when she reached them.

It was even stranger that Falyn closed the door behind her.

"5-0?" Cole asked as he walked in from the kitchen.

"You do something to get us busted?" Curtis teased.

"I'm not the one who got thrown in the drunk tank that time," Cole reminded his brother.

"...invasion...on a jobsite...whereabouts," came the disembodied voice of the police officer through the open sliders.

I strained to hear more, ashamed that I was being nosy, but cops didn't stop by every day. What could they want with Falyn? God, I hoped nothing bad had happened to her. We hadn't been talking as frequently as we used to. Something could have happened, and she hadn't felt comfortable telling me about it.

"...not me...my rights...go down there," Falyn's replies were just as sporadic.

"...alibi?" That I heard loud and clear. Were they asking Falyn for an alibi or telling her that their suspect for whatever happened didn't have an alibi?

The boys didn't seem bothered by the fact that their housemate was talking to the police. Nor that it didn't sound like a cordial conversation.

"Come back with a warrant," Falyn said loud enough to be heard in full.

"You don't want that, Falyn."

The front door opened and she said again, "Warrant."

"We can make this easy if you'll—"

"Goodbye." Falyn closed the door in their faces. Her forehead rested against the door before she seemed to realize she wasn't alone. She whirled around to face us, her face red and eyes large. "Sorry."

"What's up?" Cole asked, looking concerned. Perhaps he wasn't as blasé about this as I thought.

"Nothing. No, there might," she paused, letting out a breath. Her fists clenched and unclenched. "No, nothing."

"What do they need a warrant for?" I heard myself ask.

Her eyes shot to mine. It looked like she might cry. I rose from the couch in a knee-jerk reaction. I'd never seen her cry. She and I were alike that way. We'd rather chew glass than cry, and I sure as hell didn't want to see her cry.

"Something went missing from a house we worked on."

"Seriously?" Cole perched forward on his seat. "Which one?"

"Don't know."

"Why aren't they talking to Natalie?" I asked. That seemed more logical than coming to one of the crewmembers. Maybe that had been their first stop.

She shrugged and looked away. Her sad eyes turned almost guilty before leaving mine. "Do you mind if we cut tonight short?"

I looked at the guys. She hadn't been talking to them. They lived here. She'd been talking to me. She looked sad and embarrassed, and she wanted her friend to leave. I didn't want to leave. I wanted to wipe those looks from her face, but I was a guest. I didn't have much choice.

"Can I do anything?"

Her sad eyes went wide in amazement before she shook her head. "We'll try it another night."

As I walked toward her, she had a hard time keeping my gaze. The guys watched for a second then made some excuse to go into their rooms. They really weren't as clueless as they seemed.

"Are you okay?" I laid my hand on her arm and rubbed softly.

"Yeah." But her tone suggested otherwise.

"Did they accuse you?"

"I was at the house. They're following all leads."

"Do you want me to stay? We don't have to watch baseball."

She swallowed roughly. She was going to cry. Jeez, I couldn't just leave her. They had accused her just because she'd worked in a house that had something stolen. Before I realized it, I leaned forward and pulled her in for a hug. She didn't exactly fling herself into my arms, but she did finally settle in. It was still surprising to have her face pressed against mine, her hips and other body parts lined up with mine. I was just remembering all the benefits of hugging someone my size when she pulled away.

"Thanks, I'm good. I should let Natalie know."

She was pushing me out the door without physically pushing me out the door. Her eyes hit mine, and I thought I could read so much more than gratitude in them. So much more than guilt or embarrassment. I thought I could read how much she wished we didn't have to stop hugging.

"Falyn."

"Some other time, if you want."

That seemed to have two meanings. I wasn't sure which one I wanted more.

17

Her door loomed before me. It had been a week since we'd ended the evening so abruptly. I'd left messages but hadn't heard anything from her. Vivian was being evasive, too. I didn't know what was going on, but it had to be bad for both of my close friends to avoid me.

When I knocked, no one answered. Her car was in the driveway. The boys' van wasn't. She could be out with them, but for some reason, I had the feeling she wasn't. I knocked again. And again.

"What?" Falyn called from the side porch.

I walked around to the side and saw her sitting in a chair with a cigarette in her hand. She flicked dispassionate eyes at me, brought the cigarette to her lips, and took a long puff. It was such a different Falyn than I was used to seeing.

"Hi." I leaned against one of the support posts, facing her.

She tipped her head in greeting and sucked in another long drag.

"You okay?"

"Sure. You?" Her tone was light as if we'd talked last night, but it wasn't the same lightness she used when she accepted invitations to join my tours or made suggestions to hang out or agreed to help fix whatever happened to make my bathroom fan stop working. This seemed forced, polite, obliging.

"You haven't been around." Anywhere. Not here, not at softball games, not on my couch, not on bike rides.

"Work's crazy." That wasn't a lie. Vivian had said as much when I checked in with her and tried to be offhand about how much I was freaking out that my buddy had stopped talking to me.

"Can I sit?"

Her long stare made me uncomfortable. It was an easy question, but she seemed to be considering it. For the first time, it felt like she didn't want me here. "Sure," she finally said.

I eased into the seat, hitching it around to face her. The evening air brushed over us. Warm for June, but my shorts and sleeveless polo were virtually all-weather for me. A forest of pine, spruce, and aspen trees surrounded Glory's side and backyards. In the distance Aspen Mountain stood tall and proud. The perfect little spot.

"You don't seem like everything's okay," I offered, flicking my gaze between her and the colorful plant at the edge of the yard. "I hate when people say that to me, but you really seem like something is terribly wrong."

She let out a long sigh, stubbed out her cigarette, and immediately pulled another from a half empty pack. "Bad week. I've been thinking about moving back."

"What? No." I jerked forward in my seat. Dammit, how could so much change in one week? "Why?"

"Nat doesn't deserve..." She shook her head. The strands of her hair didn't move as they usually would. Either she hadn't washed her hair this morning or she'd worn a hat at work. "I'm not sure this is a good fit for me."

"Did something happen with one of the clients? I know she has you going out on electrical jobs, but I thought you liked that." She did. I knew that. She preferred being an electrician to working regular construction. She hadn't done either back in Denver. So why would she be thinking of moving back where she wouldn't get to do the work she loved?

"I did, do, it's just..." Another pull on her cigarette. The stench permeated every molecule on the porch and made my eyes blink away a slight sting. "Nothing. A feeling."

I considered this. It couldn't be one of the guys. They were all joking around that day I helped out with landscaping, but perhaps she felt left out. "Maybe it's just a bad week. I don't like making decisions when things seem bad at first. It could right itself."

She nodded and finally seemed to give me her full attention. Her lips tugged up in the start of a smile. "I meant to call you back. I just—" Her gaze shot over my shoulder and an obscenity flew out of her mouth.

I craned my head around at her sudden alarm. I recognized the familiar markings of two police cars as they pulled into her drive. Again? No wonder she was so stressed.

"Time to go, Mol. I need to deal with this." That steely façade slipped back into place.

"I want to stay. Help if I can." Knots formed in my stomach. I disliked this front Falyn put on but hated that she felt she had to put it on.

"I wish you wouldn't." Sadness poured from her eyes and posture.

"Falyn Shaw, we have a warrant to search the premises. Stay where you are." One of the officers came up onto the porch and addressed me. "Ma'am, do you live here as well?"

"No, just a friend."

"I.D.?" He asked as his partner joined him on the porch. A man in a suit came up behind them. He looked familiar, but I couldn't place him.

"Why?" I asked as Falyn said, "She came to visit one of my housemates."

"Sit tight." The officer turned back to the man in the suit.

"What's going on," I whispered to Falyn. "Do they think you have whatever was taken?"

Her breath hitched. "They're going to look."

Were they crazy? Just because she was in the house where something was stolen didn't make her a thief.

"Can she leave?" Falyn asked. "She doesn't live here and has nothing to do with this."

The police officer stared hard at her before checking with the man in the suit. Then he looked back at me. "You can go."

I watched Falyn. She looked resigned but not worried. She also looked like she wanted me out of here to spare her more embarrassment. Such a different attitude from the woman I'd been getting to know. A much tougher, much harder version of herself. When threatened, I could become a little like that. The least I could do was cut her some slack.

"Call me later?"

"Sure," she sounded dismissive for the cops' sake.

I weaved through the four officers on the porch to get down to my truck. Once inside, I called Vivian. If this had something to do with Natalie's company, she should know.

"The police are searching Falyn's place," I said as soon as she answered.

"What? Right now?" This was the appropriate amount of distress. Vivian didn't go for steely fronts.

"She just told me to leave. She's acting like it's no big deal." Or Falyn the Android was acting like it was no big deal, I should say.

"I better tell Nat."

"Do you know what's going on? Are they searching Nat's place, too?"

"She wasn't at the jobsite. Just Falyn, Miguel, and Cole."

"Are they searching Miguel's place?" I was grabbing for anything that would make sense of the police getting a warrant to search someone's house without other evidence. It seemed like they could make the same case for a party guest or housecleaner.

"I don't know." A loud breath whistled across the line. "Listen, I know you guys...well, anyway, it's not my place to say anything."

What was that? Vivian didn't hold things back. That wasn't like her at all. "What's not your place?"

"Nothing," she was quick to assure. "Just give Falyn some time to deal with this."

"Okay." She was right. I'd be freaking if the cops were searching my place. I could give my friend the space she needed to work through this odd turn of events. "I'll talk to you later."

"Molly?" Vivian paused and cleared her throat. "I know you want to fix this, but really, just give her a little time."

Why did it feel like Vivian knew more about the woman who'd become my good friend and whom I'd had a sexual relationship with? Nothing about that felt right or good.

18

Palming the c-notes, I finished shaking the hand of the father before his two girls wrapped their arms around me in a sandwich hug. They'd been fun and adventurous but a lot of work. They'd also been with me all weekend. A long exhausting weekend that I was glad to have over. I'd earned the next two days off, and the two hundred dollars the father had tipped me.

I dragged the shop vac over to the van and began cleaning it out. Wayne and one of the new guys put this off until their next shift, which often meant that if someone needed the van first thing, they were stuck with cleaning someone else's mess. Drove me nuts.

"High energy those two, huh, Mol?" Ron asked as he came out the back of the store after closing for the night. "You wiped?"

"They were cute, but that father is in for a wild ride once they reach their teenage years."

"Don't I know it. My Beth was hell on wheels once she hit fifteen. I wasn't sure either of us would survive."

I smiled. His daughter was Ron's pride and joy even during her teenage years. Now in college, I missed having her underfoot at the shop on weekends. She'd liked me even when she was being a teenage hellion. "Any news from Greece?"

"She's still enjoying it. I'm the best dad in the world."

I had to laugh. It had been his wife's idea to let Beth spend the summer in Europe. He didn't want her to go. "You are, Ron."

He beamed and took the vacuum from me after I shut it off. I put the clean floor mats back in place and dumped the collected trash into the bin on the way back into the store. I checked the schedule on the board, noting that I was leading a hike on Thursday, white water rafting on Friday, mountain biking on Saturday, kayaking on Sunday, and hiking on Monday. All good activities, but I wasn't looking forward to it. I still had three to four months left of these summer activities, and I was already getting a little tired of them. Or maybe it was something else I was tired of. Two days off would help.

I flipped through the contacts on my phone. I could use a drink with a friend. My thumb hovered over the listing for Falyn. No, she was going through some stuff right now and clearly didn't want me around. Vivian and Dwight were on their annual international shopping trip to pick up new design ideas and elements. Kelsey liked to chill out at home on weeknights. James was taking a conversational Spanish class. Nobody looked good as I scrolled through every name. Monday nights were hard to motivate people into anything. That was one detriment to my job. I worked weekends when most of my friends had them off.

Tessa. Hmm. I could try her. If she wasn't taking clients around for showings she might be free.

I pressed the call button and waited for it to ring through. "Hey, Tess, you free tonight?"

"Yeah, let's do something fun."

I felt a smile come over my face and breathed in a sigh of relief. At least someone was free tonight. We made plans to meet as I zipped up my backpack.

Outside, the street was fairly quiet now that the ski areas were closed for the season. Summer tourists customarily arrived Thursday or Friday afternoon and stayed four days. Shops closed earlier, restaurants took one or two days off a week, and fewer people window shopped. It was easier to scent the air, pine and bark and lushness. A crowded town dampened the luster of the mountain freshness.

Crossing over to South Mill, I made my way into Tessa's favorite bar. I preferred the one closer to my place with over twenty beers on tap, but this place had passable mojitos. After ordering our drinks, I debated placing a food order, too. Tessa always had the same thing here, but I didn't want to be too assertive. She had enough of that with Kathleen.

"Molly-Bear!" Tessa exclaimed as she wove through the tables to get to me.

"Hi, Tess." I stood to hug and kiss her hello. The gentle brush of lips didn't cause my heart to flutter. It most definitely didn't set me aflame like someone else's kiss had.

"I'm so glad you suggested this. I had a tough weekend with three open houses yesterday and signed up two new buyers."

That actually sounded like a good weekend for her. She needed buyers. They were more work for her, but buyers almost always closed a deal. Sellers could fire her after three months if she didn't close the deal.

"Kathleen called while I was showing a couple around my West End place."

My eyebrows rose. Kathleen had been giving her the cold shoulder since they broke up. "So you finished with the showing and called her back?"

"Huh?" Her eyes flicked away. "Oh, no, I took the call."

I pushed back in my chair. "You what?" During a client showing, she took a call from her bitch ex-girlfriend who'd been ignoring her for months? Clients didn't like when they weren't the sole focus of their realtor. Tessa knew that. Tessa lived by that.

"She called me. Finally!" Excitement made her light blue eyes glitter.

"What did your clients think?"

"Huh? Oh, well, they weren't my clients, just a couple going through an open house. They weren't buyers anyway."

"Did they have a realtor? Did you try to interest them in other properties?" These were all things she'd normally do, had done many times. Tessa was good at her job. So was her business partner, Rachel. I knew Rachel wouldn't be happy to hear that Tessa blew off potential new clients to take a phone call from her ex.

"What?" Her gaze flicked away in thought. "Oh, you know, I didn't think to ask. They weren't acting like buyers. You know everyone wants inside one of the Victorians in the West End. They were probably just neighbors who wanted to snoop."

"But you don't know that for sure." I wasn't sure why I was so upset about this. It seemed like I cared about Tessa's career more than she did right now.

"I have their names on my list. I'll contact them tomorrow. But she called!"

She was so exuberant I wanted to be happy, but I wasn't. "Great." I mustered my best fake smile.

"Isn't it? She wants to get together and talk."

"Tess," I began then stopped. What? *Don't let that bitch manipulate you anymore? Don't hang your hopes on something that isn't going to get better? Get over that user?* "Be careful."

"Of what? She sounded happy, like her old self."

I shook my head. Falyn had been right. I was working toward a losing goal. Even if Tessa was interested, I'd be nothing more than a rebound. She obviously needed someone like Kathleen whether it was Kathleen or not. I didn't fit that role.

"You're right. Hope it turns into something."

"Me, too," she said dreamily then went on to tell me every word Kathleen said and what she hoped would happen when they met for drinks.

Not once in all the time she talked did she ask how I was doing or why I'd called for a night out or how my weekend tours had gone. She was normally a lot more considerate, but she obviously functioned better as a couple.

Scratch one more potential off my list. It seemed like I'd gone through every possibility in town and the next town over. Maybe my old tour company in Seattle was hiring. I much preferred small mountain resort towns to city life, but college had been fun there and the tour outfit was good enough. There were a lot more single lesbians. Single lesbians who weren't looking for a rebound. And single lesbians who weren't my buddies that caused confusing emotions whenever I was around them.

19

A doorbell interrupted my closet organization. I'd been reduced to closet organization for my evening's activities because I couldn't interest anyone in going out on a Tuesday night. It needed organizing, and I'd make some donation center very happy tomorrow when I dropped off all my gently used but mostly forgotten clothes. A benefit to wearing cargo shorts and company shirts half the year was that a few pairs of jeans completed my wardrobe the rest of the year. Some of these clothes followed me here from college. It would be good to be rid of them.

The doorbell sounded again. I growled, wanting to shout through the connecting wall to my neighbor's unit. She was always home by now and always entertaining at this hour. If I heard her doorbell, surely she could. Then I realized it was my doorbell.

I dumped a pile of old sweats into the nearly full donation bag and went to the door. Falyn waited on the landing looking tired and a little sad. I sucked in a breath, feeling a flush come over my skin.

"Hi. Are you busy?"

"No. Come in." I stepped back to let her brush by. The smell of smoke wafted off her. Guess she'd upped her once a week habit to every day. I shouldn't be disappointed. It wasn't my body, but the odor wasn't great.

"I'm sorry," she said, her tone and expression showing every bit of her sorrow. "I've been a little wrapped up and a lousy friend. Please accept my apology."

She was just full of surprises tonight. "It's okay. You don't have to apologize. I don't know how I'd be if the police were hassling me for no reason."

Her hazel eyes skated away from mine, searching the apartment before coming back with a determined look. "It doesn't excuse me blowing you off. I'm sorry for that."

It seemed like she was leaving something out. Not that it mattered, I was just glad to have her here tonight. So glad that I hugged her.

She went rigid for a second then relaxed into my arms. My face brushed against her hair. The smoky smell blasted me as if she'd blown it right into my eyes, but I didn't care. She felt so good. Her long arms squeezed me to her, hands gripping my sides. Her heart beat against mine, heavy thumps that felt as good as her hug. We held each other for a long time, letting it release our tension.

"The Rockies are on," I said when she started to pull back. "We can make your fabulous burritos and watch."

She started to smile but concern clouded her expression. "What's wrong with your eyes?"

My hand came up, fingers touching eyelids that were somehow wet. Odd, I wasn't sad. I was just the opposite now that she was here.

"Oh, jeez, you're allergic to cigarette smoke, aren't you?" She gripped my shoulders and stared at me with sorrow. "Why didn't you just say so when you found out I smoked?"

I blinked my watery eyes to clear them. Allergic to smoke? Was that a thing? I knew it bothered me and I could smell it from yards away, but allergic? "I don't think I am."

"But you can smell it on me, can't you?" She stepped back. "I'm sorry, Molly.

"It's okay." I closed the distance between us. "I never noticed it was a problem. I just thought I didn't like the smell."

"It affects you pretty badly." Her hands came up to cup my face, thumbs brushing away the moisture from under my eyes. "Well, that's the best motivation I could have for quitting."

My eyes popped wide. She'd quit so it wouldn't bother me? Amazing, and one of the main reasons I liked her so much. "You don't have to do that."

"I will. I don't like it anyway. It's just a habit I picked up in...a bad habit. It doesn't help with stress as much as it used to." She brushed some stray strands of her hair off her cheek. They fell into place at the wave near her ear. No hat hair today, nothing but bouncy, shiny blond tresses. "I'll head home to shower and change. Do you want to come over and watch the game there?"

She might change her mind if she got back to her place. If I went over there again, she might decide to push me away like she had the last time. I couldn't risk that happening. "Use the shower here. I've got clothes you can borrow."

She squinted and tilted her head. "You sure?"

"Yeah, I'll get the stuff for dinner started. You know where the spare towels are." I felt my face get hot and looked away. Yeah, she knew where the spare towels were. The last time she was here she'd used one, put it in the laundry, and woken me to say goodbye after we'd made love most of the night. "I'll set out some clothes for you."

She studied me for a minute. Perhaps she was also remembering the last time she'd used my shower, or maybe she was thinking the same thing I was. If she went home, we'd lose this fragile reconnection. "Okay."

The shower flipped on as I was pulling tomatoes, cheese, and lettuce out of the fridge. I almost started humming, thinking about how happy it made me that my friend felt comfortable here. That she'd shower because she knew the smoke bothered me. That she wanted to stay.

I ventured into the interrupted chaos of my closet to find a Rockies jersey and my best pair of shorts and set them outside the bathroom door. I turned and hurried back to the kitchen, fighting the desire to open the bathroom door and place the clothes inside. My glass shower door wouldn't hide anything. I'd be glued in place staring at her wet, lean, sexy, showering body.

Friends. Buddies. Chums. Pals. No looking or thinking about naked, sexy, wet, friend bodies. Or how her hipbones created these enticing little dips that drew my eyes to the soft, trimmed curls on her mound. Or where her collarbones stood out, pointing to that lickable hollow at the base of her throat. And the upward tilt of her squeezable breasts. I should have stayed awake to study her longer. Touch her longer.

No. Bad buddy, bad.

I reached into the fridge for the avocados I'd picked up hoping she'd follow through on her promise to make fresh guacamole some time. She could do it tonight. She liked cooking. I didn't unless I was helping her. Typically I lived on whatever I could grill, sandwiches, and frozen dinners.

I started chopping the tomatoes when the bathroom door opened and closed. She'd found the clothes. I tried not to imagine her wrapped in a towel, but it was difficult. Had I done this with other friends? Did I picture Vivian naked when we'd first met? I know I'd never crushed on her because she was way too gorgeous for me. I never knew why I did that. I was interested in any woman who was a four to an eight on my scale. When they were tens like Viv, it was like my brain shut off the attraction part. No, I never pictured Vivian naked. J&B, sure, many, many times, and I definitely wouldn't bed them. So there, it was a normal thing for me. Attractive woman, picture her naked.

Falyn appeared looking far better than I ever did in my baseball jersey. "You got a lot done." She smiled and took a spot next to me. She smelled like my soap and rosemary scented shampoo, both familiar and comforting. "Better?" One eyebrow rose as she glanced at me.

"You didn't have to."

She studied my eyes, which no longer felt itchy or watery. "Yes, I did. It won't happen again."

I wanted to tell her not to quit smoking for me. I wanted to tell her that she shouldn't worry about how I reacted to smoke on her clothes and hair. I wanted to tell her that it wasn't my business what habits she kept or lost, but I didn't because no one had ever changed their habits for me. No one. And to think she'd try felt really good. Like I was as important to her as she was to me.

That was it, what felt so good about her. I was as important to her as she was to me. I'd never had that either. I felt myself turning to stare at her. Her hair was still wet and looked sexy. Her lips pressed tightly together in concentration while she peeled the avocados. Her contoured jaw tilted down as she worked with her graceful hands.

Heat pulsed out from my chest, flooding my arms and face. My heart twitched and started pumping double-time. Sparks swirled in my stomach. I gripped the counter for balance. This wasn't how I'd felt about any of the tourist flings. It wasn't how I'd felt about the snowbirds I'd been involved with. It wasn't even how I felt about my crushes. This was substantial.

"What?" She noticed I'd stopped slicing the tomatoes. "Did you cut yourself?" She turned and reached for my hand, tenderly inspecting each finger.

"No," I said in a daze but didn't pull my hand back.

"Oh, good, you scared me. Cole got a jolt today, and I probably went all grey from the scare."

The news put the flare of lust in check. "Is he okay?"

"Yeah, he just forgot to throw the breaker first, but it scared both of us. Natalie must have lectured him for a half hour after that."

I chuckled. Natalie was pretty obsessive about safety. "What do you mean all grey?"

"I've been heading that way for a while now."

My eyes flipped up to her damp hair. The blond looked darker wet. I wanted to reach up and run my fingers through the strands curled over her collar. "You don't dye your hair?"

"Two years now."

"No."

"Same color, just covering the white streak."

"Premature grey. Hot-Ness!"

She laughed and my heart pumped faster. I hadn't been kidding, but I let her think I had been. "Just wait, lady. When you get ancient like me, you'll want to remember what your natural color is before you start dyeing."

"You're only four and a half years older."

"Your body will give out, you'll groan when you sit and stand, you'll say things like 'when I was a kid,' and you'll think you're too young to go grey."

"You're definitely too young."

She gave a wistful smile and went back to stirring the Spanish rice she had in a pan. I tried not to stare, but it wasn't every day I learned I had actual feelings for someone. Feelings that we'd both decided couldn't be explored. Or shouldn't be explored. Or something like that. What had we decided? Oh, yes, not to sleep together because we were better as friends. But that was when sleeping together was just sex.

"Okay, really." She stopped stirring and focused completely on me. "What's up? Did your weekend go okay? Any assholes?"

She asked. Tessa, my friend of many years, hadn't asked. Hadn't cared enough to ask. I'd known Falyn months rather than years, and she cared enough to be concerned about my work. I really needed to figure out what do to about her.

20

Vivian asked me to pick her up at the jobsite. Her brother needed her car for some reason and Natalie was giving her nephew driving lessons later. Viv felt like dinner out, which we hadn't done alone in a while.

I skirted past Natalie's truck, two other trucks, an SUV, and Falyn's bike on the now paved driveway up to Vivian's house. Guess I was early since the whole crew was still there. It would give me a chance to inspect the project a little longer.

Viv's nephews darted out of the house as I hit the bottom step. I broke into a grin. I had a little love affair going with these cuties. Their mom, Cassie, appeared in the doorway after them, waving hello.

"Hey, guys." I stopped to say hello. "You helping your aunt build her place?"

"She needs us to help," Teddy told me.

"I'm sure she does." I patted the seven-year-old's hard hat and scooped up his younger brother, Mason, for a surprise squeeze. He giggled and squirmed out of my arms.

"C'mon, Ms. Molly, you got to see what we did." Mase tugged on my hand.

"We're late to meet your dad, boys," Cassie told them, coming forward to give me a quick hug. "Aunt Viv can do the show and tell."

"Okay," Mason agreed easily. He never whined. If I ever had kids, I'd want one just like Mase.

"Viv's upstairs with Sammi." Cassie herded the boys down the driveway. "You can still make it to Viv's b-day cookout, can't you? The usual gang will be there, and Nat's entire crew is showing up."

I'd switched with one of the new guys so I could take Sunday off. Cassie could throw a mean birthday bash, but I was really looking forward to spending the day with Falyn. Since I worked weekends and she worked on my days off, we hadn't had a whole day to hang together.

"Wouldn't miss it." I waved and stepped up into the house, spotting Miguel first and saying hello.

He looked up as he dropped another stack of sanded boards at his feet. "Good to see you, Molly. You here to help?"

"I'm here to steal Viv." I watched as Tyler and Curtis nailed the boards horizontally on two of the walls. I'd seen Vivian's drawings for this room. The boards would be whitewashed, making the room feel more beach cottage than rustic, which suited Vivian's style perfectly.

I reached for my cellphone and snapped a picture for my mom. We liked exchanging snapshots of whatever was going on around us on our weekly calls. Sometimes she'd just send a picture of what she made for dinner. She could play really dirty, too. If a photo with an entire Polish feast appeared on my phone, she was almost guaranteeing I'd jump on a plane. No one cooked her native Polish food better than Mama.

"Wait, let me take my hat off." Tyler whipped off the hat and patted down his hair. He stepped directly into the view of my camera and posed, flexing his arms while holding up the board for Curtis to nail.

Curtis moved to block Tyler's face with his nail gun, shooting me a winning grin. "Who's getting the pics?"

"My mom. She won't be coming up until after you're done with the place."

"I'm available for all kinds of modeling gigs," Tyler joked as I snapped one last picture of the downstairs and started for the staircase.

Upstairs, I found Ramón and Natalie installing glass pocket doors in Vivian's studio slash Natalie's office. In the guestroom, Cole and Falyn were fiddling with the receptacles. I smiled at the size of the room, just large enough to accommodate their nephews but not large enough to encourage the rest of Vivian's family to use the room as their own private ski lodge. Typical Vivian.

"What's up, Molls?" Cole greeted.

"Hey, guys," I said, stopping to watch their progress.

Falyn tipped her head with a smile. She concentrated on finishing what she was doing before looking at me. "You just stopping by?"

I watched her long fingers deftly straighten the switch and grab another screw to secure it in place. Before meeting her, I'd never found construction work alluring. Now I couldn't pry my eyes away. "Viv and I are getting dinner. You want to come?"

"I'm going for a bike ride with Lena and Brooke tonight. Thanks, though."

I felt a twinge of disappointment, but happiness broke through when I realized that she had made some other good friends in town. No more talk of leaving town if she had lots of friends anchoring her here. "Hunter Creek's a nice trail. If you don't go tonight, we can try it next time."

"Hey, you snuck in." Vivian poked her head out of the bathroom. She and Samantha joined us, loaded down with sample tiles.

"Not quite ready, I see."

"We're trying to decide on tiles for the bath up here."

"Crucial," I joked and received a shoulder smack.

Falyn and Cole laughed but went back to work as soon as they caught Vivian's mock glare. Samantha winked at me and hustled back into the bathroom.

"Mama wants pics," I said, capturing the view from the open balcony to the first floor.

"How is Morela?" she asked. "They're still coming in November, right? They'll be able to see it finished."

"Yep, and she will be expecting a tour." Usually I went to Phoenix to visit my parents, but I'd be turning forty in November, so they were headed this way to celebrate. "You want in?" I gestured with my camera before lining up a shot that included Vivian.

I turned the camera back to the guestroom and raised my brow in silent question at Falyn. She started to shake her head, but Cole cut her off by throwing an arm around her shoulders and posing them both. I snapped the shot before she could come up with a reason why she'd never shown me a photo with her in it despite seeing every photo album I had. "Thanks, guys. My mom likes to see who I'm hanging with." And was especially curious about Falyn even without knowing that we'd been intimate once.

"If we're lucky, she'll cook for us when she gets here," Vivian told them. "You thought Tamiko's gyoza was good, wait till you have Morela's pierogi."

"Pierogi?" Ramón asked. "Are you Russian, Molly?"

"Polish," I told him, feeling the pride of my mother's immigrant status puff me up. She'd come to America at eighteen and worked as a hotel maid for ten years before she met my dad in a Polish community center. Their marriage came far later in life than her culture would consider acceptable at the time. Everyone else in her family had gotten married by the time they were nineteen. I loved that she'd bucked every tradition without disrespecting any of them. I hoped to do the same.

Falyn glanced over and winked. She knew how much my parents and their heritage meant to me. She didn't feel the same way about her ethnicity. She was a mix of Scandinavian, Dutch, English and some others she wasn't sure about. Yet she let me drone on and on about my mom's story and visiting Poland to meet her side of the family. She listened and asked questions and encouraged me to talk all I wanted about something she didn't find important for herself. But I did, so she liked hearing about it. She was the best kind of friend.

"First generation," Vivian added. "Her mom's got the best accent."

That was true. I'd been guilty of calling Mama just to let her accent soothe me.

"Will you'll bring some for us to taste?" Ramón asked.

"I'll invite you over for dinner when she's here," I promised then turned back to Vivian and gestured to the sample tiles. "Which one are you going with?"

"Natalie?" Vivian got her attention. "Got a sec?"

She set the door she was holding against the wall and went to Vivian with a dreamy smile. Now that's what a woman in love looked like. I might not be completely sure of my feelings where Falyn was concerned yet, but I didn't look like that.

"Which do you like better?" Vivian laid out the tile samples in the light from the French doors to the balcony off the studio.

She watched Natalie carefully. Falyn and Cole had stopped working to watch her, too. Something was going on, but I couldn't put my finger on it.

Natalie looked at each sample. Three were different marbles, one was glass mosaic, and another travertine. They were all beautiful and looked expensive, but one of Vivian's many design talents was finding expensive-looking materials at budget prices. My eyes immediately went to the marble with the greenish tint in the veins.

Natalie considered each then looked up at her girlfriend. "Are you asking because you like all five equally and want my preference? Or are you asking because you think I should have a say in decisions like this?"

Vivian's lips quirked, a motion I'd seen many times over the years. Natalie had guessed exactly what she was thinking and she was tickled by it. "I've been having my way with everything in here."

"You're allowed. This has been your dream since you went to design school, hon."

"Yes, but it'll be yours, too. You should get some say."

I swallowed the pang of envy I felt. Vivian and Natalie would be moving in together when the house was done. Something Vivian had wanted since I'd known her. Romance and love and companionship, all of which Natalie provided. It never occurred to me to think about moving in with someone before dating at least a year, but I didn't think anything of them going for it. Odd that I felt more sure of their relationship than I had about any of mine. My eyes shot to Falyn. Well, maybe not all my relationships.

"I got to choose all the materials we used in the structure. You even redesigned the master bathroom for me," Natalie continued.

"But that was as much for me as you," Vivian said and I found myself nodding in agreement. Who wouldn't want a two-sided shower, back to back vanities and cabinets, a large soaking tub, and separate toilet rooms? I'd seen her do something similar at Lena's house a year ago, but she'd outdone herself for her own house.

"You're letting me use reclaimed wood and the best materials."

"You really don't mind if I make all the design decisions?" Vivian reached out and grabbed Natalie's hand. They looked good together, but better, they were good together.

"It's been your dream, Vivi," Natalie said sweetly.

I almost rolled my eyes. Was anyone really that sweet to the woman she loved? Okay, yes, Natalie was. I'd had a year of proof to know that. None of my girlfriends were ever that sweet. I was expected to be the sweet, accommodating one.

Falyn shot me a look that said she knew exactly what I was thinking. We'd just witnessed another nauseating moment between our two friends but were both secretly happy about it. Yet another reason she and I made a good pair. Of buddies, of course. But maybe more. In time.

21

We strolled through City Market using one cart for our groceries. Before meeting Falyn, I really didn't like grocery shopping. It was mundane and tedious. Not being a cook probably added to the boredom of collecting the same kind of food every week. With Falyn, it was an event. Something to do together.

"Did I forget the boys' beer?" She glanced back and rifled through her half of the cart.

"You did," I confirmed. "But shouldn't the boys be buying that?"

"We finished their case last night. I'm not leaving them with an empty shelf."

I felt a smile pull at my lips. Her courtesy was one of the things I liked most about her. Making simple things fun was another checkmark on her list of appealing attributes. Grocery shopping, folding laundry, even biking around the neighborhood. I'd come to think of my bike as a work tool only. With Falyn, it became a fun activity again. She didn't care if we were biking mountain trails or streets. She just liked to ride her bike, and I liked riding with her.

"You want spaghetti for dinner?" she asked. "I think the guys are home, so I better get double."

"Triple," I inserted. They ate a lot. Normally I'd be disappointed not to have Falyn to myself, but she made hanging out with her housemates almost as enjoyable as spending time alone.

"Let me run back and grab their beer."

"Are you making the sauce, or should I get a jar?"

"Jar?" She gave me a scathing look at the idea of tomato sauce from a jar. She and my mom were going to get along great. "Thanks for the reminder. I'll grab enough tomatoes for the sauce tonight and a practice run on the dip I'm bringing to Cassie's. Meet you over in the bakery aisle for the garlic bread."

Garlic. No kissing tonight. Not that I should be thinking about kissing my buddy in the middle of the grocery store or anywhere for that matter. Yet, more and more lately, I was wondering why we weren't kissing and why we'd shut down any sexual intimacy. We were sharing other intimacies. She certainly knew me well enough. She even knew how I'd react to things almost before I did. I'd never had that with friends or girlfriends before.

I wheeled the cart out of the aisle and started for the end of the store. I recognized one of my neighbors. She had her toddler with her, so I was saved from having a long conversation. After a quick hello, I made my way to the bakery section.

"What's up, Molly?"

Ugh. Cherise. Not my favorite chick, but small town rules demanded politeness. Especially since she was one of an even smaller cluster of lesbians. If I wanted to continue hanging out with J&B, I had to act like I liked Cherise since they were friends.

She was still in her police uniform, which was another thing I didn't like about her. She was the typical power-hungry authority figure. I'd seen her put a tourist through roadside sobriety tests just because she thought his vanity license plate was obnoxious.

"Hey, Cherise."

"Shopping?" Her brown eyes twinkled like she'd made a deductive conclusion.

"Getting groceries," I confirmed unnecessarily. What else would I be doing in a grocery store? Giving a poetry reading?

"Haven't seen you in a while. What have you been up to?" She ran her fingers through her short, dark blond hair. Curious how the same shade did so much more for Falyn.

"Working mostly." It was best to keep things brief because—ah, yes, there it was. Her walkie crackled to life.

As usual, she put up a stopping hand and leaned down toward the mic on her shoulder to hear whatever the dispatcher was calling out. She wasn't on duty, but she liked that it made her look important.

"Do you need to respond?" I asked, stroking her ego as she would expect.

"No, unit three has it." If memory served, unit three was Kevin. She knew I knew Kevin. Why not just say that Kevin was taking care of it?

"Well, good to see you." I tried to push past her, but she stopped me.

"You heard from Brandy recently?"

Ah, so this was the reason for her sudden chattiness. She liked Brandy. She wanted Brandy, but J&B's competitiveness kept her from being able to keep a hold on Brandy. They'd been together a few times. Brandy wasn't enamored. Cherise was.

"She's in Denver for the rest of the summer like usual."

Cherise knew this. J&B vacated Aspen during the non-skiing months. They had a standing summer sublet in Denver to work at some clothing boutique. They liked the discount and the city but returned each winter to be ski instructors at Snowmass where they raked in more tips than I did all year.

I studied Cherise, wondering why she was asking me about this. She must have thought bringing up Brandy would make me mention her to Brandy the next time we talked. Like we were in homeroom, and I was going to tell Brandy that Cherise was crushing on her when I saw her in geometry class later.

"Oh, yeah. Might have to head up there and hang out soon."

Yippee for her. Why did she think I cared about this? We weren't exactly buddies who confided in each other.

"Did you grab the French bread?" Falyn asked as she came up behind me.

Cherise's eyes narrowed when she caught sight of Falyn. "What's going on here?"

"Have you two met?" I glanced back at Falyn. She was rooted to her spot three steps away, muscles tense. Only her eyes moved, first from Cherise to me, then from Cherise to the front of the store. She looked ready to bolt. After the police visits to her home, any cop must make her nervous.

"Oh, we've met." Cherise's expression went from suspicious to superior. "What are you doing hanging out with an ex-con, Molly?"

What? What kind of bull was she throwing my way now? "What are you talking about?"

"She didn't tell you?" She gave me a haughty grin. "This is classic. Brandy's going to love hearing about this."

Falyn gripped my elbow and tipped her head, indicating she was ready to go. I wanted to leave, too, but I didn't like Cherise getting mouthy about her. I was about to fire back when I recognized that hurt look on Falyn's face. She was getting choked up, and I didn't want her to feel cornered.

"Let's go." I turned my back on Cherise.

"No, you need to hear this." Cherise's big hand grabbed my forearm to stop me. She was two inches shorter, but she had the hands of a giant. "Your little friend here did time."

I spun around. She looked serious, not like she was trying to push my buttons. She tended to exaggerate or come on too strong in some situations, especially when she was meeting new people. "What the hell are you talking about?"

"We pulled her in for questioning on a recent B&E. Or didn't she tell you that? Yeah, your little pal here did what?" She glanced at Falyn with question in her eyes. "A dime for multiple burglaries."

"I'm leaving," Falyn stated before I had a chance to respond. She darted up the aisle and straight out the door.

"What's with you, Cherise? That's not funny."

Her mouth dropped open. "I know it's not. That's why I told you. She's obviously been lying to you, but you need to know about her. We don't have the evidence this time, but she's a thief."

"Are you serious?" I used my hardest tone to let her know I wasn't joking around. I allowed her and many of my friends to have fun at my expense because I could take it. But this wasn't something to joke about.

"She was part of a burglary ring in Boulder like ten years ago. She went to prison for it. Didn't you know?"

No. I didn't. If it was true, I felt like I should. It couldn't be true, though. I knew Falyn. She wasn't a person who would do that. She worked hard. She enjoyed the little things in life. She didn't care about money or possessions. No, nothing about what Cherise said matched up with the woman I knew.

"Is this another one of your elaborate jokes? Just own up to it now, because if you don't, I'll never speak to you again."

Her hands came up in a defensive gesture. "I'm not. I swear. I was surprised to see her with you. I know we haven't always been good friends, but she's an ex-con and you deserve better."

Her radio crackled to life again, and this time, she acted like she had to take the call. I watched her abandon her cart and hit the exit at a trot. Normally I'd make fun of the trot that would hardly save her any time, but it didn't even cross my mind. That was how much what she'd said screwed with my head.

Twice, I'd watched Falyn deal with the police. If what Cherise said was true, she had every opportunity to tell me she'd gone to jail and she hadn't. What did that say about how "close" our friendship was?

22

Groceries in hand, I approached Falyn's house hesitantly. I didn't want to have this discussion, and yet, I did. Cherise could have been lying or exaggerating. It was the only explanation for what she'd told me. None of what she said meshed with the Falyn I'd been getting to know and certainly not the Falyn I was starting to have feelings for.

The door popped open before I reached it. Curtis shot me a wide smile. "Hey, Mol."

"Hi, Curtis. Is Falyn around?"

He grabbed two bags to help. "Lena called about a blown breaker at her place. Falyn's over there trying to fix it. You want to wait?"

"Thanks." I followed him inside.

"This is a lot. You doing her shopping for her now?" Curtis kidded.

"We were shopping together, but I got tied up. Thought I'd drop the groceries by."

I didn't normally lie so easily. I could see how someone could, though. Maybe this explained Falyn not saying anything. If she didn't say anything, that is.

We unloaded her groceries, chatting about the progress of Vivian's house. Curtis seemed very happy when the beer appeared and oblivious to anything that Falyn might have said when she came home. She could have walked off whatever upset her enough to leave the grocery store. That thought made me feel slightly better.

After setting the last of her vegetables into the crispers, I wasn't sure if I should be here. I almost didn't want to know if what Cherise said was true. I wanted to go back to believing that my friend had told me everything important about herself.

Falyn arrived home before I made up my mind. She set her toolbox in the mudroom. When she looked up and saw me, she froze for a second and her face fell. I hated myself for making her feel whatever regret she was feeling right now.

"Hi," I greeted. "I brought the groceries."

She blinked, frowning for a second. "You didn't have to do that. Here, let me get you some money."

"That's okay."

Her eyes narrowed, either suspicious or angry, but she got over whatever it was and disappeared into her bedroom for her wallet. I hadn't come over here to get paid for groceries. She needed them, and they were already in my cart. I just had to load them and deliver.

She surfaced with three twenties and stuffed them into my hand. It was about a dollar more than what I'd paid for her share. I wondered if it was a guess or if she really kept a running tab on everything she added to the cart. "Thank you for bringing them over."

I tried to catch her eye, but she was busying herself with checking the refrigerator. "Falyn, please."

Her shoulders tensed as she turned to face me. A look of resignation accompanied her stiff shoulders and tightly strung movements. Her gaze flicked to Curtis in the living room. He seemed caught up in a TV show, but I could tell he was aware of us. She tipped her head toward the sliders.

I followed and took my usual seat. Her eyes glanced toward the street then over at Spence and Mei's driveway. Almost like she was expecting someone to appear and interrupt us. Her cats followed us onto the porch before she could close the door. The skinny one, Dancer, bounded onto my lap while Tusk wound around her chair and settled against her feet.

Falyn appeared to be waiting for me to speak as she watched Dancer and the street. She reached for a pencil on the chair arm and started rolling it between her fingers. The gesture made it clear she was craving a cigarette. I felt bad for being the impetus to her quitting. If any conversation needed a stress reliever, this would be the one.

"Is what Cherise said true?"

Her eyes showed momentary surprise. "At least you're giving me the benefit of the doubt. I appreciate that."

"I always give my friends the benefit of the doubt." I didn't understand people who didn't. It was the main job of being a friend.

"Cherise is your friend."

"No, she isn't. We're friendly but not friends." I made sure I caught her gaze. "She was saying some pretty heavy stuff."

She reached down and picked up Tusk. As a delaying tactic it worked well. Tusk took her time winding around Falyn's lap to find a comfy spot.

The wait got to me. "Was any of it true?"

"You already know the police were here."

"Yes, but it doesn't mean what she said was true." I sighed. She wasn't making this easy. I scratched behind Dancer's ears for something to do. "Just tell me. Were you in prison?"

She met my gaze head on. "Yes."

"For how long?"

"Five years, one month, six days."

Jesus. It was true. That she knew to the exact day made my heart ache even more. "For what?"

"Burglary."

So far Cherise hadn't lied. I'd never met anyone who'd been to jail, let alone prison. This was unbelievable. She'd been to prison and stayed there for five years.

"Like people or homes?" I forced myself to continue. Part of me didn't want to know. Part of me wished she'd lie to me because I couldn't get my brain around this.

"Robbery refers to people. Burglary is of a premises."

I didn't ask for a legal lesson, dammit. Why couldn't she just tell me everything? I didn't want to be made to feel like I was in the wrong here. "So, homes?"

"Yes."

"How many?"

"Twelve."

"You stole from twelve homes and went to prison for five years because of it?"

"Something like that."

"Something like that?" I jerked forward, forgetting that I'd jostle Dancer out of my lap. "Now's not the time to be flippant."

She took a deep breath and released it. Tusk jumped off her lap and joined Dancer at the sliders. She stretched over to let them back into the house. "Do I look flippant?"

No, she didn't. She looked sullen and hurt. I felt the same way. How could she not tell me this? I reached out and laid my hand on her arm. I needed this connection. She didn't rip her arm away, which was a good sign.

"So what does 'something like that' mean?"

Her mouth opened then shut, swallowing roughly. Her eyes grew watery. "It means that I stole from twelve homes, but the police only knew about eight before the statute ran out on the others. It means that I was sentenced to eight years, but I got time off for good behavior and paroled for two years, so I spent a little over five years in prison. It means that once I got out of prison, trying to find a place to live or a job wasn't much easier than just staying in to serve the full term."

Every statement she listed made my stomach hurt more, but I still had to know. "Why didn't you tell me?"

She let out a disgusted snort. "Because I didn't want you to think the way you now think of me."

How was I thinking of her? I wasn't even sure. How could she be? "You didn't think I'd want to know?" My throat went dry. "We've been close friends for months now, and you've been lying this whole time."

"I didn't lie."

I swiped my hand through the air. "Technicality. You could have said something when the police came by."

She shook her head and blinked hard, causing a tear to spring from the corner of one eye. Her hand swiped it away instantly. "What would I have said? These guys are accusing me of doing something I've never done before because I once did something similar?"

"No, but you could have said that they were hassling you because of your record."

"And that would have solved what for you?"

God, she was frustrating. I expected, I don't know, pleading? At least something that showed she was sorry she hadn't said anything. "I just can't believe you didn't tell me."

"Be realistic. How would that have gone? 'Nice to meet you, Molly. I was in prison for five years.' Would you have hung out with me if you'd known from the beginning?"

She had me there. I honestly didn't know how I would have reacted. Would I have given her a fair shake? I would like to think I wouldn't have prejudged her, but I probably would have. Prison wasn't like finding out a friend had an arrest for pot possession in college. This was a big deal.

I tried swallowing the lump in my throat. A second tear raced down her cheek. I felt my eyes well up in sympathy. "Natalie knows?"

"Of course." Falyn raked a hand through her hair before letting it drop to her thigh with a slap. "Even if

she hadn't known me when it happened, I would have
told her. I wouldn't put her business in jeopardy. It's
something I have to list on the application for my
electrician's license anyway."

"So some random people at the electrical licensing
board know about you, but you don't tell the person you
hang out with the most?" I knew I was bordering on
petulant, but so many things were bugging me right
now.

She flicked resigned eyes at me again. "That's right.
Strangers know more about me than you do, Molly."

Her voice dripped with sarcasm, but I wouldn't
relent. "It feels like it."

"But it's not true." She shook her head and sighed.
"The way I am now isn't how I was before I went inside.
I was consumed with materialistic shit, keeping up
appearances, trying to please my money-hungry
girlfriend, and basically an ass to a lot of my clients
because they thought they could disrespect me. I'm not
that person anymore."

She certainly wasn't. Other than her car, bike, and
tiny TV, she didn't have much in the way of possessions.
She didn't even have an iPod or a computer of any kind.
She was fine with listening to the radio in her car and
never talked about wasting time on the internet. She
didn't care about trendy styles, and she seemed to
stretch every minute out of her off time. Most of all, she
didn't have a money-hungry girlfriend. At least I
assumed she didn't.

"Did you do it for your girlfriend?"

She studied me for a full minute. The tears were
gone. Despondency was all that remained. "I'd love to
say yes, but I made the mistake. I let myself get caught
up in what she wanted and what her friends had. Every
time I went out on a job, I'd deal with these assholes
who had so much expensive crap and no regard for a
worker like me who made it possible for them to enjoy

all that crap. I convinced myself that I was doling out justice. Assholes shouldn't have what they had. I was there to help in that process." She snorted derisively. "I was wrong. I was the asshole. I was the bad person." She sounded so heartbroken. So sorry. Like she wished she could go back in time and undo everything, even if it meant a harder life for her.

"I don't think you're a bad person."

Her hazel eyes flicked over to meet mine. "You didn't know me then. You know someone else entirely, and that's why I never told you. There's no good way and no good time to say, 'I was a callous shithead, who did so much wrong.' Not to someone who's become so important. I didn't want you to know that I was ever that kind of person. I'm sorry if hearing this now changes how you feel about our friendship. I never wanted that."

I shook my confused head. Too many thoughts muddled my feelings. I couldn't get a handle on how to deal with this. It wasn't like she'd changed from two hours ago. She was still the same Falyn who called me the other night because she knew I wasn't looking forward to dealing with my lousy tour group on their second day. She was still the woman who listened to me blather on and on about those jerks without once interrupting me.

And then she wasn't. She was the woman who'd been my friend for months and somehow managed not to tell me about something that consumed more than seven years of her life. I just couldn't reconcile that.

"Does Vivian know?"

"I assume so. I never told her, but I'm sure Natalie has."

"What about the guys on your crew?"

She shrugged. "I didn't tell them."

That meant I could at least talk to Vivian. Why she hadn't told me, especially after she knew I'd slept with

Falyn, I didn't know. If I'd found out something mind-
blowing about Natalie, I sure as hell would have told
her.

"Okay."

A flash of hope came into her sad eyes. "What does
that mean?"

I wanted to keep that hope there, but I wouldn't lie.
"I don't know."

She pushed up from her chair, pacing the length of
the side porch and back. She looked at me and sighed. "I
understand."

I stood to meet her. I wish I understood. I couldn't
believe how much it hurt to learn these things about her
and to learn them from someone else. She hadn't
trusted me enough to tell me. It didn't feel fair or good.
"I need some time to think."

Her mouth nudged open. A formidable expression
came over her face. "Right. Well...okay then."

That was a brushoff if I've ever heard one. I wanted
to assure her that I wasn't trying to blow her off just to
get away from her. I honestly needed time to process
this. I didn't like feeling bad for making her feel bad
about something she'd caused. I should be the indignant
one.

"Yeah. Okay then," I repeated her brushoff, not
bothering to hide the hurt from my eyes as I walked
away.

23

Natalie was still working on the house when I drove up to talk to Vivian. The rest of her crew was off, but she would probably go well into the night. I wanted to smile because I knew how much this house meant to Vivian and would mean to Natalie. They'd be done a month early at this pace.

I stopped just inside the door, taking in all the changes. The place looked almost done to me. Natalie and Vivian probably had a million finishing details on their punch list, but it looked like every drawing Vivian had shown me of the final phase of her dream home. If I weren't so disturbed by what just happened, I'd be happy just standing here.

"Hey, Molly." Nat came in from the kitchen to greet me.

"Hey. Is Viv around?"

Her brown eyes showed curiosity at my urgent tone. "She was taking care of Mason and Teddy, but she's probably at the cabin by now."

"Great, thanks." I turned to leave.

"Is everything okay?"

I paused to look at her. I liked her a lot, but we weren't buddies. We could be, but she placed a lot of importance on my friendship with Viv. She didn't want to force her way into it, which made me like her more. It was always so obnoxious when a friend's new girlfriend just assumed she'd become my best friend, too.

I studied this woman who let Viv and me stay as close as we'd always been without showing any passive-aggressive resentment. We didn't have heart-to-hearts, but she knew Falyn well. Maybe she could provide a different point of view.

"Falyn was in prison."

Her chin dipped once. "She told you."

"No, a cop told me."

"It bothers you." Not a question. Natalie didn't really question people. She observed and made comments if asked.

I might as well be just as frank. "It does."

"She's not that person."

Exactly what Falyn had said. "You don't worry?"

I didn't have time to feel mortified by the implication of my question before Natalie answered, "I don't. She's the electrician that taught me everything I know about electrical work and the woman who looked out for me on jobsites. She's more concerned about my business than her own job. She'd sacrifice circumstances in her life to ease mine. I know she'll never do what she did again. I know it, but best of all, she knows it."

That rang true. So why was I having such a hard time? It just hurt to know that this woman I'd been growing to care so much about hadn't told me something that anyone would consider a crucial part of her. Hurt a crazy amount, actually.

"Did you know her girlfriend at the time?"

Her face flinched in distaste. "I met her a few times. Didn't like her."

"Was she the reason?"

"No one can force Falyn to do anything."

I knew that, too. Why did I feel so sure of things about her and now so unsure of things about her?

"What was she like?" Why was I asking that? Of all the things to ask.

Natalie bit back a smile. "Pretty, short, busty, and flighty."

Everything I'm not. "Was Falyn in love?"

"They lived together. I don't know if she was in love with her. She'd hired on with an electrical contractor by then. We didn't see as much of each other after that."

"I just..." What? Why couldn't I figure out how I felt about this other than confused and angry and upset and hurt and, and, and.

"Don't like that she was in prison, or didn't tell you about it?" she finished for me. She shrugged and gave a small smile. "You may not like either, but everything she's gone through makes her the person you like today. That should be worth something."

It was, but still, it wasn't enough. My trust in her had faltered. She'd had a major life event, had the opportunity to tell me about it many times, and chose not to share that with me. What if something else major came up?

I thanked Nat and took my leave. Vivian might add a different perspective. At the very least she could help me with these muddled feelings.

"I found out about Falyn's record today," I said as soon as Vivian opened the cabin door to me.

The smile she wore slid off her face. She pulled me in for a hug. "How do you feel about it?"

"Why didn't you tell me when I called about her place being searched?"

She pulled away with a grimace on her face. "Natalie asked me not to tell anyone. But even if she hadn't, it really was up to Falyn to tell. How would you like it if I told her some things I know about you?"

Nothing was as major as going to prison for five years. Excuse me, five years, one month, and six days. Then two years on parole.

Vivian's gaze sharpened and her mouth twitched. "You don't think you have anything as major as her history?"

Dammit. I hated when she could read me so well. That was the thing about her. She wasn't judgmental, which meant she could present both sides of any issue objectively. It could tick me off when I wanted her firmly on my side.

"Do I?"

"Have you told her how many women you've slept with?"

I took a step back, shaking my head. She wasn't judging. She'd had a couple of tourist flings herself. Not nearly as many as I had. Okay, yeah, maybe my number might be shocking, but I've been single for almost forty years. Obviously, my number would be higher than someone who got married at twenty-two or was a romantic like Vivian. Not that any of that equaled a prison record. "That's not the same thing."

"No, it's more relevant."

"How in...how?" I blew out a long breath. She was just trying to push my buttons. She did it because she thought I was too intense and needed distractions from time to time. "More than a prison sentence?"

"What does her being in prison have to do with your relationship?"

Dammit. She was right again. "Okay, nothing, but what does my sexual history have to do with her?"

A laugh slipped out. "She was one of your sexual relationships, and based on how you're reacting now, you want her to be your future sexual relationship." Her lips tipped up in a knowing smile. "Singular, as in the only one you'll ever have again."

No way. That wasn't what was happening here. "Don't romanticize."

"I'm not. The only reason this upsets you so much is because you're really close. If Tessa told you she was in prison years ago, would you really care other than if it caused her harm?"

Tessa in prison. It would bother me, yes. I wouldn't have wanted her to suffer through that. It probably wouldn't change how I felt about her unless she'd done something really horrible. What had Falyn done? She'd stolen things from people who could afford to lose those stolen things. Not a decent thing to do, but she hadn't killed or physically harmed anyone.

"I can guess how you're thinking here, darlin'. You don't like that she made the choices she made to land her in prison, but you think her not telling you is a betrayal of your trust." She paused, considering me for a long moment. "That's usually a walk-away for you."

She hit that right. I didn't handle betrayal well. It was the disrespect that bothered me more than the betraying action. If a girlfriend cheated on me and told me about it right away, I just might forgive her. Maybe. Slim chance, but maybe. If she went around town soliciting our friends to keep it quiet while she continued, I'd kick her ass out with zero regret or sorrow.

"But you don't want to walk away. I see it as plain as the hurt on your face."

I felt tears threaten. I'd never been this teary before, but in the space of two conversations I was becoming a weeper. "I don't."

"You're in love with her."

I took three steps back this time. I had feelings for her, yes, close friendship, but love? "Now you're just talking crazy."

"Let's see." She held up a hand and started counting with her fingers. "It's more than like, more than lust, more than caring, definitely more than friendship. You're on the cusp; admit that at least."

"I hate when you're like this." I sighed, exasperated by pretty much everything at this point. At least I'd moved away from the gnawing feeling of dread and hurt that attached itself to me as soon as I walked off Falyn's porch.

"You love when I can express your feelings for you." She gave me a brilliant smile.

I laughed because there was nothing else to do. "Know-it-all bitch."

She joined my laughter. "Repressed jackass."

I grabbed her in a hug to keep her from saying more. She wrapped around me and held on for as long as I wanted.

24

Our eyes met across the street, then Falyn bolted around the corner of the Opera House. Great. Just what I needed to add to my conflicted feelings. Guilt to go with the irritation and disappointment. It was bad enough when she didn't show up at Cassie's for Vivian's birthday barbeque yesterday. I still didn't know what to do about my feelings or our friendship, but I hated that she had to miss out on the fun with some of her crewmates and other friends. I also didn't want her avoiding me at all costs.

I crossed the street and walked past the beautiful structure. When I reached the corner, there was no sign of her. She must have sprinted back the way she'd come. Or maybe she'd had her bike with her. Either way I wouldn't catch up with her on foot. If I wanted to catch up with her.

Why couldn't it be a week ago? Why did I have to run into Cherise? Everything would be so much better if I never learned the truth. No, that's not true. Everything would be so much better if Falyn had never had to go through that whole experience. Then again, both she and Natalie were convinced Falyn wouldn't have been the person I care about without it.

It bothered me so much when I didn't know how to feel about something. I never spent a lot of time thinking about my feelings. Vivian was right. She could always voice my feelings before I even knew what they were. I should trust her on this. It burned not to be able to call Falyn or see her. The burn flared hotter when I thought about how much I wished she'd told me. That she didn't feel like she could trust me enough to tell me. I trusted her with everything I had, including an intimacy that I'd never shared with anyone else.

Well, screw that. I hated this feeling.

"Molly!" Kelsey called from behind me just as I'd taken my first determined step.

Oh, for the love of all that is holy. What is it with this town? Can't I walk two steps without running into someone I know?

I had to turn around. Ignoring Kelsey would make me feel like a jerk. If I made it quick, I could get back to trying to resolve things with Falyn. We had to talk this thing out. Tomorrow Wayne and I were taking a group out on ATVs to a camping spot for four days. If I didn't talk to Falyn tonight, it would have to wait almost a week.

When I turned and spotted Kelsey's boyfriend and Jenna with her, I knew I'd be on this street for a while. I sighed, lamenting the small town life I usually loved. "Hey, guys."

"Hi, Molly," Jenna greeted enthusiastically.

She could make me feel a little uncomfortable at times. Vivian thought she had a crush on me, which couldn't be true because she was straight and married. If she were a lesbian and available, she would have been my type. My former type, I should say. I needed to adjust my view on that, obviously.

The same thing would have happened with Jenna as with all the others I thought were my type. She'd be fun and affectionate for the first couple of months, then she'd start to complain about how I had too much whatever because I was too intense or serious or involved or whatever else she thought was just too something. She'd want me to continue with the fawning and attention lavished on her without considering that I might want some of the same treatment. It usually took something like a Valentine's day to go by before I'd see the relationship for what it was. I'd buy flowers, candy, and jewelry and take her to dinner. She'd just accept it all with nothing more than a thank you. No one had ever given me a Valentine's gift. Like being butch meant I didn't need one.

"Hi, Jenna. How's Jay?" I liked to remind her of her husband before she started getting grabby.

"He couldn't be bothered to dine with us," she complained. "You should have come. Kelsey called you."

"I just got off work."

"Hang out with us now."

"I'm beat, but thanks."

Kelsey eyed our exchange with a smile. She knew better than to try to get me to go out right after work. I always needed a shower and a half hour to shake out the stress of having everyone's lives in my hands for whatever activity they were unqualified to perform.

"Next time," Noah put in. He was a nice enough guy. Not good enough for Kelsey in my opinion but nice enough.

"See ya." I backed away, hoping they'd let me go.

"Mol!" Tessa got out of a parked car up the street.

I shook my head. Damn this small town. "Hey, Tess."

"Hi, folks," she said to Kelsey and her gang, coming to a stop before us. "Did you have a good tour today?"

Thoughtful Tessa was back. "They were good, thanks. Buyers or sellers today?"

"Both. I should close a deal tomorrow if I can get Natalie to give a bid on some work that needs to be done."

"Congrats," Kelsey offered.

"Thanks. Oh, hey, I was going to call you. Rachel and I will be having an open house at the new office once Vivian moves out. We'd like you to cater."

Kelsey's eyes widened. "You're moving into Vivian's office?"

"Yeah. She's moving her office to her cabin when the new house is done. She and her brother wanted to bring in some rental income and asked us to list it. We snapped it up before anyone else could look at it. We're saving twenty percent a month on office rent."

"Smart thinking," Jenna told her. "Are we invited to the open house?"

"Absolutely, and bring all your house buying friends." Tessa looked back at Kelsey. "Can we count on you to cater?"

"Of course. Just let me know the date."

"Make those crab cakes again, sweetie," Noah encouraged.

I could tell I was about to lose a half hour of my evening, maybe more. They'd talk about menus and house sales and dealing with customers at Jenna's restaurant and the insurance claims that Noah processed. It was pointless conversation but made everyone feel connected. I never minded before, but now that I had a purpose tonight I was bothered by it.

"I know you just got off work, but will you grab a drink with me?" Tessa asked after the eternal conversation about menus and such finally wound down.

I glanced at my watch. It was rude, but I couldn't help myself. Noting the hour and the fact that Falyn got up earlier than I did, I figured I wouldn't have time to get over there and have the kind of discussion we needed to have. Might as well get drinks with a friend. "Love to."

She looked relieved, and I scolded myself. My friend wanted to spend time with me, and I was worried about whether or not I could cut it short to get over to another friend's house. I needed to put that on the back burner for now.

We made our way to her favorite bar, passing two acquaintances on the way in and losing another ten minutes catching up. Tessa was bubbly throughout. It was such a change from our last few visits.

I went up to the bar while Tessa snagged a booth. When I joined her, I made an observation. "You look happy, Tess."

"Thanks, I am. I have news."

I felt a smile pull at my mouth. My friend was happy. Finally. "What's up?"

"Kathleen is moving back in."

My shoulders fell. Not the happy I'd hoped for her. Even if I was no longer interested in pursuing a relationship with her, it didn't mean I wanted her back with someone who wasn't good for her. "Really?"

"Yes! We had a long talk and went on a couple of dates. It's been so great, Mol. Just like when we started."

I wanted to keep my mouth shut. This was none of my business. When they were together before Kathleen dumped her, I never had a problem with them as a couple. I didn't even have a problem with Kathleen as a person. I didn't like her as much as I liked Tessa, but I didn't have a problem with her. I just couldn't let four months of constant crying on everyone's shoulder go without some discussion. "Did she apologize? Did she tell you why she broke it off? Did she say she was sorry she broke your heart?"

"Molly!" Tessa exclaimed, ruffled by my nonsupport.

"Well? She broke up with you for seemingly no reason. You were a great girlfriend, and she just left. Now she's finally realized how great you are and wants you back. So basically she got herself a sanctioned four month sexcapade, and she still gets to come back to you."

"That's not fair." Her brow pinched. "I was miserable without her. I love her so much."

I should shut up. This wasn't going to make the situation better, but damn, I hated that she was going to be taken advantage of. "Did she admit to seeing other women?"

Tessa's chin tucked against her chest. She didn't need to say anything. I already knew about two of Kathleen's hookups. They were tourists who looked me up every time they visited. When I declined because I wasn't into that anymore, they found Kathleen available.

"Did she, at least, tell you she loved you?"

Blue eyes rounded at me. "She isn't like that. She doesn't even tell her parents she loves them."

I took a gulp of the mojito I'd ordered. The cool liquid slid down to my belly and helped numb my thoughts. "And that means she loves you? She doesn't tell her parents, so she doesn't need to tell the woman she shares her life with? It's all the same to you?"

"Why are you being like this?" Hurt flashed on her face.

"I want you to be happy, and she hurt you so much."

"I have to forgive her, Mol. I have to. She's been my life for three years. I want her back."

Breath pushed out from my chest. I'd said what I needed to say. I no longer felt locked up around her, like I was keeping my feelings or thoughts from her. We could be friends without anything secretly bothering me.

"I hope she makes you happy, Tess."

Her face brightened. She flung her arms out and pulled me in for a hug. She felt curvy and pliable and she smelled flowery. All the things I'd always been attracted to. Not one of them affected me tonight. Vivian was right. My type had changed.

Part III

Falyn

25

Someone was watching me. I shivered in the evening air, sure of it. The sense was something I'd sharpened in prison. Needed to in order to watch my back. It settled over me like someone standing too close in a pitch black room. I glanced around as I loaded my groceries into my backpack. Nobody turned away from me in a rush. No one seemed to be looking at me either. I shook off the sensation, figuring I must have lost the power sometime over the last two years.

The bike ride home helped to subdue my unease. I was probably just being paranoid. Either way, it was nice to store the bike in the garage and not feel like someone was right behind me. Now I just had to figure out what to do tonight. The guys had dates and Natalie was busy with her nephew. I could see if Lena wanted to go for a ride or maybe Ramón was up for some darts at the bar.

I wanted to call Molly. Had wanted to every day since she walked off my porch, but the chances were great that I'd never get to call her again. Seeing her last night on the street was startling. That Molly stopped dead in her tracks when she saw me wasn't the greatest feeling in the world. I did the only thing I could think of to make it easier for her. I fled, crisscrossing streets all the way home.

I wish I could put myself in her shoes, but mostly I wish she could put herself in mine. When would it have been all right to tell her? Before we became friends? That would be inappropriate. The moment we became friends? That would have made her rethink a new friendship. After I'd grown to deeply care for her? That would have put us in the exact spot we were in. I could have said something after the police first came. Anything. I was a wreck, nervous, sick to my stomach, afraid that I was headed back to prison even if I was innocent this time. I might not have been able to get all the words out, but I should have said something. She might have walked away, especially if I couldn't get everything out. She might have stayed and grilled me with questions, which probably would have triggered a claustrophobic feeling for me at the time. Hoping it never came out was stupid. I get that now. But no other option worked either.

I shook my head, thinking about our miserable situation. All I could do was hope that Molly would decide to forgive me. I couldn't change what I'd done years ago any more than I could change not telling her about it.

Walking out of the garage, I glanced over at the street when I heard a car approaching. I'd been doing that every night, hoping it might be Molly's pickup. It wasn't Molly. It was the police, two cars worth. Again. What now? Honestly, this was hardly better than those assholes in Denver who knocked on my door every week.

The cop from the supermarket encounter hopped out of the first cruiser. The smirk on her face showed delight. "Shaw, long time, no see."

The police van emptied out. Suddenly there were six cops in my driveway. I didn't go through this the first time. Two officers had arrested me, and I'd made bail by the end of the day. They'd searched my place while I was being arraigned. I'd never faced a wall of cops led by someone who appeared happy to ruin my life.

"Last week you worked on a house on Red Mountain Road." She threw the smirk over to her colleagues before looking back at me. "What? Cat got your tongue?"

"That wasn't a question," I retorted, dread filling my stomach.

"Were you working at a home on Red Mountain Road last week?" she sassed back.

"Yes." For one of Dwight's clients. A small electrical job that took one evening. What happened now? Something got misplaced, and the police think they have the case solved because I'd worked there?

"What's the address?"

"Don't remember. My employer has records." I'd learned never to offer anything without a lawyer present, and my dry mouth wouldn't allow it anyway.

"Oh, we've double-checked those records."

I waited, the dread twisting into a tight ball in my stomach. Out of the corner of my eye, I saw the neighbor who lived across from Spencer and Mei step out onto her porch to stare at our little impromptu police party. Just what I needed, another person to judge me.

"You need to respond," she insisted.

"Actually, I don't, or are you not familiar with Miranda?" Being cornered always made me lash out. It was definitely the wrong tack to take with police, but this woman seemed to delight in spoiling my relationship with Molly. I couldn't help the sass. "And you keep stating things, not questioning."

"You bit—"

"Cherise," another cop cut her off then addressed me. "We're here to search your place."

My knees felt weak, but I stepped over to block their path. "Not without a warrant, you're not."

"Have something to hide?" Cherise sneered.

I bit back a reply that would anger them more. Soon, I'd need to hire an attorney. This was obviously going to keep happening, and not every cop was as stupid as Cherise.

"Warrant," I turned and started up the front steps.

"You sure you don't want to cooperate?" the other cop took over.

"You're going to search my place whether I cooperate or not. I'd rather make it all legal."

"Stay where we can see you," Cherise told me.

"Unless you're arresting me, you can't keep me here." I'd had a lot of time to read legal books in prison.

"Warrant is on its way," the other cop told her.

I shook my head. They'd gotten a warrant before they questioned me. I felt like I might throw up. Would this ever stop? I made a foolish move eight years ago, gave up five years of my life and endured two years in near squalid conditions. I'd lost my friends, the respect of my family, and dealt with humiliation on a daily basis. I paid for that mistake. Over and over, but it looked like I would continue paying for it.

Another cruiser slowed to a stop in front of the house before I made it inside. They really worked fast here.

"Hold it, right there, Shaw," Cherise called out. "Your warrant." She thrust it into my hands and brushed past me to the door. When she found it locked, she glared at me. "Open it or we kick it in, and I don't want to do that to Glory's house."

I pushed out a calming breath. I didn't want to do that to Glory's house either. I unlocked the door for her, very happy the guys were on dates tonight. "Will you let me get my cats into their carrier before you begin, please?" They'd gotten a little spooked last time.

Her head jerked back, surprised at my more cooperative tone. Her eyes softened for a split second. She must be a cat person. "Yes. Kevin, you're with me," she said to another officer. "We'll secure her pets then begin."

As soon as I had Dancer and Tusk in their carrier, which Cherise searched first, I was escorted back out to the front porch. They wanted me in sight of at least one officer at all times.

I left a message for Natalie to call me. She hadn't been with me on this job either. I'd been there with Owen and Cole for one day. I wondered what had gone missing this time. But mostly, I wondered how this happened at another house I'd worked. Were burglaries the norm for this idyllic little town? I thought it was a pretty sheltered place, but with all these rich homes, it might be a mecca for thieves.

Speaking of Owen, he appeared on the street past the cluster of trees lining Glory's property. Lena's dogs were pulling him along. He studied the police cars blocking my driveway and the officer standing next to me with the same patient eyes he used on the jobsite. "Everything all right, Falyn?"

"Fine," I responded because I was embarrassed that this was happening again. He'd asked me about it the first time, but to witness it live now, well, just sucked.

"Would you like me to sit with you?"

Kind man. I'd gotten to know him a lot better each week, on the job, as my neighbor, and on occasional excursions where he'd join Lena or Natalie in something we'd do together. I wanted to say yes, but I couldn't. My tongue felt leaden and heat burned my face. I didn't want this to be happening, but I was powerless once again.

Spencer came out of his house to survey the scene. I wanted the porch to open up and swallow me whole. His gaze took everything in before he strode toward the street, stopping beside Owen. He looked completely different from the casual guy who'd hosted a cookout last night. Tonight he looked professional and serious. Even his greeting was serious. "Hello, Falyn."

"Spence," I responded, feeling the burn turn up another ten degrees. I'd spontaneously combust from embarrassment soon.

"Mr. Mayor." The officer standing with me almost saluted Spencer.

"Hello, Brent. What seems to be going on here?"

"Um, you should talk to my incident commander, sir."

"Yes, I should." Spencer advanced toward us.

What the hell? I liked Spence and he seemed to like me, but what was he doing getting involved here? Did he think that because I lived in his friend's house he needed to get mixed up in this? What could he really do?

The officer with me ducked into the house and brought Cherise and Kevin back with him. They both stood ramrod straight in Spencer's presence. I knew he was the mayor, but he seemed kinda casual about it. It was such a small town I assumed it was more of a figurehead position.

"Mr. Mayor," Cherise addressed him as he stepped up onto the porch.

"Why are you conducting a search of my neighbor's home?"

"Sir, with all due respect, we have a warrant."

His eyes narrowed. "Does this relate to the burglary last evening?"

"Yes, sir," Kevin inserted.

Spencer took another step until he was right in front of them. Jeez, he could be intimidating if he wanted to be. "Did you question Ms. Shaw before getting the judge to sign off on a warrant?"

"If you knew about this case, you'd know we have very good reason to be here right now," Cherise told him.

"I do know about this case. I was briefed on it this morning by your boss's boss. If you'd bothered to question Ms. Shaw, you'd know she has an alibi for the time of the incident."

Cherise went pale, but she bucked up quickly. "Alibi's aren't always reliable, sir. Friends are willing to lie at first."

Spencer shook his head, his mouth a grim line. "Falyn was at my house at the time. She and Owen, here, were helping me grill most of the night."

Holy hell. The mayor just alibied me out. When Cherise brought up the address, I assumed the burglary happened while I was there or shortly thereafter. If they'd asked me where I'd been last night, I would have told them.

"Pull your people out of her home now."

"But, sir," Cherise started. "She might have been working with someone."

"Do I need to get your chief and the judge on the phone?"

I swallowed hard, tears of relief springing to my eyes. I knew the relief would be short-lived because they'd find some reason to come back, but it felt so good having someone stick up for me.

Cherise called everyone off the search. She brushed past me, bumping my shoulder on the way. Juvenile and as bad as some of the antics I had to endure in prison. I didn't care, though. She was leaving, and I had a legitimate alibi for one of the two burglaries they wanted to pin on me.

"Spence," I started but didn't know how to finish.

Owen joined us and settled an arm around my shoulders. "Being prejudged doesn't feel any good. I put up with it in the military for years. No matter what the police think, I know you wouldn't do these things. You are in a good place here with good people, and you'd never betray your friendship with Natalie."

Tears filled my eyes as this man I didn't really know somehow seemed more sure of my actions than I was. I turned and hugged him fully, thanking him first then Spencer. For a night, I could relax. I wished it could be with my closest friend, but having these guys for support would suffice.

26

Things were tense on the jobsite. Natalie was stressed for me, Vivian fed off her stress, and the rest of the crew kept throwing glances my way. After last night's search, I had to tell Curtis and Cole about prison when I saw them at breakfast. They reacted casually but were curious. Like all guys, they wanted to know the nitty-gritty of prison life. I cut the discussion off after a half hour and offered to move out. I had enough saved to swing something on my own until Vivian's house was done, but I was relieved when they backed off and told me to stay. The rest of the crew found out by morning break as I secretly hoped they would. At least I didn't have to tell anyone else.

Luis came into the master bedroom with a light fixture. He passed it up to me on the top step of the ladder. "Did Harp know before you got here?"

"Yes." I was keeping to one word answers so as not to encourage those other questions. *Did you have to beat anyone up in there? Ever run into trouble in the shower? Was it easier since you're a lesbian? Did you join a gang inside?*

"You cased the houses you worked then ripped them off later, and Natalie still hired you? Did you have dirt on her or something?" He wasn't being an asshole. He was asking the same questions all the contractors asked when I applied for jobs after prison. *You stole from the homes you worked on. What makes you think I'd ever hire someone like that?*

"Natalie has a way of seeing the good in everyone."

"Verdad, chica." He snickered and gripped the ladder I was on. "We used to work for a real dick. Harp could always make him be more reasonable. After we left, the guy was stupid enough to vandalize the first house we worked on. She didn't even get mad. Can you believe that?"

Thankful we were off the prison topic, I grabbed onto this one. "Yeah, actually. Nat tends to internalize. She probably thought her actions brought on the vandalism somehow. Plus, she doesn't waste energy getting angry about things she can't change."

"Wish I was like that," Luis said. "I punched the dude as soon as he made bail."

I gave a short laugh then sobered up. Not a wise move on his part, but I could see it wasn't just a reaction to the vandalism. He'd probably wanted to punch his old boss many times.

"Listen, Fos," he said as I secured the wiring to the new fixture. "I like you. Like having you on the crew because we're bringing in more money with you being an electrician and all. More money means bonus pay for us."

"But?" I offered for him.

"If this goes wrong for Harper—"

"I'm gone," I cut him off. "She's my friend first and has been for twenty years."

He glanced up at me with earnest brown eyes. Luis was maybe five-seven but hauled more than Tyler at two inches over six feet. *"Bueno."*

Vivian came in to check on our progress. She took a long look at the height of the fixture before nodding. "Looks good."

"Thanks, Viv, I've been working out," Luis joked, flexing the bicep on his free arm.

She tried not to smile, but it was pretty difficult. "Natalie wants a word when you're done, Falyn."

I finished securing the faceplate and came down the ladder. "Will you take the sconces out of their boxes, Luis?"

"Copy that," he acknowledged.

I followed Vivian outside to the project tent. Natalie was sorting through the plumbing fixtures, checking them off the list. She smiled at us when she looked up.

"How're you doing?" She wasn't asking about my progress on hanging the lighting fixtures.

"Okay." It was an automatic response. I was still upset about the coincidence of a burglary occurring at two homes I'd been in, pissed that the cops were trying to convict me without any evidence, and heartbroken that my now closest friend in town was disappointed in me.

"I want you on this crew."

My mouth nudged open. This was an unexpected discussion.

"Permanently, in case you were thinking otherwise."

Had Molly told Vivian that I was worried about the burden I posed to Natalie's company? If these accusations kept happening, her reputation was at stake. She already had to carry a bigger insurance bond because she'd hired an ex-felon. I really didn't want to jeopardize her business.

"I appreciate that, Nat, but we'll have to reevaluate when the house is done."

"Vivian just picked up another major renovation starting in October. It'll take six months, then we'll be back to smaller jobs. With an electrician, we'll be able to pick up more work. You're part of this team, and I would like you to stay."

"Nat," I started, knowing I had to have the conversation that would doom my spot on her crew. "What if this happens again? Think about it? Some bratty teen might borrow her mom's jewelry, lose it, and blame it on the construction crew who was in the house."

"Without evidence, they can't do anything to you. And they'll never find any evidence."

She seemed so sure of that. Cherise was pretty determined last time. I wouldn't put it past her to make evidence appear in my place. It was a lousy thing to think about a police officer, but she wouldn't want to be embarrassed again.

"Tessa has a small job for us if you're up for it."

Panic bloomed in my chest. Nothing would happen as long as I kept working on Vivian's house. The two thefts occurred on separate jobs. I didn't want to tempt fate again. "It's electrical?"

"She's got a sale pending on rewiring a media room. I'll go with you."

I felt better about having Natalie along. At least she'd get proof of her faith in me. "If you want to take the job, yeah."

"Do you mind if we go after hours? I don't want to be away from this project. I'll give you comp time later."

I didn't have any evening plans, hadn't for a while, so I was all for working. "Sure."

"Great." Natalie nodded and squeezed my arm. "My graphic designer is coming by later to take your order for winter shirts. I always go with Henleys and fleece pullovers, but the guys like long sleeved t-shirts and sweatshirts. David will show you everything that's available. Choose what you want so you're geared up to stay on."

When Natalie made her mind up about something, I guess she made it happen. I let out a breathy laugh, not believing how lucky I was to have this woman looking out for me.

27

Making the turn onto my street, I spotted someone sitting out on the porch at home. I wasn't in the mood for company tonight, especially not if the person was a police detective. After three days of extra hours on Tessa's job, I was bushed. Even thinking about how I might avoid the person was too tiring. I could only hope it was one of the boys' friends.

Cole's van wasn't in the driveway. I had just enough time to rethink the effort to avoid when I spotted a brick red Tacoma parked at the curb. Molly's pickup. My heart started pumping faster. God, I'd missed her. She might be here to yell at me, but she was here. We had to work this out. If we didn't, even as much as I loved working for Natalie, I wasn't sure I could stay here. Not if I kept running into this wonderful friend who wanted nothing more to do with me. It was hard enough sticking to our agreement to keep my hands off her. Not being friends would be that much harder.

She stood to meet me when I came up the steps. "Hi."

"Hi."

She swallowed and looked away. The hard lines of her face got harsher in the dipping sun of the evening. "Do you have time to talk?"

"Always." I set my toolbox in the mudroom and gestured her inside.

She shook her head and pointed over her shoulder to the side porch. Her eyes darted past the open door where I could hear Cole speaking on his cell.

I followed her and took my usual seat. My mouth felt all cottony, and I needed to wash away the sweat and grime from the workday, but my eyes were riveted to the sight of her. "I've missed you."

Her brown eyes became shiny. She nodded, which I hope meant she agreed. She had on long khaki shorts, the only pair she had that weren't cargo style, and a short sleeve button-front shirt. It was her dressiest casual look. That she was wearing it to visit me made my heart skip.

I let out a deep breath. "I'm sorry I didn't tell you." I didn't know what else to say.

"I can't understand why you didn't." Her fingers fiddled with the hem of her shirt. "I mean, I can, sort of. It would have been scary and hard, but you should have trusted me."

I ached to grab her hand and feel it squeeze mine in return. "I do trust you, Molly. Please believe that."

"It felt like it, but then this happened."

"I want you to understand." I stood to pace, a calming habit that I picked up in prison where space was a luxury. "Everyone has regrets and some people even make major mistakes. Only a few of us do things that we're ashamed of. Not embarrassed or guilty. I'm talking about real shame." My hands started to shake when I felt the shame creeping over me again. "I'm disgusted by what I did. I didn't want anyone to know about it, but it's part of me. I know I can't run from the shame forever."

She rose from her chair as I came close. Her strong arms swept around me. I nearly burst into tears at the feelings it stirred up inside me. "You shouldn't be ashamed that you went to jail."

"I'm not. Don't you see?" I pulled back to look at her, feeling my eyes prickle with tears. "I'm ashamed of what I did to those homeowners. Yes, they were rich jerks with lots of insurance, they were never there when we broke in, and we only took things that didn't have sentimental value, but no one should feel violated, even if it was just their homes, even if the feeling was only temporary. For a short time, they didn't feel secure in their own homes. It's disgraceful that I helped to cause that feeling."

Her thumbs came up and wiped at the tears that escaped my eyes. "I hate that this hurts you so much."

I tucked in against her face. "I hate that it hurts you."

She kissed my head and caressed my back. After a full minute, she let out a shuddering breath. "I'm over it."

I squeezed her tight. Her lighthearted tone wasn't entirely truthful, but I appreciated the effort.

"Just know you can tell me anything in the future. Okay?"

I nodded and gave her a last squeeze before pulling away. "Thanks."

"I'm serious, Falyn. Anything." Her brown eyes seared into mine, tattooing the notion on my brain.

"I know that now."

"You better because I can't go through the last couple weeks again. You mean too much to me."

Warmth spread through me. It felt so good to hear that. "How much?"

"Don't push it," she mock snapped, and I knew in that second that we'd be okay. "You need a shower."

"I know, but you couldn't wait to talk to the smelly version of me."

She laughed and my whole world eased. I forgot all about the police searching my home twice and Nat's crew still being a little skeptical. Not when Molly was finally here again, making my life better.

"Grab your shower, and we'll figure out what to do for dinner."

"Like you're in charge of me," I muttered, so happy to be able to joke with her again. I reached over and twirled a loose curl on the crown of her head. "I like your haircut." Short, but sharp. The dark strands formed an enticing rippling wave and showed off her small ears completely. Her standard tiny hoop earrings were replaced by onyx balls tonight. Sexy as hell, the complete package, hair, earrings, sparkling eyes, slamming bod, and understanding, beautiful woman.

"Thanks." Her head tilted to the side. "Viv always tells me I get it cut too short."

"Viv needs glasses."

That got a broad smile. "You charmer."

"I can cook, too."

Her smile turned to a laugh. "You still haven't made me that eggplant parmesan you're always boasting about."

"I only make that for very special people."

"I'm a very special people."

I grinned at her tease. "Really? A special people, huh?"

"To you I am."

I let my smile fade. That was so true. *The* special person for me. "You are."

She sucked in a breath at my serious response. We'd been kidding, and now I was telling her how much she meant to me. Well, not everything she meant to me, but a good start.

She reached her hand out to cup my face. I pushed into it and let the memories of the last time she'd touched me like this flow through me. She stepped closer, searching my eyes. "You're special to me, too."

Her face moved forward to brush her lips against mine. Just like last time, the brush set off fireworks inside me. I wasn't going to be satisfied with just this. I moved to deepen the kiss, opening my mouth to her hot, sweet lips. She met me with the same gusto, tongue surging forward to stroke mine. My arms went around her shoulders, fingers gripping the broad expanse. Hers came around my waist and shifted my t-shirt to get at the skin beneath. Goosebumps broke out under her scorching fingertips. I trembled and pressed harder against her. Her thigh pushed forward, jolting me to my core. A moan poured into my mouth as her hands flexed on my skin. My hand slid down her back, seeking the same bare contact. Her body felt just as good this time. This kiss somehow felt better. Something I didn't think could be possible.

"Oops, excuse us."

We broke apart at the interruption. Glory and Lena stood at the edge of the street, a leash dangling from Glory's hand. Lena's pit bull had managed to sneak up on us, which wasn't hard to do considering how involved that kiss was. He pushed his snout into Molly's leg, knocking her back a step.

Lena turned a shrewd smile away. She'd been trying to get me to admit to the nature of my relationship with Molly every time we got together. Her friend Brooke was pretty relentless with the inquisition as well. It had been fun trying to deflect their questions. Based on what she just walked up on, she'd no longer have to ask.

"C'mon, Kitty," Glory called, slapping her thigh to entice the wayward dog off the porch.

Kitty, which was a crazy name for a male pit bull, ignored her. He never missed the chance to get a rub from me or play tag with my cats. He went to the porch door, searching for them. He didn't seem to mind that his game of tag was their game of claw target practice. Lena's other dog was much smarter, sticking close to whoever walked him rather than becoming my cats' favorite toy.

Molly chuckled and helped to push Kitty into motion back to the street. "How ya doing, guys?"

"Good, Mol, thanks. We'll be getting out of your hair now." Glory tugged on Lena's hand to get them moving up the street with the dogs. Lena looked like she wanted to get in a tease, but Glory and the dogs were already taking a step away.

"Not exactly great timing." Molly grinned at me, her eyes flicking back to the street with a shake of her head.

"No, but I did need a shower."

"And I did need that eggplant specialty of yours."

"For special people in my life." I smiled and stole another kiss before using the slider to get inside. My heart was pumping hard, and I felt giddy for the first time in, well, my whole life.

28

That feeling of being watched came over me again. I glanced around the neighborhood but couldn't find the source. Natalie was showing me her apartment, which was actually a small guesthouse of a Tudor mansion. She was proposing to make it my place. This had been my second biggest worry about staying on here. Other than being falsely accused, not having affordable housing once we finished Glory's renovation was making me reticent. Sure, Natalie paid a lot more than I was making in Denver, but the rental market here would eat up a lot of that gain.

"Who lives here?" I asked as we passed between the mansion and her guesthouse.

"He's an author. Uses the place as a writing escape sometimes."

"Is he famous?"

She grinned. "Very, but he keeps to himself. I finally got to meet him a couple months ago. Before that, we always communicated by email."

I followed her into the small space. It was basically the size of the great room in Vivian's house but split into different areas. A small kitchenette lined one wall. An island with two stools served as the dining table and separated the area from the living room. There was a sleeping loft above the bathroom, laundry, and office. Standing here, coziness squeezed around me. Small spaces helped me feel secure.

"You sure you're leaving?" As soon the words came out, I wanted to take them back. Nothing was worse than having friends who didn't support your relationship decisions.

Natalie didn't seem bothered by my faux pas. "Yeah. I've never been more sure."

"I'm glad, and I meant leaving such a beautiful spot here, not concern for you and Viv."

"I know." She gestured around the place. "What do you think?"

"It's really great." I checked out the bathroom. "What does the owner think of you bringing in someone else?"

"He's grateful not to have to bother with finding someone."

"Would he be if he knew I did time?" Not many landlords in Denver were.

"We can tell him or not. It's your decision. You've got Glory as a reference. He trusts her judgment above all."

"Tell him. I don't want to be living in fear that he'll kick me out the second he finds out." If I settled in here, I wanted to be able to stay.

"It's more likely he'll want to use you as research for his next book than be upset about it."

Great, more questions. The guys still asked random questions at breakfast every once in a while. It was more of a game now to deflect than it was annoying.

"Is the rent doable?"

"He wants someone to look out for the property and occasionally repair things. I offered what I was paying when I split rent in Basalt, and he went for it. It's definitely affordable."

"Natalie, I can't thank you enough." Relief rinsed through me.

She held up a stopping hand. "You looked out for me way back when I had no one."

"The summer job and place to stay were enough. Keeping me on isn't necessary." I hated saying it because I loved the job, but I had to give her permission to let me go. This couldn't be an obligation for her. She was too good a friend to do that to.

"Fos," she started and reached out to grip my shoulders. "I want you here. We need you here. That renovation Viv took on will float everyone's salary for two years even if we never picked up another job."

"Wow."

She shrugged sheepishly. "Wait till you meet the client. Remember that reality star's house I told you about? This is one of the other women on her show. She got jealous of all the extra screen time her costar got because of the reno, so she's doing the same thing but with more money."

I let that filter through my brain. It seemed like a ridiculous reason to buy a house, but if it kept Natalie's business worry-free for another two years, more power to the dingbat. "You never said if you and Viv show up on TV?"

"We did in the first episode. Viv and Dwight a lot more than me and the guys. For this next reno, Viv negotiated appearance fees." Her face split into a grin. "I've got the smartest girlfriend ever."

I laughed at her easy statement. "Not bad looking either."

"She's hot as hell, Fos." That statement came even easier. It felt like old times, chatting about a date she might have had the night before. Once she got past the crap her parents loaded onto her, Natalie had some fun. I'd been proud that she was discovering herself, almost as proud as I felt of her now that she was an established business owner.

"Far better than that first girl you introduced me to." It was fun to reminisce without feeling bad about my past.

"Oh man, Carla? I can't believe you remember her."

I didn't remember her. I remembered Natalie telling me about her. She'd had a bloom of color on her cheeks and wild excitement in her eyes when she pulled me away from the crew to tell me about her first date. "You were so cute about having this girlfriend, and you were so young. I couldn't not remember."

"I hit the lottery of a lifetime with Vivian, and I'm not just talking about her looks." The same wild excitement bubbled to the surface, but this time it was enhanced by radiant love.

I smiled and pulled her in for a hug. "She's done the same with you, Natalie."

"Thanks." She returned the hug. "Molly's pretty great, too."

I stood back and searched her eyes. I hadn't told her anything yet. "What makes you say that?"

"Even if she hadn't told Viv about your recent change in relationship, the woman showed up on the jobsite all turned inside out about you. That doesn't happen to someone who's just your friend."

I caught the faint smirk on her face. "How long you been dying to tell me about that?"

"Hey, you used to pepper me with advice about my dating life all the time."

My mouth nudged open. "You were a baby with no experience. It was my duty to fold you into the sisterhood and steer you right."

"Fine, don't tell me then." She tried to make it sound like a sulk, but Natalie never sulked. "Just let me say that Molly's great, and you guys seem like you'd work."

I felt my head nodding without thinking about it. I glanced around the house again. "I like the place."

"I'll call the author and hopefully everything will work out." She gestured to the couch. "Want to stay a while and watch some TV?"

"Vivian's not coming over?"

"She and Dwight are out dancing."

I thought about how Dwight moved. He was both fluid and athletic. He could easily be a dancer. "I'm going to have to pass for tonight."

"Hot date?" Her eyebrows waggled.

"Very," I smiled and slipped out the door before she could try teasing me. Molly was waiting back at her place.

On the drive over, I thought about tonight. We'd only seen each other a few times since the night we made up. Every night ended with a kiss or several kisses that got hotter and hotter, but so far, we'd kept our clothes on. As if we both realized that getting naked a second time would mean the next step for us. No going back to being just friends. I was okay with that. I was pretty sure she was, too.

"How's the place?" Molly greeted me at the door to her apartment.

"Perfect."

She pulled me inside and kissed me hello. God, what she could do with her lips. Just like that, I went from feeling excited to see her to hot and breathless to see more of her.

"That means you're all set to stay in town, right? No more worries there?" Her hopeful eyes searched mine when she stepped back.

"She's got to get the author's okay." I didn't realize until that moment how much I was hoping she would get his approval. I didn't want to leave my job or Molly.

"He will. Glory likes you and, according to Nat, this guy listens to anything Glory says."

"Keeping my fingers crossed."

She held up her own crossed fingers. "Oh, hey, Kelsey called. She and her boyfriend are playing pool tonight. She asked if we wanted to join."

"I like Kelsey. She's funny."

"But?"

"But," I started, thinking about it for only a moment.

Her pupils dilated before my eyes. Breath came faster from the lips she was alternately biting and licking. The action spiked my pulse and that was all it took.

In the next second I was pressed up against her. "I can think of something more fun to do tonight."

29

Her smile kicked up a tornado in my stomach. "Yeah? Me, too." She gripped my sides and walked us backwards to the couch. Halfway there, her lips found mine.

"God, you're a good kisser." I barely held back the moan that had been threatening since she'd touched me at the door.

"You're a good everything," Molly whispered.

"Bedroom this time," I insisted, not wanting to have to break apart at any point tonight to fall asleep later.

Molly's laugh vibrated against my neck where her lips had wandered. I shivered and clutched her arms. She spun around and reached back to pull me with her. I wrapped my hands around her waist from behind. My pelvis cupped her exceptional rear as we walked glued together.

She reached out for the remote to flip on her stereo as we made our way into the bedroom. Someone I'd never heard but instantly liked sang to us about love. How very appropriate.

I took control once we got to the bedroom. She got it first last time. It was only fair I had my turn first this time. Her wide eyes showed both surprise and delight when I pushed her onto the bed. I didn't let her think about wanting to protest before I straddled her and started working on her sleeveless shirt with what looked like a million buttons.

"Why did I wear this shirt?" Molly's hands mixed with mine to get it free of her body.

I laughed and leaned down to kiss her as I got the last button free. I pushed it off her shoulders and sucked in a breath at the black cotton bra she was wearing. Her small breasts were tucked away. I couldn't tear my eyes away from the hidden gems.

My hands cupped them, forgetting about getting her naked right now. She leaned back, allowing me to do whatever I wanted. Damn, that was sexy. A woman so secure and so generous that she didn't need to rush this experience.

"Feels good, Falyn," she breathed out.

I kissed a trail down her neck to her chest. One of her hands came up to grip the back of my head. I flicked the front clasp of her bra and watched her breasts come into view. My lips immediately went to the closest nipple. With one lick, it puckered and stiffened in my mouth. I moaned at how responsive her breasts were. She seemed to enjoy this as much as anything I did to her.

The hand gripping my head reached down to pull up my shirt. I didn't want to let go of her nipple, but I needed to be naked with her. Decisions, decisions. I popped off her nipple with a loud slurp and helped Molly pull my shirt over my head. She eased my hips back until I was again standing. She took her time pulling my jeans and panties off. Her eyes lingered on what she revealed. The look hot and penetrating.

"Stand up, Mol."

Her eyes pinged up to mine. She saw the urgency I'd been trying to hide. She stood so I could get her all the way naked. Every glorious inch of her toned and, in some places, buff body. If it was possible to look better the second time I saw her even though nothing had changed, she somehow pulled it off.

"You're beautiful," I whispered.

Her eyes widened before a smile graced her lips. I would bet money that no one had ever told her that before. Handsome, striking, hot, sexy, all those things, but the kind of women Molly usually went for would expect to be called beautiful not expect to find Molly beautiful.

My hand skated down her chest and mapped out the ridges of her abdomen. It flexed as she reached around to undo my bra. I felt instantly free.

"You are even more beautiful," Molly told me before bringing her lips to mine and pressing her gorgeous body against me.

My hands slid up her sides and raked fingernails down her back. She trembled in my arms, moaning into the kiss. I'd been worried that the second time wouldn't live up to my memories of the first. How could it? It was the best sex I'd ever had. But knowing everything I knew about this glorious body in my hands, I knew this time would be better. And the next would continue the trend.

I coaxed her back onto the bed, crawling up over her as she inched up to the pillows. Her eyes watched me study her, again confident enough to let me take my time. Her breasts called out to me and I couldn't resist. I leaned down to kiss one then the other. Breath hissed out in a sexy exhale she couldn't keep in.

"I love what you do to my tits," she sighed, closing her eyes as my tongue lashed against one hard bud. She practically vaulted off the bed when my teeth closed around it and applied pressure.

I loved what I was doing, too. In fact, I was beginning to love pretty much everything about this and her. "So sensitive."

"God, yes," she said through a clenched jaw. She brought her hands up to squeeze my breasts. Her index and middle fingers tightening around my hard nipples and pulling toward her. Damn that felt good.

I lifted a leg and settled it between hers. Her thighs, burning hot, clamped my knee between them, hitching up to get me prone. "Impatient."

She pulled on my nipples again, making it so damn hard to concentrate. "Don't hold out, foxy."

"Oh, I won't, hot stuff." I glided up her body and shifted to the side.

"Where are you going?" She tried to roll to line our bodies up, but I held her in place.

"Right here. Let me have my way this time. You got first go last time."

She frowned. "And last time, you were on top of me. That worked. Like really worked."

I chuckled at the desperation clogging her tone. She was worried that I wouldn't bring her off. "I know what I'm doing, Molly."

"But you did so well last time."

I tilted up and over, kissing her worried mouth. My tongue dove inside, winding around hers in a teasing little chase. A hand slid over her breast, flicking her nipple as my thigh pressed against her center.

When she rocked her hips for more friction, I pulled away. Breathless and amped up, I tried to keep from spontaneously climaxing.

She groaned in frustration. "You stopped."

"I'll say it again," I told her, bringing my hand down her flat stomach before rotating to glide over the soft bristles of her mound and skating along her wet, plump lips. "I know what I'm doing."

We both groaned when my middle finger delved through then back up to her engorged clit. Molly's hips lurched up toward my hand, wanting more pressure. I ignored the hint and lightly began to rub circles over the slick bundle of nerves.

"Harder, Falyn."

I continued with the same pressure, liking the sway of her hips as she reached for what she wanted. I set my palm on her trimmed mound and kept circling her clit.

"Harder," she moaned again, tilting her hips up. "I need it."

"No, you don't, Mol. I'm not going to almost hurt you again."

"It's the only way." Her voice was strained.

I gave a soft laugh and kissed her mouth again to ease her tension. "We're learning a new way. Soft and light and teasing and so, so good."

My finger continued its swirling dance over her pulsing clit. I dragged my mouth over the column of her throat, pulling skin between my teeth at the bend of her neck. My hips brushed against her thigh and I seized up, holding back my climax. I couldn't believe I was that close and she hadn't touched me with her hands yet.

"Oh God, Falyn," she groaned, her hand coming around my back to grip my side and the other moving up to cup a breast. "I'm close. How are you doing this?"

"You're doing this. Feels good soft, doesn't it?"

"Yes!" she shouted when my finger went from circles to swipes. "Falyn, ahh, God, Falyn."

"Yeah, Molly, you're right there."

My finger drummed lightly against her clit. I tilted my hips down for full contact on her muscular thigh. Goddamn, I had to last longer than she did this time. I went back to circling again as I slid up her thigh. Her hands gripped my hips and helped me rock against her.

"Come with me," she cried as she climaxed against my hand.

I was mesmerized by the violent jerking of her head and torso as she came harder than any of the times before. When her thigh twitched against me, I forgot how mesmerized I was and exploded with my own fierce orgasm. My body roiled and rocked through the spasms. I tried to stay upright and wring every twitch from her.

Her hands pulled me down on top of her, and the extra stimulation set off another mini-climax for me.

"Molly, oh God, you're amazing." My face pressed into her neck and kissed softly while I shuddered through everything she'd done to me.

"You should be giving master classes on your technique," she mumbled against my forehead.

"I'm glad I didn't have to bruise you this time."

"You didn't last time either, but this was incredible." Her lips skated over my face. "I'm not walking away from this tomorrow, foxy. You better not want to either."

I tilted up to look into her eyes. "Not going to walk away."

"I'm not talking about a friends with benefits thing, either." Those intense brown eyes got my heart pumping. They would never hide how much she cared about me.

"I get it, and I'm in."

"How in?" She smiled and her eyes flared.

I swallowed to keep my mouth from drying out. "All the way in."

She nodded and tipped her head up to kiss me. "Me, too."

30

Her hand slipped into mine, the feel both soft and strong. I looked over and caught her smile. She squeezed my hand once then let go, placing hers on my back to guide me ahead of her on the sidewalk as another couple passed. That had always been my role. Always taller than my dates and girlfriends, always adjusting my stride to match theirs. It felt odd having Molly make these same gestures, her face bobbing beside mine at the same height. Odd, but pretty wonderful, too.

"What next?" she asked. Normally she had suggestions. She knew this town much better than I did, but she was asking what I wanted to do. Yet another question I'd usually ask my dates.

"What do you feel like doing?"

She smiled, knowing I'd just done what she was used to doing. Lust flared in her eyes. What she wanted to do became suddenly clear, but I was having too much fun edging the pleasure and forcing her to edge. I doubted anyone had made her do that. I loved being different for her in all ways.

A familiar face drew my attention across the street. A man stood in front of the library, acting as if he owned the street. His familiarity was slightly clouded being older with less hair and more flab. When his eyes met mine, I came to a sudden halt. Molly's shoulder brushed against me, surprised by my standstill on the walkway. Someone grunted behind us as a couple had to make their way around our little roadblock.

Brock Porter tipped his head and disappeared into the evening stream of pedestrians through town. My mouth popped open, disbelief hanging in the air.

"What's wrong?" Molly's hand came up to glide over my back. "Did you roll an ankle?"

I swallowed hard, tension tightening my chest. I blinked to clear my head, staring at the spot where I'd seen the man who'd recruited me for the burglary team. He'd gotten five more years than I had. How was he out? Was he really out or was my imagination playing tricks on me? A lot had happened in the last month, and stress always made things a little too vivid for me. Nightmares had plagued my dreams recently. It was possible that I made someone on the street look like Brock.

"What is it?" Molly searched my line of sight.

"Nothing," I said then thought better of it. Should I tell her? Our relationship was just getting to solid ground again. The subject of my record and storied past wasn't a good one for us. Keeping something from her, though, might be a more ill-advised.

My eyes scanned the area again. He wasn't there. A few guys with the same color shirt walked among the slow moving pedestrians. I must have imagined it. Even if he was out, he couldn't be here. He'd be tied to Denver like I was on parole. He didn't know anyone in Aspen. My eyes had to be playing tricks on me. Paranoia and relief mixed together to make me see things that weren't there.

"Nothing," I repeated, shaking my head. "Thought I recognized someone, but it was my imagination."

Molly tipped her head once. "Everyone starts looking familiar after a while. There aren't that many of us in town."

Yeah. That had to be it. It couldn't be someone from a town four hours away after so many years when there was nothing but bad memories left between us.

"So? What do you feel like doing?" Molly wriggled her eyebrows, suggesting more than the agreed upon dinner date. Her playful question snapped me back to the wonderful present.

"Hmm," I stretched out coyly. "We could head back to your place and…"

"Yes." Her eyes glittered.

"Watch another episode of that show that Viv and Nat were on."

Her laugh was loud enough to startle a guy passing by. "You didn't even like the show."

"I didn't get it. How can the word 'housewives' appear in the title when only two of them are actually married?" I joined her laughter, remembering the numbing feeling I experienced while watching the first episode of the most pointless show I'd ever seen. The six minutes that Vivian, Dwight, Natalie, and Miguel appeared as the star walked through the renovation, acting like she was the one doing most of the work wasn't enough to make me want to see the rest of the show. "And how can they spend more time out of the title city where they were supposedly housewives? Shouldn't they just call it Bratty, Spoiled Attention-Whores?"

"Hey, those attention-whores made our friends a pretty penny on that contract."

"I know, but come on. I assume Viv manages to make it through the season without killing anyone. She sure looked like she might lose it with that bimbo."

"You should have been here when they were going through it. She needed a night at the bar three or four times a week. It was great."

"I'll bet."

"The show's not on until Thursday." She reached out and slid her hand down my arm like she couldn't go another second without touching me. I really liked this about her. Her touch set off all kinds of delicious sensations inside me. "That leaves us with a big gap in our schedule tonight. What else did you have in mind for tonight?"

"Hmm," I repeated, loving the look of anticipation in her deep brown eyes. "How about we take the bikes up Smuggler Mountain?"

Her face fell for just a second. It was pretty cute to see her get all worked up and not get what she wanted. She'd learn that she needed to voice what she wanted instead of leaving it up to me to decide. I liked winding her up too much.

I leaned forward and kissed her lips quickly. "You had the chance to tell me what you wanted to do. Next time, speak up, hot stuff."

She laughed and cupped my nape to bring me in for another kiss. "You're too much fun, foxy."

31

Dwight and Molly were bickering again. It was far more entertaining than any television show I'd seen recently. They had bickering down to an art form. It didn't seem to bother them that the bickering was always about inane stuff.

"Just be thankful that Natalie let Falyn borrow her truck. Otherwise, you'd be riding the jump seat in my king cab, and I know how much you hate that." Molly reached back to smack one of his long legs to emphasize how uncomfortable he would have been if we'd taken her smaller pickup.

"I am grateful, but I'm also thinking it would have been better if you'd just loaned me your truck to pick up the armoire and you two skipped the trip." He leaned forward and rested his elbows on the backs of our seats. "I could have found more stylish clothes for you without any whining. I wouldn't be about to go into a western store for the first time in my life. And I wouldn't be arguing with you for the entire afternoon."

I knew we'd horrified him with our shopping habits in the mall. I chose some casual clothes to retire my worn-out khakis and Oxfords. Molly got some nice things, too, but apparently they weren't stylish enough for the clotheshorse that was Dwight. Since neither of us liked shopping, we appeased him by purchasing a few of his choices and letting him drag us through some shops for him.

It felt so good to have the funds to build on my fairly nonexistent wardrobe. I would be paying rent soon, but Natalie's place was the best of all worlds, affordable and decent and roommateless. With the new contract, I wasn't worried about her keeping me on out of obligation. I could afford some new clothes and needed to expand my work wardrobe. All summer, I'd been forced to run laundry every three days for a clean pair of jeans to work in.

"You're not putting me in a dress, Dwight," Molly shot back.

We all laughed at that. Molly in a dress. Something would be terribly wrong with the world. I didn't wear them either, but I had worn a few skirts for weddings and funerals in my lifetime. I doubted Molly had ever been in a skirt before.

"I could put you in something other than cargo shorts."

"I have jeans."

"And cargo pants. Let's get you into something that doesn't have useless extra pockets."

"Shoulda left your ass at home," Molly muttered, turning back and catching my grin. She slid her hand over and grasped mine.

"You would have left that first store with two pairs of pants and three shirts that didn't fit if I weren't here," Dwight told her.

I watched his slim face break into a smile that wasn't at all smug when he saw Molly's hand in mine. I was overjoyed that none of her friends objected to us together. I thought protective Vivian might have a slight issue or maybe Dwight. They both liked me, but Molly was their good friend and I was an ex-felon. Even her parents, whom she'd made me talk to on the phone, seemed thrilled about me. When they said they were coming up for Molly's birthday in November and wanted to get to know me, I nearly threw up. It wasn't the fact that her birthday was still months away, it was meeting her parents. I'd dated my ex for more than a year before she had me meet her parents, and that was only once I'd upgraded to a condo lease and let her furnish it. Molly just wanted me to meet the two most important people in her life because we were together.

"They would have fit fine," Molly assured him of the clothes she'd picked.

"They were a size too big, and I'm still waiting for you to thank me for making you try them on."

And the bickering continued. Neither seemed to mind that I couldn't stop chuckling after almost everything they said.

I pulled the truck to a stop in front of the western store that scared Dwight. I didn't make a habit of going to western stores either, but it was the only place I could find that had both a wide selection of work clothes and work boots in the same place.

"God, please make this stop," Dwight moaned before sliding out of the backseat. "I swear, woman, if you try to get a sleeveless western shirt with snaps, I'm storming out of here."

"Hey, good idea," Molly teased as she slipped her arm around my waist.

I had to agree with Dwight on this one. I much preferred her formfitting t-shirts, sleeveless polos, and short sleeve button-downs to a western shirt. "We'll keep her in sight at all times, Dwight."

Molly shot me a surprised look but smiled when she saw that I was kidding to keep the peace. "Drop your guard, D. We're here for Falyn."

And almost everyone on my crew. When they heard where I was heading this afternoon, they each gave me a boot order and cash to cover it. No place in town sold work boots, and the shipping costs online were too expensive. They took advantage of anyone running out to Glenwood Springs.

We pushed through the door. I went straight for the work boots section. Dwight lingered by the rack just inside the door. Molly came with me until she spotted the kind of shirts he'd kidded her about and made a beeline for the rack. Jeez, those two.

"Can I help you?" A tall, beefy guy in complete western garb came up to me.

I waited for him to ask if I was shopping for my husband because a lady like me couldn't possibly need work boots. That happened often enough in the past. When it didn't come, I relaxed and started in on my list. His eyes widened. I needed boots for everyone on the crew except Miguel, whose wife had picked some up on her last trip.

"How-dee, Cowboy." Dwight joined me as the guy retreated to the back room with my list. "Maybe this place isn't so bad." He looked around and spotted Molly pulling shirts from a rack and holding them to her chest. "Oh, no. No!"

She grinned and slipped into the dressing room before he could reach her.

"Is something wrong?" The cowboy was back with a stack of boot boxes in his arms.

Dwight's attention split between him and the atrocity Molly was trying on. "Not anymore. How are you this fine day?"

I thought the cowboy would give him a suspicious look and step back when he figured out that Dwight was flirting, but instead, he just smiled. "Doing well, thanks. How about you? Something I can help you find?"

"I'm just here for support." Dwight gestured to me then glared over at the dressing room. He noticed the numerous boxes of shoes the man had put down and looked back at me. "Didn't know you loved shoes so much."

"I don't. The guys on the crew asked me to pick up new boots for them while I was here."

He looked surprised. "You're too nice to them, Falyn."

"I was already going to be here, and Nat let me off early with her truck so we could fit in your armoire and Viv's chairs. Remember?"

"Yeah." He rolled his eyes at the cowboy and got a lingering smile in response.

"What do you think?" Molly stepped out of the dressing room in a red, black, silver, brown, and green patterned sleeveless western shirt with shiny chrome buttons. Gold piping darted everywhere. Other than the wonderful flash of her amazing arms, it was probably the most hideous shirt she could find.

"Lord, help me now." Dwight pushed a hand through his cropped brown hair in exasperation.

Molly came toward us to model off the shirt. "Looks hot, right?"

Even the cowboy, whose only job it was to sell these kinds of things, couldn't help but join in our amusement at how awful the shirt looked. "Perhaps another color."

"Another color won't make him this uptight," Molly declared.

"Ha!" Dwight exclaimed.

"Help me decide between these three styles, Dwight," I encouraged him to look at the boots the cowboy had unpacked before he could go into Round Twenty with Molly.

"Those, definitely those," Dwight said with one glance, pointing to the six inch brown pair with a steel toe and good electrical rating. "And tell Luis that they didn't have these in his size." He held up the standard tan work boot that Luis preferred. He pointed to the black steel toe that Tyler liked. "Would you grab those in his size?" He looked at the cowboy.

"Dwight, he specifically asked for the tan ones," I protested.

"He'll thank me later. Those others are more comfortable anyway. He's just being stubborn." Since they were cheaper and he had mentioned he liked

Tyler's boots once, I figured I'd let Dwight take the blame if he got angry.

Molly came over as the cowboy went to get the other boots. "Beefy Cowboy's checking you out, D."

He smiled and gave her a fist bump. I thought I'd seen the look, but I was a little out of practice. These two probably spent many hours in bars together and knew what to look for. "He'll be mine before we leave this place."

Yep, these two were definitely friends.

"You need workpants, too, Falyn?" she asked as she headed back toward the dressing room to change out of the shirt. "I'll check the racks for you."

My heart warmed. She was so attentive, even when we'd just been friends. It was such a change from my other relationships. I was always the attentive one. To have that for myself was pretty incredible. And to have it appreciated so much by her was prize worthy.

"I'm happy for you," Dwight said in a low voice, squeezing an arm around my waist. He tipped his head at the dressing room. "Happy for her, too. She's needed someone like you, and the stubborn numbskull couldn't see it."

I should probably have some witty retort for him since that was how he and Molly communicated, but I couldn't come up with anything other than honesty. "Thanks. I've needed the same and was just as unconvinced about it."

"Lesbians," he sighed and shook his head but perked up immediately as Cowboy came back with the other boots for Luis. "Those will be perfect. Now, we've got to put her in workpants that don't look like they were made for a man. Help me save her style, will you?"

The cowboy laughed with me as they went to the women's section, leaving me to try on the boots that Dwight liked best. My foot slipped into one and felt like it was being massaged. Okay, maybe not massaged but so much better than the cheap boots I'd been wearing all summer. That I could afford them now and had a reason to get them tightened my throat.

Molly appeared beside me and sat down, bringing a hand up to rub my back. She smiled sweetly at me as if she could read my mind. She probably knew how much being able to buy boots for a job I loved at a place forty miles from home meant to me. Four months ago, I wouldn't have been able to afford them, let alone be allowed to leave the area to make this trip.

"They look good. Feel good?"

I nodded, still a little choked up that this was my life now. Great job, good friends, and amazing girlfriend.

"I'm glad we did this, even if we had to bring Dwight along." She gave me a squeeze. "Happy?"

I glanced over at her. My heart swelled. "Happy."

"Me, too." She leaned in for a swift peck that had both a calming and sexy effect.

"I leave you two for a second," Dwight interrupted with a mock sigh. Several pairs of pants draped over his arm on hangers. "Try these."

I shared a look with Molly before following his order. Unlike her, I found it was best just to follow his suggestions rather than fight him every second. Molly rather enjoyed the arguing, which was funny because she didn't argue with Vivian or me at all. She must expend it all on Dwight.

"That furniture place closes in an hour, Dwight. Don't make her try on every pair in the store."

He checked his watch as I slipped out of the boots and grabbed the hangers he was holding. "We'll make it. They like me there. They won't mind waiting an extra few minutes for us."

After trying on the pants both Dwight and the cowboy had picked out, I chose enough to make it a full week without having to do laundry. At the register, the price for my stuff would have alarmed me just months ago. Before I went to prison, I would have handed over a credit card without even checking the receipt. I wasn't at that stage yet, and planned never to be there again, but I was happy that I could fork over the cash without having a seizure.

Outside, Molly and I piled the bags into Natalie's locking toolbox in the bed of her truck as Dwight ran into the coffee shop next door to get us some beverages for the rest of our trip. We were just about to get into the truck when a familiar voice stopped us.

"Look who it is!"

We twirled to see Joanna and Brandy getting out of a car. Molly groaned beside me. Dwight came out of the coffee shop with a panicked look when he spotted them, afraid we wouldn't make it to the furniture store in time.

"What a small world," Brandy exclaimed, coming closer. "We were just on our way back for a long weekend and here we run into you so far from home. Are you world travelers now?"

"Hey, guys." Molly received hugs from both.

They did the same to me and Dwight before focusing on me. "We were going to call you, sexy thing. Spend Saturday night with us. We'll hit a bar or two and have some fun."

My eyebrows rose. It wasn't a blatant come on, but still. "I'm busy." I stepped closer to Molly.

"But we're only here till Sunday. Don't make us wait till the slopes open," Joanna ordered.

I shook my head with conviction. "I'm busy for the winter, too." This time I slid my arm around Molly's waist.

She grinned and slipped an arm around me. She looked pretty proud, and it felt wonderful. Especially when their jaws dropped.

"You two?"

"Yep," Molly stated. What I liked best was that she didn't feel the need to make the point further. No extra squeeze, no kiss on the head, no slipping around me to make out in front of them.

"You said to give her space. Look what space did,'" Brandy accused Joanna.

"Don't blame me," Joanna cried.

Dwight sighed loudly and tapped his watch. "Great support, ladies. Why don't we take this up another time?" He opened the back door of the truck, prompting Molly to leave my side and head to the passenger door.

"Who would have known?" Brandy asked Joanna but looked at me as if I'd explain.

I didn't need to explain. Molly turned out to be the best type of woman for me, and I wasn't about to question it. I shrugged, waved goodbye, and got into the truck with my ideal girlfriend and her bickering friend. We had an armoire to rescue.

32

Ramón and I moved the sofa two inches back per Vivian's instructions. Installation day at her house and it was the first time she hesitated on any decision. We'd repositioned the couch three times now.

She looked at the couch and over to the fireplace and back at our position. "Good. Curtis, move to your left."

I turned to see Curtis heft one of the beautiful chairs Vivian had chosen for the great room. Luis followed his move with another chair. Miguel and Cole were maneuvering a mattress up the staircase for the guestroom. Natalie and Tyler were right behind them with the tempered glass tabletop for Vivian's studio worktable.

The huge smiles Vivian and Natalie wore were the best part of the day. Miguel and Luis warned me that install day was the only time we'd see Vivian's temper flare onsite. They laughed about it, having endured what they'd described as a bipolar boss for years before joining Natalie's company. Vivian's temper was like a pillow fight compared to an MMA match, they said. No one's temper had shown yet today.

I followed Ramón out to the furniture truck. There wasn't a lot left to bring in. Mostly it would be arranging to make sure everything was placed where Vivian envisioned. In a few hours, what she'd been calling her dream home would be put together. I could feel the excitement rolling off her in waves.

"Are you coming to the housewarming party on Saturday night?" Ramón asked.

I grabbed the other end of a custom ottoman as he started backing out of the truck. "Planned on it."

"Bringing a date?"

I chuckled. The guys on the crew liked ribbing each other about their dates. Only Miguel and Owen were married. They'd been guessing about my status for weeks. Even Cole and Curtis weren't quite sure what was going on with Molly since we stayed over at her place a couple nights a week and didn't show a lot of affection in front of them. Not because we were embarrassed but because neither of us was a big displayer of affection. Yet another perk of dating someone like me instead of the usual femme, lovey-dovey type.

"My date's already invited."

"Oh, really?" He grinned as he set the ottoman down, looking over at Vivian for her nod. "Do we know her?"

"You'll see her on Saturday."

"C'mon, Fos, give me a hint. More importantly, does she have a hot friend that she can set me up with?"

I laughed. Molly did have quite a few friends. "Can't get a date?"

"Everyone else is bringing someone." He glanced over at Vivian. "You're inviting single *chicas* to your party, right?"

She motioned with her hand for us to move the ottoman back a little. "You'll be happy, Ramón."

"Oh, yeah, *guapo* is getting lucky."

"I've got a hundy says he strikes out all night," Tyler called down from the balcony overlooking the great room.

"Your nickname for yourself is 'handsome' and you think women are going to be okay with that?" I asked incredulously.

"It's one of many," Miguel shared as he passed by. "There's no shortage of ego with this one."

Ramón went into a long conversation in Spanish with Miguel, only half of which I caught. I'd been picking up Spanish a bit at a time all summer, but it was mostly job related conversation. This was all over the place, and I didn't have a hope of following it. Natalie spoke up in flawless Spanish, telling them to get back to work. Or I assumed that's what she said because we all started back out to the truck again.

By the end of the afternoon, the home was almost entirely put together. Now it was just the personal items that Vivian and Natalie would have to unpack to make the home theirs. When I got into Curtis's van, I had the impression that Natalie was going to do something special on their first night in the new house. I smiled, thinking about what I'd do for Molly on our first night in our new place. Then I smiled harder thinking about how I'd just had that thought.

I had the boys drop me off at the supermarket. I wanted to make Molly dinner at her place to celebrate finishing the project. Seeing the look on Natalie's face made me want to have my own private celebration with my special someone.

"Meet me outside," a voice I hadn't heard in eight years said from behind me in the produce section.

I turned to watch a man walk past a stand of apples and out through the automatic doors at the front of the store. I didn't recognize the white hair, but I'd followed that gait many times into and out of a home we'd broken into.

My heart rate spiked. Sweat bloomed under my arms. The basket in my hand grew heavier and the muscles in my arms seized. This couldn't be happening. I'd left that life behind. I'd survived the hopelessness of prison and frustration of parole. I was on the other side of the gloominess, and in the space of one sentence, I plunged back into the darkness.

202 – Lynn Galli

I looked around. Everyone else was going about their shopping like their lives hadn't just been jolted. Like grocery shopping was the only task at hand instead of facing something terrifying from their pasts.

I found a place to set my basket down. I couldn't ignore Brock. I didn't know how he'd found me, but I would bet he'd been in town for a while. I'd bet even more that he was the source of my feeling of being watched over the past few weeks.

When I cleared the doors, Brock wasn't around. For a moment my heart lifted at the prospect that I'd again imagined it. Then I saw him at the far edge of the parking lot. He waited until I saw him then disappeared behind the building next door. I had no choice but to follow him.

"Missed ya, Shaw." Brock leaned casually against the brick building as if I'd seen him every day for the last decade. His face looked the same but with wrinkles. Prison hadn't been as kind to him. No trace of his brown hair was left. He'd gone all white, despite being only a year older than I was.

I checked out every inch of the space around us. We were alone on the sidewalk. I didn't know for how long. Just saying hello to him when I was on parole would have put my status in jeopardy. I wanted to punch him for how casually he was putting our freedom in danger.

"Doesn't look like you missed me much since you have yourself a sweet little deal going here. Wanted to keep it all to yourself."

"What the hell are you doing here?" Anger and fear clogged my throat. The heat of the August sunshine felt like it was baking my skin.

"You don't sound happy to see me." He made a disbelieving sound. "Last time we saw each other was before my trial."

"What are you doing here?" I repeated.

"You seem pissed, Shaw. No love for the man that made you rich?"

"You didn't make me rich." Not even close. It was a nice take, but with a girlfriend who could burn money like a wildfire, I didn't hold onto any of it. "And you still haven't answered my question."

"You know, I always thought it was funny how you, of everyone on the team, had the biggest gold-digging girlfriend. I thought mine was bad, but yours took the cake. Heard she cleaned out everything you had as soon as you went inside."

"Fuck you," I seethed at his cavalier tone. The devastation I felt at her betrayal was second only to how I'd felt when I found out one of the burglary crew turned state's evidence against us. Brock knew how that felt, too, and here he was making light of someone else who'd screwed me over.

"Hey, we've all been there. Mine lasted three years then got bored. It's always best to keep some people you trust on the outside to handle your shit when you get pinched. Did you hold onto your sweet car at least?"

I didn't want to have this conversation with him. I didn't want him to be here. If that police officer who kept "bumping" into me on the street showed up tonight, I doubt I could talk my way out of her suspicions this time.

"You pulled those jobs?" I already knew and dreaded the answer.

"What jobs?" He gave me a sinister grin.

"You broke into those two homes I worked on." I turned away and started pacing. Damn and damn and damn again.

"Not sure what you're talking about, Shaw. If you're interested in starting our little business venture again, I could round up a team."

I stared hard at him. He'd done it. I knew that as much as his tone confused me. Normally he'd brag about

204 - Lynn Galli

everything he'd done. Shutting him up was the hardest thing to do in our planning sessions. "Not interested."

"Really?"

"Leave me alone, Porter. I'm done with that life." And everything about that life. I didn't want it or need it, and that allowed me to be the best version of myself.

"No one is ever really done. You're judged and treated with disrespect everywhere you go now because you did time. Gets tiring, doesn't it?"

Yes, it does, but it isn't enough of a reason to get back into the life. "I don't know what you're doing here, but I'm out of it."

"You're in the same ideal position as you used to be. We could have something even better here. I've strolled around town, cased a few places. With your access to the interiors, you'd know exactly the places to hit. I can get everyone together again. We're all out now. Not Kaplin, of course, can't have another snitch on the team."

"I'm serious, Porter. I'm out. Don't contact me again." I started walking away.

"No one can escape this life, and you don't want to miss out on this."

"What's that mean?" I turned back at his threatening tone. I was practically sweating clean through my clothes from the nervousness and the heat.

"Point us in the right direction, that's all. You don't even need to be on the crew. Just give us a heads up on the places."

"No."

"Shaw."

"No, I won't do it. And if I were you, I'd leave town soon. The police already suspect me when one of those places is hit."

A faint smile drifted across his lips. "Yeah, I saw them headed to your place once. See what I mean about not being able to get out from under this life?"

I wanted to punch him. He'd intended for them to suspect me. "You asshole."

"Had to give you a little incentive. At least give me credit for making sure you had an alibi."

"I'm telling you now I don't want any part of whatever team you're putting together." I got right in his face. "Go back to Boulder and pick up there."

"But it's so nice here and a lot more money."

"They'll find you." Not if they kept looking at me every time, but I could at least make the threat.

"Next time, I might not make sure you have an alibi."

Dickhead. "I'm not helping you."

He shrugged, giving me nonchalance. "Next time, maybe something will turn up in the search."

"One phone call and you're back inside. Unlike me, you're still on parole." It was the only card I had.

He snorted in disbelief. "Don't make me regret giving you this offer, Shaw. We were a good team before. We'll be good again."

"Back off. If I see you again, I'm calling you in."

A smile drifted over his face. "Sure."

He sauntered off like he was on an evening stroll, enjoying his vacation in this beautiful town. That sense of being pushed into a corner pressed hard against me. I could only hope that he'd figure out I was serious.

33

Molly already had her key out before we hit the top stair of her condo complex. We were coming back from Vivian's housewarming party that had turned into an engagement celebration. I'd been right about Natalie having something planned when we left the house on installment day. She'd proposed to Vivian in some grandly romantic event on a beach or something with rose petals and ice cream or something. I didn't really follow the narrative because it was the result that mattered. Vivian sported a beautiful engagement ring, and Natalie wore her happiness in every word and gesture.

"If I weren't so caught up in you and I didn't think Vivian would kill me, I'd kiss Natalie for giving my friend everything she ever wanted in love."

"Caught up, huh?" I teased, winding my hands around her waist and bringing her to me.

She tilted her forehead against mine and pulled me closer. "Pretty damn, yeah." Her lips coasted over mine, tantalizing now with a promise for more as soon as she got the door open.

Except when she opened the door, her apartment was in disarray. Her bookcase had been tossed, books and knickknacks spilled over her couch and floor. The speaker set she kept on one of the shelves was dumped on the floor, the iPod gone. I glanced at the kitchen table where she kept her laptop and the iPad she just got. Neither were there. All of the kitchen cabinets were open, broken glass and dishware sprawled onto the counters.

Molly squeaked in dismay beside me. Her hand braced against the open doorway, shallow breaths moving in and out. This was what it was like for those twelve homeowners I'd burgled. The descriptions really didn't bring the devastation to life like seeing it happen.

My eyes took in the chaos of her small apartment. I knew her bedroom wouldn't be spared. This wasn't the kind of job I pulled. We weren't messy. We could avoid being messy since I'd already cased the homes. Still, this was amateurish. Overly.

Molly stepped inside, wariness in her eyes. "I can't believe this."

I couldn't either. I knew she didn't keep cash here. They got away with a TV and some portable electronics? They'd get maybe a few hundred for the effort. It was dangerous to hit a condo building because the halls were often monitored by cameras with offsite backup and nosy neighbors. Her second floor unit didn't make for a clean getaway either.

"Molly." I grabbed her arm, shocked to find it trembled under my fingers. I pulled her in for a hug that I needed as much as she seemed to.

"This is unbelievable."

"I'm sorry this happened."

She pulled away and gave me one of her intense stares. "I'll call the police."

"Wait," I said as a thought formed fully in my brain.

She gave me a quizzical look. Her finger hovered over the call button on her phone.

I shook my head, not wanting to voice what I'd been thinking. "I think if you call the police, they'll find something that isn't yours."

"What do you mean?" Her eyes looked around the room as if something might suddenly animate and attack her.

"I told you I ran into that guy the other day." I hadn't gone into everything that Brock had said, but I did want to be as forthcoming as possible with her. She seemed to need that to keep the trust. "I think he did this."

She shook her head and took a step back. "Why?"

"I think," I cleared my tight throat and restarted, "He wants to take away my choices so I'll work with him again."

She reached out and cupped my face, stroking her thumb along my cheekbone. "How does this fit in?"

"He hinted that if I didn't start back up with him, something incriminating might show up in my possession. I'm betting that he thought you'd find this alone and call the police. They'll give the place a cursory search for fingerprints and find something from one of those jobs. They won't suspect you, especially if the cop who responds is Cherise. She'll think I stashed the take here." I shook my head and swore.

"Jesus, Falyn. Who is this guy?" Her hand slid down my neck to grip my shoulder.

"He was the planner. We had three others, but we all listened to the planner. He wants to get us together again, and he's trying to force me into it."

She made another sound of disbelief. "This is the kind of guy you worked with?" Her arm waved around her place.

Guilt swamped me. This was exactly the kind of situation I never wanted to face again. Molly didn't need to see this side of me because it no longer existed.

"We never left a place looking like this." I stopped before I said anything more. She didn't need to hear what I'd done or not done. Not now, not in the face of this. "I'm really sorry."

Tears sprang to her eyes. A hand came up to wipe at them angrily. "Why didn't you call the police the second you saw him?"

"Because I'm not in the same position as you. They'd believe you. They'll just think I'm rolling on my conspirator for a deal on something I've already done. I told him to back off, that I wasn't interested. I hoped he'd just leave."

"But he didn't. He broke into my house, went through my things, took my things."

"Yes."

"And you're saying we can't call the police now?"

"I don't know." I wasn't sure how to handle this. "Let me look around first."

She crossed her arms, gripping them tightly. She was afraid and angry and frustrated and facing something she'd never faced. And the only person with her was someone who'd caused these reactions for many others.

I turned away, afraid of the disappointed look I knew would soon develop. My eyes searched everywhere he touched. There wouldn't be any fingerprints, or I should say, the only other fingerprints besides Molly's would be mine.

If he wanted the police to find something, it would have to be fairly easy to find because they wouldn't do a search. Yet it wouldn't be out in the open because any thief would take whatever it was.

I went to her bedroom, a place I'd felt so comfortable. Molly followed slowly behind. I couldn't blame her. She probably didn't want to see what he'd done. I let out a sigh when I entered. A lamp from the nightstand and her alarm clock lay on the ground. The closet door was open, but otherwise, nothing was amiss. Big clue that something was wrong here.

"Do you have a safe?"

Her head shook. "I don't have anything really valuable to safe keep."

"Jewelry box?"

"No. I just keep some earrings and the one necklace I have in—"

"Your sock drawer?" I guessed.

Her eyes went wide. "Bad idea?"

"It's actually smart to keep things in an innocuous place." I looked around again and noticed a wood carved box on the top shelf in her closet. "What's that?"

Her eyes flicked up. "A gift from my mom. She put some old photos and newspaper clippings from my high school soccer and softball days as a birthday present one year."

"Will you look inside it, please?" It was the only place that a good officer would ask about when assessing the damage.

Molly stepped over and pulled the box down. She opened the lid and gasped. The box tilted in her hands and sitting right on top of the news clippings was a diamond bracelet. Retail, easily ten grand, fenced nothing more than one. It was from the second house. I'd seen the homeowner wearing it. The second house where I had an alibi.

"That isn't mine."

"I know." I sighed, dropping onto Molly's bed to gain my thoughts.

"How?"

"That was taken from the second place, the one where I have an alibi. He's warning me. Even if the police found this, it's still only circumstantial, which can be trumped with my alibi. If he'd left something from the first house, he'd be telling me he was pissed. He's still trying to recruit me."

Her eyes squinted in confused anger. "We have to do something, Falyn. This is awful."

"I know, but I don't know what to do. Short of hurting him, which was never my deal."

"A lawyer?"

I let out a breath. "I think that's the only option I've got. I can't be seen with stolen property."

"I'll call Mei."

I knew my neighbor was a lawyer but didn't know what kind. "Does she do criminal work?"

"Not really, but she'll know someone who does."

I bit my lip and nodded. Molly gave me a small smile and pulled me up from the bed and into her. "I'm so sorry about this. I thought this was over for me."

"I'm sorry this is happening to you."

I gripped her tight, not wanting to let go. I should be distancing myself from her. Brock had no qualms about using her against me. Things could turn wrong for her on his next attempt, whatever it was.

Once again, I found myself in a situation that didn't make me comfortable or happy. The last time I gave up seven years because of it. I really didn't know if this time would end any better.

34

My neighbor scheduled the appointment with the criminal defense attorney for me. Mei even managed to get me a free consultation. That never happened with criminal attorneys.

The attorney didn't mince words. She shared a practice with another defense attorney, who seemed to trade on his sharp looks and even sharper suits. She dressed nicely, but not designer custom. Her jewelry was minimal, and she took notes with a disposable pen not a Cartier. It was an interesting juxtaposition. Her hourly rate scared me, but she didn't flaunt the hourly rate in her office or, I would guess, the courtroom.

"When they get here, let me do all the talking unless I nod at you," Yolanda said as we sat around her conference room table for our second appointment.

"How did you get them to come here?" We were waiting for the detective in charge of the burglary investigation. The police always preferred to question people in their interrogation room, yet here we were in her office.

"I told them I had a client with information about an ongoing case. If they wanted it, they'd have to come get it." Her smile was made up of what looked like a million sparkly white teeth. The image of a shark came to mind.

I took a cleansing breath. My chest felt tight and I was perspiring again. I wanted this over, and yet, I didn't want to be involved. What Yolanda was proposing wasn't much better than what had happened to me the first time, but something had to be done. I couldn't let Brock coerce me into illegal activities.

Cherise was the first one through the outer doors of the office. My stomach sank at the sight of her. A guy nearing retirement followed her in. He was in plain clothes and looked like someone who sold vacuums rather than busted criminals.

They were shown into the conference room, each shaking Yolanda's hand and ignoring me. Cherise couldn't keep up the act for long. Her brown eyes kept shifting to me with accusation.

"It's not like you to be so vague, Yolanda," the man who'd introduced himself as Detective Tanner said. "Don't keep us in suspense."

"My client has information about two burglaries you've been investigating."

"I knew it!" Cherise exclaimed.

"Officer." Tanner cut her a look.

"She's trying to cut a deal. I knew she would," Cherise explained.

"She doesn't need to cut a deal." Yolanda spoke only to Tanner now. "Let me say this up front. She has no direct proof, but she is in a position of knowledge based on experience."

"In other words, she has nothing solid," Tanner countered.

"She has more than you."

He blinked. In another setting he would have flinched. Yolanda knew how to push all the right buttons. "She expects immunity for her involvement?"

"She's not involved."

"Then how does she know anything?"

"Your perpetrator contacted her."

"She's associating with him."

"He contacted her to work with him."

"I knew you weren't working alone," Cherise said directly to me.

"Officer, my client will not respond to you," Yolanda said in a chilly voice. "And you'll take care in your accusations. From what she's described, I have enough for a harassment claim against you."

Cherise leaned forward in her chair, fingers gripping the arms. "I haven't—"

"She does not want to pursue that course right now, but we're keeping her options open." Yolanda spoke as if Cherise hadn't said anything.

Cherise slanted a murderous look at me. I kept my eyes trained on Yolanda.

"Go on," Tanner said.

"My client was confronted on the street by the man responsible for the two burglaries you questioned her about. He did not admit to them directly, but he did reference them in his recruitment chat. He also mentioned that if my client didn't comply, he would make sure his next action would lead directly to her."

"There hasn't been another burglary," Tanner said, glancing at Cherise for confirmation.

"Yes, there has." Yolanda paused, letting that sink in. "The apartment of Ms. Shaw's girlfriend was broken into last night."

"Girlfriend?" Cherise turned fully toward me. "You're with Molly now? Oh, no. Not once I have a talk with her, you won't be."

"Officer." Yolanda waited until Cherise brought her attention back. "That is exactly the kind of harassment I'm talking about. You will not abuse your authority to affect my client's quality of life. Am I understood?"

Cherise huffed, knocking her hand against her partner's shoulder and gesturing to me. When Tanner didn't immediately back her up, she slumped down in her seat.

"Now, as I was saying, my client and her girlfriend entered the apartment after being away most of the evening and found it burgled. Here is a list of the items missing from the apartment. Ms. Sokol is available for a statement. You are free to investigate the premises."

"What does that have to do with this guy you're saying your client thinks did the others?" Tanner asked.

"Ms. Sokol is a direct link to my client, and there's this." She produced the stolen bracelet. "This was left in a place that Ms. Sokol would have checked in front of responding officers. We assume this is a missing item from one of the two burglaries?"

I'd told Yolanda where I'd seen the bracelet, but she thought it was smarter to let the police figure that out. Advice from defense attorneys usually kept most people out of more trouble, so I let her lead the way here.

"This is from one of the homes?" Tanner looked to Cherise, who studied it and nodded.

"And we're to believe your client didn't take this?"

"My client didn't take this. She doesn't need to be here. She's offering you her help in closing these cases."

"Again, what proof do you have that your client didn't take this?"

"You have no proof that she did."

Both of them scoffed and pointed at the bracelet in Yolanda's hand. "She's in possession of stolen goods."

"I'm in possession of stolen goods," she corrected.

"Which you got from your client."

"Which I got from my client's girlfriend." This was like listening to a well scripted rom-com from the forties where characters talked too fast and without breaks.

"Fine, let's say your client is telling the truth."

"She is."

"She can deliver this guy?"

"She doesn't know how to contact him. It's presumed he'll try to contact her again."

"Presumed," Cherise snorted.

"And if he doesn't contact her? What then?" Tanner took over.

"You'll have the name of the man behind these burglaries. He's got a record and known associates to start with."

"Or we'll find definitive evidence against your client."

Yolanda chortled, the sound rhythmic and forced. "Not now that we've had this meeting. If you decide to bring charges against my client, I get to put you on the stand and ask you about this meeting. That will give me all the reasonable doubt I need." She smirked but noticed I'd gone pale at the prospect of being tried for something I didn't do. "But we don't want it to get that far."

The detective sighed and adjusted his position, wincing when the effort produced a flare of pain from somewhere. "You propose what?"

"If you get a wiretap for Ms. Shaw's cellphone, she can record her next conversation with the man. It'll be admissible in court." Yolanda paused for no more than two seconds before pushing out a disbelieving breath. "You already have the wiretap? Really, Tanner? Did you forget to tell the judge my client has an alibi? You know I can have it pulled with one appearance, don't you?" She gestured to Cherise. "This officer is all the talk of defense attorneys over at the courthouse right now. Were you taking the day off when she rushed that bogus search warrant through?"

His chin tucked against his chest. She got him, but I felt sick. A tap on my phone meant someone had been monitoring my calls for a while now. Most were harmless, but I talked to Molly on that phone. We weren't exactly having phone sex, but they were private conversations. Yet one more thing I'd have to confess to Molly.

"I assume we'll have cooperation now?" Yolanda stated.

"All we'd get is intent. I doubt this guy is stupid enough to admit to the burglaries if he didn't before."

"What if we gave him a bait address?"

Tanner considered this. "We'd want the goods returned."

"That's up to you to find. My client can lead him to you and offer a chance for you to catch him in the act. Your cases are closed and you leave my client alone. If I find you've been issued another warrant, I'll pursue that harassment claim with or without my client's permission."

Kick. Ass. Damn, Mei sent me to a wolverine. A wolverine who charged a quarter of my monthly salary per hour, but based on this meeting, she earned the steep fee.

"You can remember to record the conversation?" Tanner asked me.

I glanced at Yolanda for a nod. "I'll try."

"Will he suspect that you're setting him up?"

I didn't think so, but he might. "I'd have to be sent on a job to the address first."

"That's how you used to do it?"

Yolanda placed a hand on my arm before I could answer. "This man is trying to coerce her involvement. The easiest way to do that is to burgle a place where she's worked. He's done it twice now."

"Fine, we'll see if it works." Tanner started to get up.

Yolanda shook her head. "You'll get the D.A. to write up a deal first."

"Your client hasn't done anything wrong, or so you say."

"My client will not have the recording or prior knowledge of the bait burglary used against her in court."

His eyes moved over me and back to Yolanda. He nodded his head once.

"By the end of the day. We don't know when this guy will contact her again."

He stood, Cherise standing with him. "It'll be done."

35

Every time I took a step, it felt like the ticking from
my bike's wheels could drown out a hard rock band.
Cleveland Street was deserted this time of night,
projecting the wheel clicks out into the silence. Now on
my third circuit through this part of town, I had the
smallest hope that Brock had pulled up stakes. I
checked my phone again. One more missed call, this one
from Cole. I'd already ditched Molly for the night, the
last two nights actually. It helped that I'd just moved
into Natalie's old place and still had boxes to unpack,
but Molly was probably getting a complex. I really
wanted to tell her what was going on, but my new high
priced lawyer told me not to say a word to anyone.

I couldn't figure out what Brock was waiting for. He
had three evenings to approach me when I was alone.
My gut couldn't take much more of this tension.

"Falyn!" Tessa waved to me from the bank across the
street. A familiar looking woman turned from the ATM
machine and slipped her arm around Tessa's waist. The
unyielding glare I received would have been message
enough. She didn't need to throw the possessive arm
around Tessa to tell me to back off. "Out for a bike
ride?"

I focused on Tessa, ignoring the back-off vibes I was
getting from her companion. "Just cooling down. Where
are you off to?" I didn't want to risk scaring Brock off
with a long conversation, but it would look more
suspicious to ignore her.

"Have you met my partner, Kathleen?" She smiled
sweetly, not sensing the hostility coming from her

partner toward me. I should be swelling with pride that I'd guessed right about their boomerang relationship, but I'd actually gotten to know and like Tessa. Based on the little I saw of these two together and Molly's judgment, I didn't want her with this creep any more than her good friends did.

"Haven't had the pleasure. I'm Falyn. I've worked on a few of Tessa's home deals."

Kathleen plastered on a smile that looked so real I had a hard time believing it wasn't. No wonder most of Tessa's friends had been fooled by her. "You work for Natalie? She's a sweet lady. Thanks for helping out. I know my baby wouldn't have closed on a couple of those deals without Natalie's work."

My baby? If Molly were here she'd probably ask how a baby was capable of closing real estate deals and why this woman felt she needed to publicly claim Tessa, but she wasn't and I needed them to move on. Damn. Molly. Did she know these two were together again? She'd be disappointed. She wanted the best for her friend. Kathleen didn't seem to be that person.

"I go where my boss sends me, but Tessa's a great client wrangler. Never have to worry about them going renozilla on us with Tessa around."

Tessa laughed and pushed against my shoulder. "Oh, you."

Kathleen's eyes narrowed momentarily before smiling again. "She rocks her talent. Nice meeting you, Falyn. Baby, we've got to move if we're going to make those reservations."

They hurried off, thankfully, away from my circuit route. Ten seconds later, the feeling of being watched settled over me again. I caught sight of Brock out of the corner of my eye. I lifted my phone to my ear and acted like I was making a quick call. My head swiveled as I talked and let my eyes land on him. He tipped his head toward the alleyway behind him.

I switched on the recorder of my phone, thankful that I'd splurged and gotten a smart phone this time instead of a simple cell. I walked my bike over and turned into the alley between the buildings. Brock was waiting with a welcoming smirk.

"I told you to leave me alone, Brock." My pulse rate contradicted my threatening tone.

"And I told you that you'd regret trying to make me leave, Shaw. Did you like my last move?"

Smug, evil bastard. "The one where you broke into my girlfriend's home, trashed her place, and took her portable electronics?"

"Hey, she left her balcony sliders unlocked. I couldn't not go in. You should talk to her about that."

"Damn you, Porter. You didn't have to do that. I said I wouldn't help you. Find some other spotter."

"But you were so good. Our take increased forty percent when I brought you in last time."

I cut him off before he said anything more specific about our criminal acts together. While the statute had expired, I didn't need the police here knowing I'd actually been part of four more burglaries than they knew about. "I can't do time again, man. I really can't. Why would you want to risk that again?"

He scoffed at my concern. "We didn't get caught, remember? If that asshole hadn't gotten picked up on something else and offered us up, we never would have been caught. The cops here are small town idiots. Their only lead is an ex-con who didn't do either job."

As much as recording that confirmation helped, I still needed an end to this. "They'll keep harassing me if you continue breaking into places I work on. Christ, Brock, that was our old M.O."

"Hey, I did you a favor. If they accuse you without evidence again, you can sue their asses for false arrest or something. We'll find a good lawyer to help. They'll lay off, and you're never going to have the take with you."

He'd really thought this through. Yolanda had made a similar case. One more false accusation could make getting anything to stick in the future impossible. Kind of like crying wolf too many times. Still, I had to convince him that my reluctance was genuine, which it was.

"I'm not doing this."

"You will, or the next time they search your place, they'll find everything."

My chest constricted with his threat. I remembered back to the last three jobs we pulled in Boulder. He came close to giving me a similar ultimatum when I told him that using my jobsites was getting too obvious. He didn't agree and gave me what he called a pep talk— what I called a warning. This time the ultimatum was clear, but I played dumb for the benefit of the recorder. "What are you talking about?"

"Don't tell me you've lost your touch over the years?" He thumped my back as if we were two buddies reminiscing about old times. "You didn't find my little surprise?"

"You mean the diamond bracelet you stole from one of those houses I worked in?" I was laying it on pretty thick. The only thing more obvious would be if I used his full name. He'd definitely be tipped off then.

"Ah, good, you haven't lost everything." He clapped his hands together. "There's a lot more from that job and the one before. Imagine what the police will think when an anonymous tip comes in that you've got the stuff stashed at your place now."

"You asshole." I fisted both hands. I'd only had to use physical violence in prison a few times, always in self-defense, but I felt like going on the offensive this time. "I don't like being cornered. You know that."

"I gotta do what I gotta do to get you on the team, Shaw. You're in the best position to make me rich again. I'll consider letting you play spotter only. If your leads are good, that is."

I shook my head and breathed out my anger. In prison, I'd learned to deflect feelings of anger before things got too unbearable. I'd do two hundred more sit-ups or pushups to get past it. Right now, I let the anger flow through me. It helped me feel less guilty that I was setting him up. We'd both gone to prison because someone else on our team turned on us. It didn't feel good, but watching Molly's reaction to her home being broken into felt a hell of a lot worse.

"Fine," I agreed. "But I want Molly's stuff back."

"There's the Shaw I remember. We're gonna be rich in a town like this."

"Molly's things," I insisted.

"Yeah, sure, whatever. It's not worth anything anyway. Gotta say, Shaw, she's a far cry from the last chick you were doing."

"Shut up, Porter. We're not going to be friends this time. You're forcing me to do this. You don't get to say anything about how I live. Got it?" I growled but should have hit him. I knew exactly what he was trying to say about Molly. He had no idea how beautiful Molly was. How good she was to me. No idea.

His hands came up but his expression was smug. "Yeah, yeah. Whatever you say. Here's my cell. Call me when you have an address. Oh, and bring the bracelet back."

I scoffed at his cavalier tone. "Call it a recruitment bonus." And exhibit A, but he didn't need to know that.

"Not a chance. I need something to live on while I get everyone back together."

"Pull another job."

"Ooh, aren't you the eager beaver." His face showed amusement. "You have someplace in mind already?"

I pretended to consider. "I just worked a place that could be good." Tessa's house with the tricked-out media room. The buyers hadn't moved in yet.

"The empty house?" He smirked and scoffed. "Right. I'm not an idiot."

"They close escrow next Tuesday. That'll be moving day, and from what the realtor says, the stuff always moves in before the homeowners."

His eyes sparkled. "Sounds promising. Let me check the entry points, and I'll get back to you."

"Spotter only, remember? I'm telling you it's a good job, and it's the only one I'll have for months."

He jerked forward, not liking the sound of that. "What?"

I shrugged helplessly. "My boss has another massive project coming up. We won't be going out on any small jobs like my old crew used to."

"Shit. What's wrong with her?" Like it was Natalie's place to provide for his burglaries.

"I was trying to tell you that things won't be the same here. It's not too late to head back to Boulder and start up there again. You already know the right neighborhoods."

"I'll risk it. I can always double up on the other two. They'll have replaced their shit by now."

I held in the disgusted snort. Every time I thought about what I used to do, I felt the shame well up inside me. Seeing how it affected Molly made me sick to my stomach. What had I been thinking? That those rich assholes wouldn't care about being ripped off? Monetarily? No. But they had been harmed. I couldn't have been thinking of anyone other than myself.

Brock let me know he'd be in touch and sauntered away. I seethed at his back, dying to run up and tackle him or side swipe him with my bike. Since neither would happen, I reached into my pocket to stop the recording on my phone.

Spinning the bike in the direction of home, I was about to step onto the pedal when I saw Molly glaring over my shoulder before shifting her glower to me.

36

The scowl on Molly's face wasn't nearly as disheartening as the look of distrust. She stormed down the sidewalk, nearly knocking over a tipsy man who spilled out of the bar in front of her. When she reached me, her eyes bored into mine then flicked over my shoulder to watch Brock turn the corner out of sight.

"You said you were working." Her voice was calm but steely.

"I said I couldn't hang out tonight." It was a trivial distinction but the truth, which was more important to Molly than anyone I'd ever dated. I would always respect that.

She swallowed hard, uncertainty clouding her gaze. "Who was that?"

"Molly," I began, but her hand came up.

"That was him, wasn't it? You described him pretty well." She swiveled and marched four steps away, clenching and unclenching her hands to help relieve the strain I heard in her voice. "He didn't leave then? Even after you told him to, even after he got back at you by breaking into my place!"

"Molly," I rushed forward to grab her clenched fists. "Please."

"I can't believe this. I thought you were working tonight. Then I run into Tessa, and she tells me you're out riding your bike. Now you're talking to the guy who put you in prison?"

The burning ball of indigestion flared and grew in my stomach. This looked bad. I knew that, especially to a woman who already felt I'd withheld too much from her.

"What did he have to say?"

My lawyer's voice screamed in my head to stay quiet until this thing was over. Brock could have ears on the street, or Molly could share her concern about my plan with Vivian and Dwight. They might tell someone else. I trusted Molly, but I knew she trusted Vivian and Dwight, too. I was so close to being done with this. I couldn't risk the plan being found out before it went down.

I gave her what I could. "He's going to give your stuff back."

"My stuff?" She looked agonized. "I don't care about my stuff, Falyn. I mean, I do, but...shit!" She twisted out of my grasp and stomped off some of her irritation. "I just, dammit, I only care about you."

As good as it felt to have her decide I was the most important thing in this situation, her anguish did nothing to help the fiery ball in my stomach. I cared so much about her, enough that I couldn't get her more involved in this jam of mine.

She turned back and laid her hands on my shoulders. They tightened in urgency. "Didn't your lawyer have something to say about dealing with him?"

I stepped up close to her, reaching to set my hands on her hips. I looked deep into her concerned eyes. "Yes, but I have to ask you..." No, I shouldn't. Could I? She'd already given me too much. Far more than I deserved. The fiery ball spread up to my throat.

"What?" she prompted, coming closer when she realized I'd gotten choked up. I loved this about her. She didn't like seeing me upset any more than I liked being upset. "Ask me what?"

"For your trust that I know what I'm doing. Please, Molly, just for a week. After that, I can tell you more.

Just please, give me the benefit of the doubt again. Next week, I'll be able to make more sense of this for you."

She studied me for what felt like an hour. Her breathing was slow and audible. She wasn't comfortable. She wanted answers. She wanted to know that I wasn't going to do something stupid again. As my girlfriend, she had a right to know.

"Please be safe," she whispered and leaned forward to press a soft kiss to my forehead.

As my girlfriend, she was giving me more than I'd ever dreamed I could have. Hope. Faith. Trust. Everything I needed, and right then, I knew I was falling for her.

37

When I opened my car door and saw the brown box, my stomach twisted. I hadn't put the box there and my car door had been locked. Brock always could get into anything. My hands shook as I looked around my new driveway, trying to spot anything out of the ordinary. I was still getting used to this guesthouse setup. The main house was about fifty feet away across an elegant patio. Its garage hid the guesthouse from the road. There was a home on each side but far enough away to make it feel as if this house stood alone. When had Brock managed to sneak up here, behind the main house garage on the extended driveway to my little house? He would have had to do some pretty interesting traversing to stay out of the author's security camera angles.

Picking up the box, I slid onto the seat. I was afraid to open it. I was afraid to touch it, but I could always wipe fingerprints. I didn't think this was a setup. Brock couldn't know about what we had planned for him today. My fingers flipped open the flaps. A sigh escaped as I recognized Molly's iPod. Good. He was keeping to his end of the bargain.

Or I thought he was. I found a note under the iPod. *Stop by the score tonight and you'll get the rest.*

The knot in my stomach twisted back the other way as if my insides were being run through a washer. He wanted me to show up when he broke into the bait house. So he wasn't above suspecting me after all.

I pulled out my cell and called Yolanda. When she answered, another difference between her and my old defense attorney, she told me to stop by and drop off the box with Molly's iPod. She would turn it over to the police as evidence. I called Natalie to let her know I would be late. As usual, she was completely supportive without requiring an explanation. It was probably why her crew had stayed with her and never complained.

"Where was this little gift?" Yolanda asked when I set the box down on her desk.

"He broke into my car and left it on the driver's seat."

"Enterprising." She pulled out the note and read it. Her face barely registered an expression. She must be one hell of a poker player. "He wants you there why, you think?"

"Probably wants another chance to recruit me. Or if something goes wrong, it never hurts to have a cohort to make a deal for a lesser charge."

She nodded, assessing. "Let me call the detective and see how he wants to play it. It's likely they'll want you to follow his instructions or Porter might back out entirely."

I sat forward in the chair. Anxiety about seeing Brock and being in a situation that might stir up the old feelings of adrenalin washed over me. I knew from several books I'd read that I should avoid putting myself into a situation that could lead to the same bad habits. Like a recovering alcoholic should not go into a bar with his drinking buddies. It just makes it that much harder to break the bad cycle.

Yolanda watched my reaction. "If the police want you to follow through with this guy's request, I'll make sure the D.A. signs another immunity agreement."

I hadn't even thought of that. I was more worried about what seeing him right before a break-in would do to me. I knew I had no inclination left to commit burglaries anymore, but I didn't even want a hint of the feelings that used to come over me prior to hitting a home.

"Sit tight at work until you hear from me. One way or another, this should be done tonight."

I saw her determination and no longer cared that I'd spent almost two paychecks on her so far. She spoke frankly and quickly and didn't bill for incidentals like copies or phone calls. My first attorney had charged all that and more, and he still couldn't get me a better deal than the one I'd gotten.

When I got to Glory's renovation, I was a little distracted. I missed a splice and forgot to add another switch in my old bedroom before I figured out that I had to get my head back into the job or volunteer to help the rest of the guys with their cabinet refinishing. That would be safer work for someone whose head was stuck on legal consequences.

Cole handed me the receptacle that we were adding. All summer, he'd been my best helper. Natalie rotated the rest of the guys onto electrical work with me so we'd all have experience, but Cole had the makings of an electrician. He'd even talked to me about the process for getting licensed after he retired from ski racing every winter.

"How much do you think someone pays for a place like this?" Cole asked as he unpacked the supplies to turn the house into a smart home. It would add a week to our electrical work here, but it would make it easier for Glory to control things in her rental from offsite.

I was shrugging in response, but Vivian joined us and answered for him. "All she needs is six weeks of vacation rentals and she'll make enough to cover her mortgage for the year."

"What?" Cole shook his head. "Damn, we're in the wrong biz, Fos. Let's pool our money and buy a place to rent out to rich morons."

I laughed. "We'd be lucky to buy a horse trailer in this town with our pooled resources."

"What could we get for renting that, Viv?" he joked.

"Probably a couple hundred a week," she deadpanned.

"Fos," Natalie interrupted. "Someone's here for you."

I glanced down the hallway to find Yolanda standing in the mudroom up front. That annoying knot started twisting in my stomach again. She must have news.

"Cole, help your brother bring in the new appliances, please," Natalie said to him, somehow knowing I needed to talk to Yolanda alone. She'd always been intuitive like that.

I waved Yolanda inside as Vivian joined Natalie to oversee the placement of the new appliances. Even with modest changes, the kitchen would end up looking different and more upscale than the one I'd been cooking in all summer. Vivian's design touches and Natalie's craftsmanship would make Glory's house elegant enough to attract high-end vacationers.

Yolanda waited until I closed the bedroom door. "I have something for you to sign."

"The police want me to show up?" I guessed as I reached for the documents she held out to me.

"Yes. Like we thought, they don't want to have the guy back out because you don't show."

I so didn't want to see him again. He'd influenced enough about my life. This shouldn't be happening to me again. Not when I finally had the sense and the incentive to walk away from it. "I don't want to do this."

Yolanda studied me. She probably had to talk a lot of guilty clients out of doing stupid things. If she was like most defense attorneys, she had a lot more guilty clients than innocent. "Legally, you're covered here."

I flipped through the document, skimming to see that it was exactly as she stated. In exchange for my agreement to show up at a crime in progress to ensure that their intended target complete the crime, I would have immunity for all actions and stolen property found on my person. Yolanda had thought of everything. I'd lose another paycheck to her, but I could now afford it.

"Show up like he asked. Take possession of the rest of Molly's things and clear out. Don't let him bait you into anything. The agreement gives you leeway, but based on what you've said, the best thing you can do is let him think he's in the clear. You're just not interested in joining him."

"Okay," I could do this if I had to.

She waited for me to say more. I didn't know what more to say. I'd do this and hopefully be done. Yolanda had warned the police that, after this was done, they couldn't just assume I was a suspect for every burglary. That was far more than I could ask for. Just one evening and the wonderful life I'd managed to somehow snare in this serene town could finally be enjoyed.

38

Late afternoon, I pulled onto a side street and parked three houses down from the target house. The police worked everything out with the new owners to bring in phony boxes and furniture earlier today. It would look like someone had hired a moving company to get the work done before moving in. Truthfully, the new owners weren't moving in until next week. They agreed to let the police open the doors for the fake movers and leave them open for Brock so he wouldn't damage the locks, doors, or windows to get in.

Letting out a calming breath, I stepped out of the car. I didn't see Brock. He was probably waiting for me to arrive first. I'd already driven past the house to get a feel for the scene. I knew the escape routes without having to think about them. I knew the best way to get to the house without drawing attention in daylight. I knew how I would approach this job if I were the one doing it. All of it came to me instantly. What didn't was the incomparable combination of exhilaration and fear and excitement I used to experience every time I approached a job. Instead I felt sick. Sick that I'd ever gone through with this kind of thing. Sick that I'd made anyone feel unsafe.

I continued past the right street when I still didn't see Brock. Going by the home you were going to hit more than once got you noticed. I didn't want to give any of the neighbors a reason to remember me.

A truck came into view down the street. I slowed my gait, wondering if Brock thought of the same approach as I had. Yes, he had. He rolled down the street in a moving truck, no wary look, no unease. That was one of the reasons I'd wanted to stop. He thought his plans were infallible. He should have taken a better look at his team.

I crossed the street and made my way back toward the house. He parked right in the home's driveway. Bold but not exactly stupid. A moving truck had already been there. Another wouldn't arouse suspicion.

"Shaw," Brock greeted as he climbed down from the truck. He was wearing a work shirt with the name "Buddy" on the tag. Sunglasses and work gloves kept his costume as a mover authentic. His hair was gelled into spikey points, unique enough that if someone noticed him, they'd remember the ridiculous hair but not so remarkable to make someone stare. "Knew you couldn't stay away."

Asshole. "You didn't leave me a choice."

"Such an attitude. You used to be more easygoing, girl. I've got a little treat for you." He walked around to the back of the truck. He unlatched the door and rolled it up.

I nearly smiled when I saw it was partially filled with his take from the first two homes. He really was going to make this easy for the cops. I understood why he had the truck loaded. More than likely it was where he was keeping his stash while he was in town. Keeping it mobile was a good idea. After today's score, he probably planned to take it to whatever fence he'd arranged. More than likely back in Boulder since that was where he'd had all his contacts. It would also give him the opportunity to bring the team back together. I wondered if they were stupid enough to want to start back up again or would they be as reluctant as I was?

"Impressive, right? Listen, you reconsider and join me on this, I'll give you a split on what I've already got." His head nodded at the stolen goods.

"Spotter is what we agreed on. Don't force my hand more than that."

"You showed because you wanted me to talk you into this."

"I showed because our agreement was for you to return Molly's stuff. Where is it?"

He sighed to show his disappointment. "I'm betting you won't be able to stay away."

"Her belongings, and don't come after me or my friends again. I'll contact you when another job comes up."

"So testy." He snorted and pointed to a small box and Molly's TV on the right side of the truck. "Anything like this comes up again, let me know right away. I watched the movers unload some good shit today. Can't believe the idiots who own this stuff are just letting it sit here tonight."

I shrugged as if I agreed with his assessment. Years ago, I would have. Now, I thought more like the homeowners. Locked house, still packed boxes, who would break in? I knew how false that sense of security actually was, but it was still a genuine feeling.

I jumped up into the truck and brought the box to the edge before going back for the television. If anyone saw me walking down the street, I'd look like I was stealing this thing, but I couldn't worry about that. I just needed to clear out.

"Help me move some of the bigger stuff." He pointed over his shoulder to the front door.

"Bye, Brock." I managed the flat screen under one arm and wrapped my other around the box. I'd take this to Yolanda's to hand over as evidence. With everything else in the truck, they could probably release it back to Molly right away.

"I'll turn you back, Shaw. Mark my words. We were good together."

Hurrying to keep from being spotted, I loaded the television into my cargo area and plopped the box on the passenger seat. I started the car and drove past the house. Brock was already inside, probably thrilled that he'd found it unlocked.

A block away, I spotted the first police car. A police van was on the cross street. I was dying to stick around and watch Brock get caught, but I was more eager to drop the evidence at Yolanda's and hear that this was all wrapped up.

"They just called," Yolanda told me when I stepped into her office. "They picked up Brock after he'd loaded a few items into the truck."

Relief swam through me. As slimy as I felt for turning on anyone I knew, I felt equally jubilant to be free of this whole predicament. Everything I'd intended when I moved here was finally free to happen. "It's done?"

"You may need to testify, but your affidavit will suffice for the parole violation hearing. Best case scenario, he realizes he can't win and takes a deal. You won't have to testify in that situation."

"That would be great." Amazing, really.

"Go home, forget about all of this. I've got Tanner's ear now, so you shouldn't have any more trouble with the police again. If anything comes up, let me know."

"Thank you."

"It's my job, Falyn, but you're welcome."

I shook her hand and left, hoping that Molly would get her possessions back soon. My stress level was so high I could crash right now, but I had to see Molly. I owed her an explanation and wanted to tell her everything now that I was free to do so.

39

I couldn't interpret the look Molly was giving me. She was probably as mixed up about her feelings as I was.

"When I ran into you last week, you had this all planned?"

"I'm sorry I couldn't tell you," I reiterated. "I know that's important to you. I would have told you everything if I could. Please believe that."

She grasped my arms, hope filling her eyes. "It's really over?"

"I'll probably have to testify. I don't know where or when."

"Falyn," she started, her head shaking as if the movement would re-jumble all the thoughts into some sort of order. "I hate that you had to do this alone."

I reached for a much needed hug. "You gave me your trust last week. That's all I needed."

"Whenever you need it, you have it." She squeezed tighter and turned her face to kiss my head. Her hands caressed my back in soothing motion that I'd come to crave.

"Thank you," I whispered, tears threatening again. I had a feeling this wouldn't be the last time her kindness got to me. She'd been surprising me all summer, and there was still so much to learn about her.

"You're welcome, Falyn. I was pretty worried, I admit."

I leaned back from her caress to search her still worried eyes. "Yolanda says I shouldn't be the cops' first stop after a burglary anymore, but I'll believe that when I see it."

"I'm going to give Cherise a piece of my mind when I see her again," she practically growled.

"She was ready to give you a piece of hers last time I saw her."

Molly looked surprised. "About what?"

"She didn't seem to like that we're together." I shrugged, still a little baffled that Cherise was the only one upset by our relationship.

Molly's face transformed into a beautiful smile. "Screw her. She's just jealous she can't land Brandy."

Brandy? As obnoxious as Brandy's attempts to seduce me were, I wouldn't wish Cherise on her. Not if Cherise was as close-minded and eager to jump to judgment as she'd been with me.

"I think she wants to protect you from me." Which was odd because they weren't good friends, but everything about Cherise seemed a bit off.

"Now that's laughable. We barely talk, and other than trying to pick up some of the tourists I dated, she never had much to say to me."

My eyes popped for a moment. Like a trained response instilled by my ex-girlfriend, jealousy flared for a second. My first assessment of Molly as a striking butch was spot on. She had a body that all lesbians would find attractive and her confidence was such a turn on. I knew she'd been with a number of women. What surprised me was the knee-jerk flare of jealousy died when I noticed the light and intensity in her eyes. Molly was completely into me. I'd never been with anyone who was this into me. I didn't think it was possible. Jealousy would never be an issue with us.

"What?" Molly asked, concerned at the changing expressions on my face. "Oh, sorry, that was a little insensitive." Her hand skated up to lay over my heart in a gesture that gave away a lot of her feelings.

"Nah," I assured her, placing my hand over hers to keep it in place. I wanted her to know I accepted her feelings and returned the same.

"Yeah. I don't want to think about your exes."

I smiled wide. A girlfriend who was as into me as I was into her. What a novelty. One I wouldn't give up anytime soon, if ever. Warmth spread through me. That was it, wasn't it? This woman, whom I never would have guessed I'd be interested in, was someone I now realized I could spend my life with. A life that wasn't even my own just a few months ago.

Molly's Epilogue

Six Weeks Later

A sound woke me. I routinely slept like the dead. It didn't matter if I was in a bed, a tent, or my car. Almost nothing woke me up.

I blinked into the darkness. It took a second to get my bearings and check the time. Early morning, very early, way too early for me to be awake. I listened for the sound again but didn't hear it. What I did notice was Falyn's warmth behind me, her hand loosely placed on my bare stomach. I felt her body heat seep into my heart, smiling at how good it felt to have a woman spoon me. I was always the spooner. I had to admit I liked being spooned. And the cats were pretty good cuddlers, too.

I shifted onto my back to get a better look at her. Her hand slid to my hip, the fingers I worshiped gripping and ungripping like she was kneading my flesh. I checked her face and noted she was frowning in her sleep. A distressed moan slipped from her lips, then another. Her leg bumped mine, fingers gripping again. This must have been what woke me.

"Falyn," I whispered and gently shook her shoulder.

She moaned louder and started hyperventilating. She seemed to be having a hell of a bad dream.

"Falyn, honey, wake up."

She woke with a start, eyes wary, hand latching onto my wrist. It took a second before she exhaled in a full body tremble and slid into my arms. "Mmm, you feel all warm and snuggly."

"You were having a bad dream."

Her head nodded against my shoulder. She ran her hand down my arm, fingering every ridge and plane. God, even this innocent touch aroused me. No one else had been able to do this to me. I always concentrated more on doing the touching, but with Falyn I got to experience the pleasure of both receiving and giving for the first time.

"You want to talk about it?" I asked, trying to fight how her touch was lulling me into bliss.

She shrugged and went back to sliding her fingers from the outside of my arm to the inside. Like touching my arm was as sensual to her as it was to me.

"You don't want to talk about it?" I guessed.

She pressed her lips to my shoulder. "It's from prison."

My hands involuntarily clutched her waist. She didn't really talk about prison, which was probably my fault. I wasn't proud of my initial reaction to hearing she'd been a convict. It must have made her reticent to tell me more. "Tell me, please, if you want."

She leaned up, shifting to put her head on the pillow beside me. I turned to my side and looked into her hazel eyes. I liked trying to count the brown flecks that made what would have been green eyes more olive. The fleck count changed every time I tried to tally them up.

"However much you want to say," I encouraged.

"My first two years were hard." Her head shook. "Awful at times, but I got into a routine and learned what was most important in there."

"Which was?" I prompted after a long pause.

"Favors and race. You needed something to trade for favors and owe a few to keep the balance. And you stuck to your own race. It was despicable to anyone who thinks they're open-minded. I lucked out and got a decent first cellmate who was black. That gave me a pass there. My custodial work partner was Mexican, which helped me there. I was pretty much covered on the race thing."

Her fingers came up to stroke my cheek and push into my hair. She ran her fingernails along my scalp. I shivered at the lovely sensation. She used her blunt fingernails to great effect on me and she knew it. None of my lovers had done this for me. None had bothered to find what would make me shiver. Sure, they tried to give me an orgasm, but they didn't seem to care what else might make me crazy.

"Keep going."

She smiled and gave another rake of her fingernails through my hair. "I was surviving. It wasn't good by any means, prison shouldn't be, but I was surviving. I started smoking because they were a good trade. Same with coffee, but you had to do both or it would be seen as your hustle."

"Hustle?"

"Thing you do to rack up favors." She stroked her fingers down my neck as mine made their way under her tank top. Her warm skin twitched in my hands. "Two years in, somebody new takes issue with me. She pretty much hated everyone, but she really didn't like me. Didn't like that I had a pass with three races and didn't seem to need the cigarettes and coffee I always had for anyone who needed a fix. For eight months, she made some part of my day awful."

I pressed closer to her. Nothing about what she said made me comfortable. I couldn't imagine trying to make it through each day in there. It seemed like an unbalanced punishment for some crimes.

"People who always needed to bum a cigarette or a bump of coffee stopped coming around. Some of the regulars who'd trade their tasteless, veggie-medley side dish for my squirrel-pigeon burger stopped wanting to trade. She got physical whenever possible. Used her gang to intimidate. The first two years sucked but dealing with her beef got pretty unbearable. Our medium security wing didn't have too many truly dangerous people. She was one of them."

My fingers automatically traced the small scar I'd found on her side the second time we slept together. I'd assumed it was an appendectomy scar. My brow drew up in question.

"No, that was an accident on a construction site. Stabbing would have transferred her to maximum security, but she wasn't above bruising." A tremor went through her. "Anyway, that's what creeps into my subconscious sometimes."

"I'm sorry, honey."

"Thanks for listening."

"What brought on the nightmare?"

She tipped her head in thought. "Not sure. I didn't get the chance to clear my mind before crashing last night. I was so tired."

We both were. It was the first time we slept together without first making love. As wonderful as our sex life was, it was so amazing just to fall asleep together without guilt that my girlfriend wasn't satisfied. I knew I loved her, probably had when Vivian first mentioned it, but last night I confirmed she was the one for me. Everything else about her said she was. She'd been my best friend since May, my lover for months, and my love for almost as long. I felt confident of her feelings for me even if neither of us had dropped the love bomb yet. That was another great thing about her. We thought the same way about sharing feelings. It didn't always have to be so blatant or talked to death.

"Then we make sure to give you time to clear your mind every night from now on," I stated, not realizing until too late that I just implied we'd be spending every night together. Up till now, we'd been spending three, sometimes four nights a week at her or my place. I was ready to change that to every night.

"Yes, my lovely protector." She leaned forward and kissed me gently. Her hand slid down my side and along my thigh. She dragged her fingers up and down. "Your skin is so smooth."

"Laser hair removal."

She propped her head up on a hand, looking at me with surprise in her eyes. "No?"

"What? I'm in shorts six to seven months out of the year. It's a lot of work to shave every day." I shrugged and smiled. "And razor burn blows. So the butch with sensitive skin went in for a totally vain deal. I know, lame and so not me, but I don't regret it for a second."

"Me, neither," she breathed. "It's so addictive. I never want to stop touching you."

I chuckled. "That works for me."

She skated her hand up my inner thigh. My hips tilted into her caress. She was so good to my body. The way she could make me climax so easily and without me being sore the next day. It was a benefit I didn't know I was missing, especially not having to wait a day or two before we could make love again.

"You feel so good," she whispered and kissed me. Her hand moved up to cup my breast. A finger flicked the nipple into a hard bud. She broke the kiss when she felt how fast I responded to her touch. "Want more?" she murmured as her lips drifted over my collarbone.

"God, Falyn, I always want more with you, but I'm good like this." My hands lightly kneaded her luscious breasts. I could picture the pale pink nipples under my fingers without needing to see them. I knew I'd never grow tired of looking at or touching her body.

"Sleepy?"

I shook my head. "Up now."

"I could make us breakfast. Then we can decide what to do with these extra hours my obnoxious nightmares provided us this morning."

I leaned in and pressed my lips to hers. She always complimented my kissing, but she was no slouch in that department. "I adore a woman who cooks me breakfast."

"You adore me whether I'm cooking or not."

"That I do."

She shoved up to her knees. "Same here, you know."

"Thought so," I said smugly and we both grinned. She adored me and she wanted to be with me whether we were making love or hanging out. My ideal woman turned out to be the complete opposite of what I'd been searching for.

She brought my hand up for a kiss on the knuckles and bounded out of bed. Her blue paisley panties looked amazing on her sweet ass. She always slipped something on before we fell asleep. It tantalized me every time I saw the panties or sleep shorts. I wondered what her winter PJs would look like. I couldn't wait to find out.

Her cats and I took an extra minute to drag ourselves out of bed. They went straight for the stairs of her loft, but I had to spend some time digging through the drawer she'd given me for something to wear. Something she would find as sexy as I found her undies. Right on top was a pair of light blue boxers. No, her eyes never flared when I wore boxers. I could easily give them up since they weren't the best option with shorts and didn't fit under my silk thermals in the winter. She'd given up smoking for me. Boxers weren't that hard a habit to break.

Hmm, let's see. She liked the black hipsters or, yeah, these green boyshort panties. She'd taken her time stripping these from me the last time I wore them. These'll do. I slipped them on, found a clingy t-shirt to wear, and headed down to the bathroom.

Falyn was scrambling eggs just how I liked them with a bit of milk and butter when I walked into the kitchen. She had coffee going for me and was cutting up mushrooms to sauté. Strips of bacon were already sizzling in a pan. I could ask her to marry me just for that. She'd taken the time to learn what I liked for breakfast on all kinds of days. For today's camping trip, bacon was a must. She was easier, cereal, oatmeal, eggs, fruit, whatever I had was fine with her. In fact, I was pretty sure that when my parents visited in a few weeks and Mama made my Polish favorite, golabki, Falyn would eat it. We wouldn't expect her to eat anything with meat, no matter how scrumptious the cabbage wrapped goodies were, but Falyn probably would so as not to offend my mom, which made her the perfect kind of woman.

I came up and slipped my arms around her. She leaned back and sighed while whisking the eggs in a bowl. Her face turned to nuzzle my neck. She was awfully good at multitasking.

"I was so tired last night I forgot to tell you my work news." She set the whisk in the sink and turned to face me. Her eyes slipped down my front and graced me with the coveted flare. A quick grin stretched her lips wide. She slid her hands onto my hips and plucked a finger under my waistband, running it slowly along my abdomen.

I could have stood here all day sharing this simple touch with her. Ridiculous, really, but damn it made me happy. I glanced up, remembering that she'd started to tell me something. "What news?"

"Hmm?" she asked in a dazed voice, her eyes still transfixed by the glide of her finger. She always looked so beautiful when she was distracted. "Oh, yeah. Nat told me that big reno we start Monday will go seven days a week."

I frowned. That would suck. We already didn't get to see each other as much as other couples because I didn't get weekends off. "That sounds like too much work."

She smiled and shook her head. "No. It means we're all rotating days off. I get to pick my days."

I think I yelped, excitedly reaching to lift her off her feet. She started laughing as I guessed what she would choose, "Tuesdays and Wednesdays?"

"I thought it might be nice to have the same days off for six months."

"It'll be awesome." I set her down and basked in the wonderful news.

She pressed a hand to my cheek. "Glad you approve."

I more than approved. We'd get to wake up late and spend an entire day or two together if we wanted. I never thought I'd consider that an extravagance, but with her it would be.

She turned to pour the eggs into a pan and place the bacon onto paper towels. It was something I could envision watching every morning for years to come.

"Want toast," I asked to be helpful. "Smoothie?"

"Please, to both."

I put the fruit, yogurt, milk, and protein mix into the blender. Before meeting Falyn, I'd never made a smoothie before. Never even used a blender, but now I was becoming an expert at making them because it was one of her preferred breakfast staples.

"What's this?" I noticed a small brown bag on the island counter.

She glanced over her shoulder. "Got that for you."

I popped the bread into the toaster, brushed off my hands, and went over to the bag. My heart tripped as I pulled it open. I reached in and took out a new set of headphones for my iPod.

"How did you...why would you...?" I was at a loss for what to say. Not one of the women I'd dated would get me something like this. I had a few rich tourist trysts try to buy me expensive earrings or necklaces. I never accepted them. The girlfriends I had would buy clothes they'd rather see me wear or gift certificates because they couldn't be bothered to figure out what they should get me for Christmas or my birthday. No one would have thought to get me something both useful and thoughtful just because.

"You said the pair you had kept cutting in and out, and you have that camping trip tonight. I know how much the iPod saves your nights on those trips."

"Falyn," I breathed out in wonder. "Thank you."

She looked surprised by how grateful I sounded. "It's nothing big, Molly."

No. It wasn't as big as her changing her work schedule to match mine, but it was a big deal to me. Every big gift had a purpose like softening me up for something I wouldn't like or apologizing for something I wasn't happy about. Little gifts or gestures said she was thinking of me when she was doing something else, when she didn't need to be thinking of me. "It's not my birthday."

"I know." Her mouth quirked up. "Do I need a reason to pick up something for you?"

"No one's ever done that for me."

"Well, get used to it." She smiled and gripped my hand. "I don't ever want to take you for granted. You have to promise to tell me if you feel that way."

I went to her for a hug. Her face tucked in against mine. "I will as long as you tell me the same."

"And no keeping score, either."

I smiled because she guessed one of my habits with friends. If Vivian or Dwight paid for dinner twice in a row, it made me antsy. Yeah, they made a lot more than I did, but I wanted things to be even between us. "Yes, ma'am."

She laughed. "I am okay with being the boss, though."

I joined her merriment. "In your dreams. That we will be keeping score on."

"Share it?"

I nodded. "Yeah, we can work with that."

Her teeth pulled her bottom lip in for a tantalizing three seconds. "I wouldn't think of sharing control with just anyone, you know?"

"Same for me."

"So..." Her hand came up and waved two fingers back and forth between us. "It's love then, is it?"

My heart sped up as an amazed laugh escaped. The way she finally said it was as original as the rest of her. She wasn't telling me she loved me. She was saying it for both of us, and it wasn't really a question.

"Yeah," I agreed, pulling her to me. "It's love."

"The kind that sticks." She smiled and nipped my lips.

"For a long, long time." I captured her teasing lips in a smoldering kiss to seal my promise.

Other publications by Lynn Galli

Wasted Heart - Attorney Austy Nunziata moves across the country to try to snap out of the cycle of pining for her married best friend. Despite knowing how pointless her feelings are, five months in the new city hasn't seemed to help. When she meets FBI agent, Elise Bridie, that task becomes a lot easier. (Special Edition includes epilogue never before in print.)

Imagining Reality - Changing a reputation can be the hardest thing anyone can do, even among her own friends. But Jessie Ximena has been making great strides over the past year to do just that. Will anyone, even her good friends, give her the benefit of the doubt when it comes to finding a forever love? (Special Edition includes epilogue never before in print.)

Uncommon Emotions - When someone spends her days ripping apart corporations, compartmentalization is key. Love doesn't factor in for Joslyn Simonini. Meeting Raven Malvolio ruins the harmony that Joslyn has always felt, introducing her to passion for the first time in her life. (Special Edition includes epilogue never before in print.)

Blessed Twice - Briony Gatewood has considered herself a married woman for fifteen years even though she's spent the last three as a widow. Her friends have offered to help her get over the loss of her spouse with a series of blind dates, but only a quiet, enigmatic colleague can make Briony think about falling in love again. (Special Edition includes epilogue never before in print.)

Full Court Pressure · The pressure of being the first female basketball coach of a men's NCAA Division 1 team may pale in comparison to the pressure Graysen Viola feels in her unexpected love life.

Finally · Willa Lacey never thought acquiring five million in venture capital for her software startup would be easier than suppressing romantic feelings for a friend. Having never dealt with either situation, Willa finds herself torn between what she knows and what could be.

Mending Defects – Small town life for Glory Eiben has always been her ideal. With her rare congenital heart defect, keeping family and friends close by preserves her easygoing attitude. When Lena Coleridge moves in next door, life becomes anything but easy. Lena is a reluctant transplant and even more reluctant friend. Their growing friendship adds many layers to Glory's ideal.

Something So Grand – Vivian Yeats has dreamed of a grand romance for herself, but her relationships always fall short of that mark. Instead, she focuses on her design business where she can control her success. After meeting Natalie Harper, the contractor who steps up to help save her business reputation, Vivian begins to think that Natalie's white hat complex could give her more than she's ever hoped for.

CPSIA information can be obtained at www.ICGtesting.com
Printed in the USA
BVOW07s0943201214

380036BV00001B/88/P

9 781935 611240